ALSO BY TALIA HIBBERT

RAVENSWOOD

A Girl Like Her

Damaged Goods, a bonus novella

Untouchable

That Kind of Guy

DIRTY BRITISH ROMANCE

The Princess Trap

Wanna Bet?

JUST FOR HIM

Bad for the Boss

Undone by the Ex-Con

Sweet on the Greek

STANDALONE TITLES

Merry Inkmas

Mating the Huntress

Operation Atonement

Always With You

A GIRL
LIKE HER

Ravenswood Book 1

TALIA HIBBERT

Nixon House

A GIRL LIKE HER

Published by Nixon House.

ISBN: 978-1-9164043-0-4

For my mother, who wouldn't allow me to be anyone but myself.

CONTENT NOTE

Please be aware: this book contains mentions of intimate partner violence that could trigger certain audiences.

PROLOGUE

MAY 2016

DANIEL BURNE FELT SMUG. This wasn't particularly unusual; he was often pleased with himself. But tonight, he was especially proud of his own brilliance—because the second-most beautiful, and eminently suitable, woman in Ravenswood was on his arm. Wearing his ring.

And the crème de la crème of the town was there to see it.

"Daniel, love," Laura murmured, leaning in close. "Do you think your dad is pleased?"

Daniel's gaze crawled over the room, past the chattering guests of the engagement party, until it settled on his father. The older man lounged against the mantle, ankles crossed, as if his only child's engagement simply bored him.

Their eyes met, green clashing with green. Daniel studied his father's face for less than a second. That was long enough to recognise the familiar disdain there.

"Yes, love," Daniel said. "He's just a bit reserved; that's all."

Laura relaxed beside him. "Oh, good. I wondered what everyone would think, since we kept ourselves a secret." She smiled. It was a beautiful smile, the teeth neat and small. Irritatingly perfect. She patted his chest and added, "You naughty man."

Daniel smiled back. He also slid a hand into the pocket of his freshly pressed, linen suit. Hidden from view, he dug his nails into his palm until he drew blood.

Instantly, he regretted it. There'd probably be stains on the silk lining now.

"Oh, I say!"

The exclamation cut through the party's quiet music and the low hum of voices. All eyes swung to Margaret Young, who stood by the window, champagne in hand. She twitched the curtains back, sharp anticipation dancing across her powdered face.

The anticipation of a shark smelling blood in the water.

"We have a visitor!" Margaret trilled.

Daniel's heart lurched. A cold sweat sprang to his brow. Surely, she wouldn't come here. Not in front of all these people. Not when she knew how important this was.

"Daniel?" Laura's voice was at once too distant, as if coming through a tunnel, and too loud. Her arm, tucked into his own, felt tight and confining. He shook her off and strode toward the window, ignoring her confused frown.

He would shut the drapes, shove bloody Margaret Young aside—

But, before he could manage either objective, two overdressed biddies pushed in front of him. They peered through the window, squinting into the growing darkness of a spring evening.

"Who is it?" one wondered aloud.

"You need spectacles," the other drawled. "It's one of those Kabbah girls. Clear as day."

"Which one?" the first asked.

Yes! Daniel wanted to scream. *Which fucking one?*

"Oh, I don't know. Whole family looks the same to me."

Daniel's patience, always whisper-fine, snapped. He bit out, "They look *nothing* alike," and pushed through the growing crowd, forcing his way to the window and ignoring the outraged cries of old gossips.

He reached the cool glass panes to see a young woman—small, dark, soft-bodied and hard-faced—striding up the drive, dragging a cricket bat behind her. As he watched, she tucked the bat under her arm and clambered on top of his car.

His mint-condition, forest green, Porsche 911.

The woman straightened up, feet spread wide on the hood for balance. She turned to look at the window, and around him, Daniel heard a sharp intake of breath. As if she'd cursed them all instead of simply setting eyes on them. As if she were there for any of them, anyway.

She was looking at him. Only him.

Another woman might take this cliff's-edge of a moment to shout out her grievance, bellow a war cry, at least scream. But this was a Kabbah girl in a rage, and so she was utterly and disturbingly silent. For a few long seconds, she stared at him.

3

Then she turned away and swung the bat.

She was strong and she was sure. The windscreen shattered on her first try. But she did not stop there.

CHAPTER ONE

FEBRUARY 2018

RUTH's favourite place had always been her head.

Inside her mind, the sort of excitement she struggled to process in real life became accessible. She could slow it down and compartmentalise it, like a TV show she controlled utterly. And she could translate it, too. That was the best part.

Ruth's stylus flew over the screen of her graphic tablet as she sketched out the story unfolding before her eyes. Not the eyes that saw light shining off the tablet's pristine glass, but the eyes that saw entire worlds beyond this one.

She'd found the sweet spot. The zone. That precise point in time and space and possibility when a story began to flow like water, and the artist was able to keep up with the current.

In the peace of her shitty little flat, Ruth's easily-shattered focus was, for once, razor-sharp.

Until the phone rang.

"Oh, for fuck's sake," she muttered. The sweet spot

became sour. Ruth was thrust out of her own head and back into the real world, into herself. The image, the story, was left behind.

For a moment, Ruth looked down at the scene she'd just outlined. Lieutenant Lita Ara'wa glared at her captain, an 8-foot-tall, golden alien, from over a huge, living desk. The desk smelled and felt like Derbyshire peat, but that was a detail only Ruth would ever know. In a moment, Lita and her captain would commence rage-fuelled hate-sex on top of the Derbyshire peat desk.

Which, come to think of it, didn't sound very hygienic. Maybe one of them should catch something...

Aaaaaand the goddamn phone was still ringing.

Its shrill chime threatened to snip the golden thread of Ruth's idea—which could *not* be allowed to happen.

Chewing at her lower lip, Ruth thrust out a hand in the direction of her phone's repeated chime. After a few unseeing, experimental gropes at the bed's rumpled sheets, she came up empty-handed.

But the phone kept ringing, loud and clear. It had to be there somewhere.

Eyes still trained on the tablet, Ruth shuffled across her bed. Lita and the captain should definitely catch something, she decided. An unfamiliar Earth disease. What could one catch from Derbyshire peat? Frowning slightly at the image before her, Ruth reached out toward the space where—if muscle-memory and instinct served—a bedside table sat.

Muscle-memory and instinct did not serve.

In fact, not for the first time, they failed her completely. Ruth shuffled a bit too far, leaned a bit too hard, and fell right off the bed.

Again.

"Ah, fuck." The cool, wooden floor of her bedroom was a familiar location, but that didn't ease the sting in her hip and elbow.

Ruth stayed still for a breath, because serious pain usually waited a second to make itself known. Just as she decided that nothing was damaged, the blasted phone stopped ringing.

And, of course, in that precise moment, she spotted the bugger. It was on the floor, next to a nearby stack of *Avengers* comics. Exactly how it had gotten there, Ruth had no idea. Perhaps she'd thrown it.

With a sigh, she scrambled over and grabbed the phone.

1 MISSED CALL: HANNAH

Oh. Any hopes of ignoring the call and returning to work evaporated. Rising to her feet, Ruth called her elder sister back.

"Hey," Hannah answered. "You're up."

"Unfortunately." Ruth pressed a hand to her belly as she stood. Sometime in the last few minutes, she'd become aware of a concerning, nauseous feeling low in her gut. She headed out into the hall, weaving expertly through her stacks of comics, and explained, "Inspiration struck."

"Well, it's good that you're awake. I wish you'd get your sleep schedule on track."

Sigh. Ruth had been gifted with a mother who did not nag. As part of the bargain, she'd been given an elder sister who did nothing but. "My sleep schedule is fine," Ruth muttered, stepping into the bathroom. "I'm not one of your —" *Of your toddlers,* she'd been going to say. Because she was

7

an insensitive, ungrateful cow. She swallowed the words and hoped they'd gone unnoticed.

"What time did you get up?" Hannah demanded. Thank God for dogged determination.

"About four."

"In the afternoon?"

Ruth ignored the question, because the answer was obvious. She yanked down her pyjama bottoms and enormous granny knickers to find the expected splotches of blood staining their crotch. "Oh, dear," she mumbled.

"Are you talking to yourself again?"

"Nope." Ruth grabbed a box of tampons from the bathroom cabinet and found it quite tragically empty. "Shit."

"You *are* talking to yourself," Hannah insisted. "Oh, Ruthie. You really should get a cat."

"Don't be ridiculous." Ruth tucked the phone between her shoulder and chin, tearing off a length of toilet paper. "Cats despise conversation."

"Perhaps a goldfish, then."

"You'd rather I talk to a goldfish?" Ruth wadded up the tissue and shoved it down her knickers. Emergency manoeuvres were called for.

"I'd rather you talked to *people*," Hannah corrected. "Real, live people. Why don't you come out with me tonight?"

Ruth paused in the act of pulling up her pyjama bottoms. She couldn't help it. At the prospect of spending a Friday night out—like, *out* out—her body froze.

There was a pause. Then her stiff joints released, her muscles relaxed, and her breath calmed just enough for her to say, "No."

Hannah sighed. Perhaps unsurprised, probably disappointed. "Not in Ravenswood. We could go to the city."

As much as Ruth hated to deny her sister anything... "I'm on deadline, Han."

"You make your own deadlines."

"And I'm a bitch of a boss." Ruth arranged her pyjamas, then headed out into the hall, grabbing a jacket. "I have to go."

"Ruth—"

"Period emergency."

That was enough to distract even Hannah. "Oh, God. Are you alright? Do you want me to bring you some ice cream?"

"I have plenty of ice cream. Bye, Han. Love you." Ruth put the phone down before her sister had a chance to say those last words back.

She didn't really feel worthy of hearing them.

~

"You shouldn't do that, you know."

Evan Miller stifled a sigh.

He didn't need to look over his shoulder to know who those words had come from. After five days at Burne & Co., he was more familiar with those cultured, charming tones than he'd like.

So Evan continued to focus on the length of iron before him, holding it up to the light, making sure that he'd drawn it out just far enough. His muscles ached and sweat trailed down his brow as the forge cooled. He was almost ready to leave, but now he wanted to find some reason to stay. Just ten more minutes, or maybe twenty. As long as it took for his visitor to get the hint.

Evan had been waiting all week for Daniel Burne to lose interest in him, and so far it didn't seem to be working. Maybe Evan was the problem. Maybe, by not rushing to befriend the boss's kid, he'd made himself stand out too much.

Daniel Burne was rich, handsome, good at his job despite the possible nepotism, and king of this small town. He probably didn't understand why Evan rebuffed his friendship. That was the problem with popular people; they needed, more than anything, to be noticed.

So it came as no surprise when, instead of going away, Daniel moved further into the workshop. He wandered within Evan's line of sight and leant against the wall, folding his arms.

This time, Evan didn't stifle his sigh. He released it loudly, a drawn-out gust that spoke a thousand words. But his mother had raised him to be a gentleman, so that sigh was the only hint of annoyance that he allowed to escape.

"What's up?" Evan asked, lowering the iron finial.

Daniel's auburn hair gleamed bright in the light of the dying fire. He tossed his head toward the line of cooling finials at the edge of Daniel's workshop. Eventually, they'd form a gate for the Markham family.

"You shouldn't be doing Zach's work for him," Daniel drawled. "If he wants to slack, let him face the consequences."

There were lots of things that Evan could've said to that. Like, *"You do know that Zach's mother has cancer, right?"* Or, *"Since I've known him 5 days and you've known him since child-*

hood, you should be more eager to help than me." Or maybe, *"Do
you have any fucking conscience whatsoever?"*

Instead Evan said, "I'm done now, anyway."

Avoiding conflict was his mode of operation. They'd
taught him that at basic training, once they'd figured out his
hair-trigger temper. *Always avoid conflict.*

It worked, partly. Daniel nodded, and didn't say another
word about Zach or the gate. But he did hover as Evan put
away his equipment and checked the forge's temperature.
And when Evan headed for the exit, Daniel was right on his
heels.

"You walking?" Daniel asked, his long strides matching
Evan's easily.

"Yep," Evan replied.

"It's been a long week. Let me drive you home."

"That's okay," Evan smiled. "I like to walk." It *was* true; he
needed physical activity like he needed air. Plus, he had to
be gentle with Daniel. It wouldn't do to alienate the boss's
kid, even if that kid happened to be a grown man.

"Oh, come on." Daniel grinned back, a wide, white-
toothed smile. Evan hadn't seen much of Ravenswood yet,
but he'd seen enough to know that the small town's inhabitants adored Daniel Burne. And if he hadn't, the easy expectation in Daniel's green eyes would've made it clear. This
man had never been told 'no', and never thought he
would be.

Those were the men you had to watch.

"Alright," Evan relented as they broke out into the cool,
evening air. It was just after five, so Ravenswood's streets
were busy. Which meant that there was an old woman

heading into the town centre on foot, and two Volvos making their way there via road.

"Great!" Daniel clapped Evan on the back, a firm slap that spoke of a camaraderie they had not forged. It was funny; in the army, that sort of immediate connection had come easy. But here, with this man, the familiarity set Evan's teeth on edge.

"I parked in town," Daniel said. "Just 'round the corner."

Evan nodded. Since 'town' referred to the centre of Ravenswood, and Ravenswood itself was about three miles long—surrounding farmland included— nothing was very far from anything else.

But Daniel managed to pack the next five minutes with a lifetime's worth of meaningless chatter anyway.

"So, where are you living? Those new flats?"

The flats had been built in 2015, but here in Ravenswood, that counted as new.

"Yep," Evan confirmed. "Elm Block." The town's habit of naming everything in sight was something he quite enjoyed.

Daniel, apparently, did not agree. His already-pale face blanched slightly, his brow furrowed. "Serious?" he asked. "Elm?"

Something in his voice had changed. It was tight, strained, slightly scratchy.

Evan slowed down, his eyes focusing on Daniel with curiosity rather than veiled disdain. "Yeah. Why?"

"That's bad luck, mate," Daniel said. He nodded his head over and over again, disturbingly emphatic. "*Very* bad luck. I suppose you had no-one in town to guide you. There's some very shady characters living in Elm, you know."

Evan's brows flew up. "Shady characters?" he echoed. "In

Ravenswood? I haven't been here long, but that doesn't sound right."

"Trust me," Daniel said darkly. "We all have our burdens to bear."

Evan bit back a snort. Apparently, he could add *Drama King* to the list of Daniel Burne's irritating qualities.

"Be careful," Daniel continued. "I'm just saying." Then he jerked his head towards a huge, blue BMW a few metres away, parked across two spaces. "That's mine."

Evan blinked at the monstrous thing for a moment, trying to come up with a compliment. He failed. To fill the silence, he returned to the ominous topic of his little block of flats.

"I only have one neighbour. Haven't met them yet, but I think it's someone elderly. They don't seem to leave the house."

"Hm," Daniel grunted. "Well—"

His sage wisdom was thankfully interrupted. As they neared the BMW, a small figure came rushing around a nearby corner and knocked right into them both.

CHAPTER TWO

RUTH ENTERED the town car park with a lot on her mind. Major highlights included:

1. Her stomach cramps, which had gone from mild irritation to knuckle-biting pain in the space of twenty minutes.

2. The indignity of waddling about town with loo roll stuffed down her knickers.

3. The absolutely extortionate price she'd just paid for a packet of substandard tampons that didn't even have bloody applicators.

4. Mrs. Needham, newsagent proprietor and town gossip, who would tell everyone that Ruth had come in to buy tampons as if they were Year Eight children instead of grown adults.

5. How much the average person might know about the theory of relativity. Because, the less people knew about it, the more she could get away with fudging the details for the latest issue of her web comic.

Was it really surprising, with all that to ponder, that she ran headlong into a pair of enormous men?

Ruth landed on the tarmac with an unladylike grunt. At least it was more elegant than the word currently burning through her mind: *Motherfucker!*

This was to be imagined, you understand, as an outraged yowl of pain.

For an instant of blissful, foolish shock, Ruth blinked down at the ground. Then she looked up slightly, just a touch—enough to see two pairs of sturdy, boot-clad feet before her. The sight of those feet, along with her embarrassment, took Ruth from mildly irritated to unreasonably angry.

But *really*. Those boots were entirely too solid and quite abominably stable. The men hadn't even wobbled. They might at least pretend to be slightly unbalanced, since she was literally on the floor. Such firm uprightness in a situation like this struck her as rude.

"I'm so sorry," one of the men said. She didn't know which, because she refused to look up at their faces. She had quite enough to process right now without bringing faces and expressions and human lifeforms into it.

But one of the men, presumably the one who had spoken, ruined things completely by bending down to her level. He could do that, you see, because *he* hadn't fallen. The prick.

He crouched before her, bringing his faded jeans into view, and then his tight, black T-shirt—what a ridiculous outfit in February—and then... well, some rather interesting musculature.

That musculature broke through Ruth's haze of unreasonable annoyance, prodding her sharply. It said, *Look at that chest! Look at those biceps! You'd better check out his face, just to see if it's equally impressive. Quality control, and all that.*

Reigning in the urge to throw a temper tantrum—she was feeling fragile, what with the tissue in her knickers—Ruth looked up.

"Holy shit," she said.

The most beautiful man on Earth frowned at her. "Are you alright? Did you hit your head?"

Ruth didn't bother answering. Talking to this guy could not possibly be as worthwhile as simply looking at him.

In fact, talking to him might ruin the effect. Or ruin her concentration, at least.

So he continued to ask unanswered questions, and she continued to watch his lips move.

They looked soft. The thick, dirty-blonde beard covering his jaw looked soft too, matching the too-long hair falling over his brow.

His bone structure, unlike his hair, didn't look soft at all. Nor did his furrowed brows or his piercing eyes, blue as a summer sky. Of course, skies were never blue in England—but she'd seen the sky in Sierra Leone, had spent hours staring up at it from her grandmother's garden. That was the best slice of sky on Earth, so she felt authorised to make the comparison.

The stranger's voice was raw and satisfying, threaded with something that might've been concern, and it soothed Ruth's embarrassment-induced irritation beautifully.

But then came a voice that brought it back ten-fold.

"Don't bother," said Daniel Burne. "She's slow."

Ruth's head snapped up, her gaze settling on the person she hated most in the world.

His smile was as cruel and as gorgeous as ever. For a moment, Ruth's heart lurched. But then she looked back at the stranger, who was still crouched beside her—who was *frowning*—and she felt slightly consoled.

The stranger was far more handsome than Daniel. How he must hate that.

Biting down on the inside of her cheek, Ruth stood. She ignored the fact that the tissue in her knickers felt slightly dislodged. She ignored the fact that there must be grit and dirt on her pyjama bottoms, and even ignored the fact that she was in her pyjamas at all, with only a jacket to hide them.

Ruth folded her arms across her chest and took a deep steadying breath, staring Daniel down. She said, "If I'm *slow*, what kind of man does that make you?"

His lip curled. "Opportunistic, perhaps."

Direct hit, of course. She'd expected nothing less.

Her jaw set, Ruth turned on her heel. Daniel wasn't worth talking to, anyway. He was beneath her notice. He was a gnat. But gnats were infuriating too, when you couldn't squash them.

"Wait!" the stranger called.

Ruth ignored him. She walked faster. She could see her car now, just a few metres away, gleaming like an oasis in the desert.

Then she heard the heavy footsteps of a man running behind her. "Miss!" he called. "You dropped your..."

Ruth stopped. Her hands balled into fists. She spat out,

"For fuck's sake," and her breath twisted before her like smoke in the evening air.

The man was right behind her now. "I'm sorry," he said. He seemed to say that a lot.

She turned to face him. He really *did* look apologetic. Maybe because she'd fallen, maybe because Daniel was a prick, or maybe because he was holding out the box of tampons she'd dropped.

At the newsagent, Mrs. Needham had asked if she wanted a bag for five pence, and Ruth had thought, *Goodness me, five pence on a bag when I have two good hands?* And said, "No, thank you."

Now she was rather wishing she had parted with the five pence.

"Are you sure you're okay?" the man asked. "I'm sorry about… Daniel's behaviour." He said Daniel's name with the sort of tone she'd use to say *kitten killer*. Maybe that's what this gorgeous stranger thought: that Ruth was a kitten.

She snatched the tampons from him, turned her back, and walked away. He'd learn the truth soon enough.

The only question was—which truth?

Ruth started her engine and pulled out of the car park with almost reckless speed. Still, she wasn't fast enough to miss an intriguing tableau.

The stranger striding away from Daniel. Daniel shouting after him.

Ruth lowered her car window, just a touch, to catch the words.

Daniel called, "You're really pissed? Over a girl like her?"

A girl like her. It was a familiar phrase, especially from Daniel's lips.

But there was nothing familiar about the stranger. He tossed a glare over his shoulder and called back, "Don't worry about it. I'll walk."

CHAPTER THREE

THE NEXT MORNING, Ruth opened her curtains and scowled at the unholy brightness of 10 a.m.

She was not made for mornings.

But today, she'd have to cope. Ruth wanted to be out of the house when the courier came; it was easier that way. Plus, a brunch date with her sister was long overdue.

She chanted those reasons to herself as she got dressed. Pyjamas, she knew, were frowned upon in public settings, so she wore a soft, jersey tracksuit instead.

Whatever.

Hannah was waiting for her at the Greengage Cafe, which held the dubious honour of being Ravenswood's *only* cafe. It was also the only place, aside from the local pub, that served food before 5 p.m. Ruth couldn't go to the pub; too crowded. Plus, she didn't mix well with tipsy locals.

So she shuffled into Greengage, sank into a dainty, white chair opposite Hannah, and tried to blend into the furniture. It didn't work very well, maybe because the chair was barely wide enough to contain Ruth's arse. Or maybe because Hannah, in her shiny lip gloss and jewel-toned knit set, was ruining Ruth's bland effect.

"Sit up straight," Hannah said. The *please* was silent. She snapped her menu shut and caught the eye of a passing waitress with ease. "What will you drink?"

"Water," Ruth mumbled. Why Hannah asked every time, she had no idea.

"And what will you eat?"

Ruth rolled her eyes. "You know what I'll eat."

"I wouldn't dare to assume."

"Don't be an arse."

As the waitress neared, Hannah's exasperation melted into a beatific smile. "Good morning, Annabel."

The teenager didn't smile back. Her tone robotic, she said, "Drinks?"

"We're ready to order, thank you." Hannah's light, pleasant voice never faltered, and her smile never wavered.

Ruth didn't know how she did it.

"We'll have a strawberry lemonade, an orange juice, and water for the table. I'll have the..." Hannah studied her menu as if she hadn't already chosen. She was always conscious of seeming *too* perfect. She knew it intimidated people. "The eggs Benedict," she said finally. "Ruth?"

Sigh. Clearing her throat, Ruth said, "Ham and cheese omelette. Brown toast, no butter. Thanks."

The waitress, Annabel, didn't even look in Ruth's direction. She shut her notepad with a little *slap* and snatched the menus from the table.

"*Well,*" Hannah murmured. "You fixed that girl's bike, once. Do you remember?"

"I don't want to talk about it."

"About five years ago. Her father wouldn't take it down to Mack's, so you fixed it for her."

"I don't want to talk about it."

"She had braces. She thought you were God on earth."

"You blaspheme too much. Mum would slap you."

"If Mum hasn't slapped either of us yet, she never will." Hannah winked one perfectly made-up eye.

Ruth laughed. That was her sister's superpower; she could always make Ruth laugh.

Sometimes, being with Hannah was as easy as ever. Sometimes, being with Hannah was like tiptoeing through a landmine of Ruth's own guilt and self-loathing.

When it was like that, things only got worse and worse. Hannah would be upset at Ruth's cold silence, and try to hide it, and Ruth would want to say, *"It's not you or anything you've done, it's me and this fucked-up tongue that won't obey and this fractured mind that won't think and the guilt I thought I'd gotten over lurking like a shark beneath dark waters. Can you forgive me for making you pretend? Can you forgive me for being yet another reason you pull up that false smile? I am an ungrateful sister."*

Today was not one of those days. Nothing dramatic occurred. Hannah wasn't *too* annoyed when Ruth refused to drink the juice she hadn't asked for. Ruth managed not to drop anything or spill anything, or otherwise command the kind of attention that made her want to jump into a grave. Things were easy.

Until they weren't.

Cameron Wright and Will Hardy wandered into Green-gage with raucous grins and boisterous words. They had been inseparable as children, and adulthood hadn't changed that. They'd also been nasty little shits, and adulthood hadn't changed that either.

Ruth wondered if they'd ever been more than a metre apart since infancy; she rather thought not. And yet, they always *shouted* to each other as though they were miles away.

Until they set eyes on Ruth. They were silent enough then. For a moment.

"Well, well!" Cameron grinned. His smile was too wide for his narrow face, so he looked like a cartoon character, mouth pasted over hollow cheeks. He sauntered over to Ruth and Hannah's table, flattening his palm against the varnished wood. He leaned over Ruth and said, "Look what we have here."

"Gentlemen," Hannah murmured. "My sister and I are waiting for the cheque."

"*Gentlemen*," Will mocked, making his voice high and tight. He came to stand beside Cameron, folding his arms and thrusting his hips forward. "Hello, Hannah. How's your stick?"

Hannah released the sort of exhausted sigh she typically reserved for misbehaving toddlers and did not answer.

Ruth stared dully at a crumb on her plate and tried to unlock her latent mutant powers. She knew she had some. They should come out under moments of extreme stress. Surely, if she could teleport or, say, tear a man's head from his body, that ability would make itself known now?

"You know," Will continued, smirking over at Hannah. "Your *stick*."

"Yes," Hannah drawled. "The stick up my arse. Don't worry, Will; I understand the joke."

The two men guffawed together, as if they hadn't told that 'joke' a thousand times over the last ten years at least.

Then Cameron turned his attention back to Ruth. His eyes roamed the front of her oversized hoodie until they settled on the place where he judged her breasts to be. Leering at a body he couldn't see, Cameron said softly, "When you gonna give me a ride, babe?"

Ruth looked up at him, her face blank, her eyes dead. "You know the rules. I only fuck guys with money."

Under the table, Hannah kicked her in the shin. Ruth ignored it.

Cameron straightened, his too-wide smile impossibly wider. "I've got money," he said, making sure his voice carried.

"So have I," Will said, more quietly. Because he was married.

Neither of them saw the manager coming over to their table, but they jumped slightly as the big man cleared his throat.

Walt Greengage put his big hands on his skinny hips and gave all four of them—Ruth, Hannah, Cameron, Will—a hard look. Then he said, "You ladies paid your bill?"

Ruth sighed. She reached into the deep pocket of her tracksuit bottoms and found a couple of twenty-pound notes. The bill was £23.65. She threw both notes onto the table and stood, unable to even look at Hannah. "We're going."

She and Ruth left the café in silence and stalked through

the town centre in the same state. Only when they were far, far from Greengage did Hannah speak.

"Why do you let them do that?"

Ruth turned to face her sister. They were standing in the shadow of the town's yarn shop, on a side street that not many frequented. Hannah *would* choose this for a confrontation, if she was too angry to wait for a completely private space.

"Are you blaming me for that?" Ruth asked.

Hannah's dark eyes flashed. Her sensible shoes tapped against the gravel street, heel to toe, one after another. This meant that Hannah was furious and holding it back.

"You know I'm not blaming you," Hannah said tightly. "But I *do* wish you would stand up for yourself instead of… instead of goading them!"

Ruth shrugged. "Why?"

"Self-respect, that's why!"

"I respect myself just fine." Ruth started walking again, slower than before, since standing still was difficult when her mind was busy. It felt like clinging to a hot air balloon's tether, trying to hold it down with nothing but her body-weight. It was far more sensible to let the balloon fly.

Hannah followed, her heels clicking sharply against the pavement. "You think I don't know that you're punishing yourself?"

Guilt plunged into Ruth's chest, a sharp, barbed arrow. "Someone has to."

"Someone *has*. So you can stop."

"I don't want to worry you, Han. That's not what I want."

"I almost wish I hadn't noticed," Hannah said, her voice suddenly soft. "I almost wish I'd stayed distant."

That was what they called it. *Distant*. Words like *depressed* were for girls with English mothers.

"Don't say that." Ruth realised that she was rubbing her own hands—wringing them, people said—and made herself stop, even though the action was calming. "I don't understand why we can't just leave," she burst out.

"Because this is our town," Hannah snapped back. "*Your* town. Just as much as it is theirs. It's our home, and we're not leaving it behind!"

"I don't see why not," Ruth muttered grimly. "It wouldn't be the first worthless thing I've thrown away."

∼

MUM WAS ALWAYS TELLING her to be more observant, but Ruth's senses and mind didn't connect like that. When she wandered out of the stairwell toward her flat, she was too deep in thought to look around, or listen, or anything like that.

So she didn't notice the courier on her doorstep until she'd almost walked right into him.

Ruth realised, with a sinking heart, that it was far too late to turn and run. After jerking out of her way, the poor man offered her a customer service smile.

"Ruth Ka... I'm sorry." He winced apologetically. "I'm not sure how to pronounce this."

"Kabbah," she said, pulling out her keys. "I was hoping I'd miss you."

The man blinked uncertainly.

"I even subjected myself to human company. What a waste. Best laid plans, and all that." She opened the front door and turned to look at him. "What is it? Do you know?"

"Um..." He looked down at the slim package in his hand. "I don't, I'm afraid. But if you'd just sign for it—"

"Must I?" Ruth asked. She'd never asked that before. It had never occurred to her that she might refuse. But the morning's events, and Hannah's reaction, had her trapped in the eye of a rage-guilt-fear hurricane, and she was suddenly and completely sick of this shit.

"You don't want the package?" the man asked uneasily. "I suppose you could, um, return to sender."

Ruth stared. "Are you serious?"

The man shifted his weight from foot to foot. He was uncomfortable. She could see the signs. "Yes."

"I thought that was just a song. I thought it was some old-fashioned, American thing..."

"You can't do it with the Royal Mail," he said, "but we at Diamond Services—"

"You don't need to give me the spiel," she interrupted. "I don't send things to people."

The man's face fell.

"Can I tip you?" she asked, because she was suddenly incredibly fond of this middle-aged, lanky stranger. "I have, um..." She fumbled through her pockets and found nothing but Parma Violets. "Hang on." Without waiting for his response, Ruth stepped inside and shut the door.

Then she thought that shutting the door might send the wrong message and opened it again. Then she thought *that* might send the wrong message, and wondered if she ought to invite him in.

That would probably be weird.

Forgetting about the door, she hurried off to the shoe box in a drawer in her bedroom. She pulled out one of her prized fifty-pound notes—she collected fifty-pound notes—and rushed back to the door, fighting the odd worry that the man might have left. Of course, he wouldn't have left. Why would he leave?

He hadn't left.

She gave him the note and said, "Return to sender. Thank you."

"I'm not really supposed to accept tips..."

"Oh," she said, and held out her hand to take it back.

He stared at her for a moment. She realised he was doing the thing people did, where they protested, but didn't truly mean it. She put her hand in her pocket and smiled. "Goodbye!"

"Ah... Bye?"

Ruth shut the door.

Good Lord, what an exhausting morning this had been. She tore off her hoodie and the T-shirt beneath, right there in the hall. The fabric had been slowly suffocating her for hours. She weaved through her stacks of comic books as she wandered back to her bedroom, peeling off more clothes as she went.

While she changed, she heard her neighbour, Aly, moving around through the thin connecting wall. At least, she assumed it was Aly—but those heavy footsteps weren't the ones her neighbour usually made.

Perhaps Aly had a man. That didn't bode well for Ruth. She'd almost certainly overhear them going at it.

CHAPTER FOUR

Evan hadn't planned to waste Saturday morning in bed, but somehow, that's what had happened. After moving in last weekend and working like a dog all week, his typically efficient body had had enough.

The series of mysterious bangs and indecipherable voices coming from the outside corridor served a double purpose. First, they woke Evan up before midday—thank God. He had shit to do. And second, they reminded him that he still hadn't met the—suddenly quite noisy—guy next door.

After a week of hearing loud, stamping footsteps at all hours of the night, and never meeting their owner in the corridor or stairwell, Evan had developed a mental image of his next-door neighbour. He imagined a curmudgeonly, older fellow who rarely left the house, referred to mobile phones and laptops as 'new-fangled contraptions', and owned a nose hair trimmer.

So, to break the ice, Evan would make his neighbour a

shepherd's pie rather than brownies or casserole. That was one of the things his mother had drilled into him: *Give people what you think they'll want—not what you want to give them.*

He bore that in mind as he cooked, following his mother's recipe. And within a few minutes, an idea occurred to him.

He pulled out his phone and called Zach.

"H'llo?" the other man's voice was subdued and thick with sleep. If Evan was blissfully ignorant of the circumstances, he might assume that a Friday night out was responsible for Zach's heavy rasp.

But Evan was not blissfully ignorant. He knew what Zach was going through, far too well. He remembered his own sleepless nights, spent with the person he loved most in the world—not to enjoy her company but to watch her struggle, to try and ease her pain. To see her fade away. Because if she had to go through it, the least he could do was bear witness.

Yeah. Evan knew exactly what was wrong with Zach. Still, he kept his voice light as he said, "Alright, mate?"

"Yep." Zach didn't try to make the lie convincing. "You?"

"Yeah, I'm good."

"What you up to?"

Evan turned to the spice rack, searching for dried rosemary. "I'm making something for my neighbour. Was wondering if you guys wanted any meals while I'm at it. That way you can keep them in the fridge or freeze them, heat stuff up when you need to. Saves time."

"Alright, Nigella." Zach snorted. But then the amusement

drained out of him in a sigh, and he said, "I think you're doing enough for me already."

Evan wondered how he'd have felt, all those years ago, if an almost-stranger had swooped in and tried to help him and his mother. He wasn't sure. But he'd been 17, rather than a grown man. Who had more pride: teenagers, or adults?

"You'll need a better reason than that," Evan said, "if you want to stop me dropping off a meal." *Or three.*

There was a single moment of tension-filled silence before Zach spoke again, the ghost of a smile haunting his voice. "You're... you're just a nice fucking guy. Aren't you?"

"Nah," Evan said. "You guys like lasagne?"

"Everybody likes lasagne."

Evan laughed. "I must've missed that global survey."

"Yeah, you must've."

"Alright; I'll be round in a couple of hours." Evan stirred the mince browning on his stove, his mind whirring through batch calculations.

Zach's voice quietened, its harsh edges softening. "Thanks, man. Thank you so much."

"Don't thank me. I'll see you later."

So that was settled. Evan slipped his phone into his pocket with satisfaction, slightly adjusting his plans for the day, He'd make three shepherd's pies and two lasagnes. He'd save a pie, take the rest to Zach's, and sit with Mrs. Davis for a while. Then he'd come home and finally meet his neighbour.

There.

Evan was a simple man: as long as he had objectives to meet, he was happy.

~

ZACH'S MOTHER was named Shirley. Evan liked her a lot.

She wore a floral, silk scarf over her head and painted her lips bright pink. She said *Darling* often and had the kind of rakish attitude that explained Zach's own boyish charm.

Although his was a little faded, a little grey, compared to his mother's. Evan wondered how he'd been before she'd fallen ill.

Shirley had spent Evan's three-hour visit lounging in bed with the air of a woman who saw no reason to get up—though Evan suspected that she simply couldn't. She had accepted the food with the grace of a queen, and confided that Zach was a terrible cook. She had made Evan laugh, and she had even made Zach laugh, though he'd been quiet and subdued throughout the visit.

She was nothing like Evan's mother, and yet, he still felt like he'd been punched in the face.

So, when he returned home to see one last shepherd's pie sitting on his counter, he wanted to bang his head against the wall.

Evan didn't want to meet his neighbour right now. He didn't want to go over with a smile and a shepherd's pie, and he didn't want to introduce himself. He wanted to drink excessive amounts of tea and make a high-calorie dinner and fight back depressing, teenage memories.

But he didn't, because that would be childish.

Instead, he wandered into the living room and sank down on the sofa, pressing the heels of his hands against his eyes. He was exhausted. Not physically, but mentally...

He couldn't meet his neighbour right now. He simply

couldn't. When his mind became heavy and grim like this, he wasn't fit company for anyone. He'd go for a run instead, batter his muscles until they matched the state of his worn-out brain, and then he'd go to bed.

His joints creaked as he stood.

The neighbour could wait 'til tomorrow.

CHAPTER FIVE

WAS THERE anything better than a Sunday evening?

Ruth was wearing her favourite set of PJs—the ones where tiny, cartoon Captain Americas chased tiny, cartoon Buckys all over the fabric. She was sitting cross-legged on her living room floor, leaning against the side of the loveseat, belly full of her mother's home cooking. Her tablet was in her lap, stylus flying.

The sweet spot had returned.

Lita and her superior officer were indeed hate-fucking on the Derbyshire peat desk, and even though Ruth preferred a fade-to-black style—it made securing ad revenue for her website much easier—she allowed herself to sketch out all the gory sexual details, just for the hell of it.

It wasn't that she liked alien sex. She just liked drawing weird shit.

Everything was flowing beautifully until, for what felt like the thousandth fucking time—but was probably only the second—she heard her next-door neighbour's front door open.

Yes; the walls were so thin, she could hear Aly Harper's door open and shut. Amongst other things.

But Ruth could've shaken off that distraction—if it weren't followed by a knock at her own door.

"For God's sake," she muttered, setting her tablet aside. "I should ignore her. It would serve her right."

The empty flat maintained a judgemental silence.

Ruth had a policy, when it came to knocked doors: she didn't answer them. She didn't enjoy speaking to people willy-nilly. Anyone who wanted to see her could arrange it well in advance, preferably via text or email.

Plus, the girl next-door was, frankly, a bitch.

But since Aly disliked Ruth as much as Ruth disliked Aly, she supposed this must be some sort of emergency. And if someone was dying—even if that someone was a bitch— Ruth rather thought it her Christian duty to pretend to care.

With a resigned sigh, Ruth slid off her glasses and got up.

She answered the door in her oversized pyjamas and fluffy sleep socks, a blank expression on her face because it was better than a scowl. Hannah would tell her to smile, but Ruth only ever smiled by accident.

When she saw who was standing on her doorstep, she wished she'd worn the scowl after all.

Aly Harper's annoying, familiar face was nowhere to be found. Instead, a beautiful man stood in her place.

Ruth's mind said, *Holy shit.*

And that jogged her memory, helped her recognise the

face. If she hadn't been so shocked, she'd be proud of herself; recognising new faces was hard.

Then again, this one was difficult to forget.

The stranger from the car park seemed even more handsome than before. Maybe it was due to the dying sunlight that spilled into the corridor, burnishing the golden strands in his dark-blonde hair. Perhaps it was the way his shirt stretched over his broad chest, or the fact that his sleeves were rolled up to display thick, tattooed forearms.

Or maybe it was the huge, foil-covered dish in his hands that tipped him over the edge of perfection. The smell emanating from that dish made Ruth's mouth water almost as much as the stranger's firm biceps.

"It's you," he said. His voice was quiet, as if he'd spoken more to himself than to be heard. A frown furrowed his brow, but he smoothed it away almost instantly, straightening his spine. Since his posture was already excellent, this had the disturbing effect of making him look like a toy soldier.

A very attractive toy soldier whom Ruth, if given half the chance, would climb like a tree.

Oh, dear.

He offered her a genuine smile, the sort usually found on the faces of ordinary and unassuming men of strong moral fibre. She had never seen such a smile on a man gorgeous enough to take over the world. The combination was unnerving.

Sex appeal or sweetness. You can't have both.

Apparently, this guy could.

"Where's Aly?" she demanded. Because she *had* heard 1B's door open. Perhaps this was Aly's boyfriend.

I hope he's not Aly's boyfriend.

The man's brows rose. "Who?"

"The girl next door."

"Oh, well, actually… I live next door. I just moved in. It's nice to meet you again, by the way." He hefted the Pyrex dish in his arms, as if she could've missed it. "I made you a shepherd's pie."

Ruth stared. Mostly at the pie, but also at the way his long, blunt fingers gripped the edges of the dish. She wondered when Aly had left, then decided she didn't really care.

Her mouth slightly dry, she said, "Shepherd's pie?"

"Yeah. Just to say hi." He flashed another of those achingly earnest smiles.

"We already met," she said flatly, clutching the edge of the door. It was sturdy and solid, its edges hard enough against her palm to keep her wits sharp.

She hoped.

At the mention of their previous meeting, a shadow passed over his face. "I *am* sorry about that," he said, and for a second, she wondered if he meant it. If he really felt bad.

The thought disappeared as quickly as it had come. This man had been with Daniel. He was probably just like Daniel. So he might say things, live things, *breathe* things, but that didn't mean he meant it.

He said, "I know we bumped into each other—"

"Precisely."

"—but I didn't even tell you my name."

Ruth tried not to worry about the fact that, despite her stony expression and clipped words, he didn't seem to be going away. He wasn't even displaying the tell-tale signs of a man who *wanted* to go away. No awkward shifting, no flitting gaze, no humming: *Well...* as a precursor to the inevitable *I'll be going now.*

He just stood there, filling the doorway with his bloody shoulders, smiling that damned smile and waiting for her response.

She remained silent. Eventually, he realised that she wasn't going to speak. He did not seem perturbed by that fact.

"Maybe we could start again," the stranger said. "I'm Evan Miller. Ravenswood newbie and occupant of 1B, at your service."

Ruth's teeth were clenched, but somehow, words leapt from her mouth anyway. "I'm Ruth Kabbah. Town Jezebel. So you should probably avoid me." *Please, please avoid me.*

"Right... what's a Jezebel?"

Sigh. "You know; a harlot. A terrible, ungodly slut and misleader of men, etcetera, etcetera."

With a sort of cheerful calm, he said, "Oh. Well, I appreciate the warning." There was a twinkle in his eyes that should've set Ruth on her guard. It was one of those conspiratorial, *we're connected, let's-keep-this-conversation-going* twinkles. The kind typically used by confident men.

Was there anything worse than a confident man?

"Anyway," he said, holding out the dish. "I hope you like shepherd's pie."

Ruth, like most sensible people, adored shepherd's pie. She said, "I already ate."

And still, his smile did not falter. His confidence did not fade away. He did not shrink.

Ruth's mild alarm escalated to full-scale panic. Because

not only was he unaffected by her usual tactics, but something deep inside her appeared to be finding that fact… attractive.

This would not do at all.

She didn't even realise she was closing the door until he said, "Wait." His movements slow and gentle, he held out the dish. "It'll keep. Put it in the fridge. Reheat at 230."

"I don't have an oven," she said.

He laughed. "That's a hell of an excuse."

"It's not an excuse. I don't have an oven."

She watched as his brow furrowed again. Most men, when they frowned, appeared intimidating at best and ugly at worst. *This* man—Evan—managed to remain disgracefully gorgeous.

"You don't have an oven?" he echoed. "What do you eat?"

"Food," she said flatly. "Now, if you don't mind—"

"Wait." His voice lost its light-hearted quality, becoming quieter, deeper. "If you're having trouble with… well, with anything, I want you to know that I'm happy to help." His eyes pierced hers, uncomfortably direct. "You can use my oven, if you ever need to. You could take my microwave, if that would help. I don't use it often."

Ruth raised her brows. "Why would I possibly need your oven? Or your microwave? I have a microwave."

He held up a hand, balancing the dish on one palm. "I wasn't implying anything—"

"I am not in need of an oven. I had the oven *removed*."

His brows lifted slightly. "I… see?"

He did not see. Which was usually just how Ruth liked things.

So why the hell did she feel the need to explain further?

"I had an accident about a year ago, and both my sister and the landlord got all pissy about the way I use ovens. Or something. So I thought, I never cook anyway—might as well stick with a microwave, a toaster, and a kettle."

"What the hell do you make with a microwave, a toaster and a kettle?" he asked, sounding absolutely aghast.

Why did his obvious astonishment make her want to smile?

"Supernoodles, usually," she said, just to watch his concern grow. "And toast. Lots of ready meals—"

He thrust out the pie. "You're going to take this," he said firmly, "and you're going to eat it. Use your microwave or something. Just eat it. When you're done, tell me, and I'll make you something else."

Ruth's brows shot up. "I really don't need you to—"

"Are you allergic to anything? Are you vegetarian? Kosher or halal or—"

"No," she interrupted. "But you don't need to cook for me."

"I do," he said calmly, "because if you die of malnutrition just next door, I'll be drowned in guilt for the rest of my life."

"That's funny."

"I'm extremely serious. Take the pie."

Ruth hadn't thought that this man, with his constant smiles and sweetness, could ever look forbidding. But now he wore the expression of someone who was not to be messed with, and his tone was equally firm. A reluctant smile tilting her lips, she finally accepted the Pyrex dish.

"Thanks," she murmured. The word was almost painful.

Then, before he could do or say anything else, she kicked the door shut.

CHAPTER SIX

IT TOOK three days for the Pyrex dish to appear on Evan's doorstep.

He came home from work one day to find it sitting there on top of a tea towel, sparklingly clean. There was no note, or anything else to distinguish the return of the dish from a fairy gift.

At least she'd eaten it. Though she'd taken her damn time.

Evan picked up the dish and let himself in, his muscles aching from another long day at work. A day during which Daniel Burne had forced himself into Evan's presence as much as possible, trying his best to be charming.

As if Evan would just forget how the man had treated an innocent woman.

Of course, for the sake of his job, he bore the ingratiating falseness. He nodded, and tried his best to smile, and swallowed down the words *Fuck off.* Honestly, that was the best he could do.

Evan put the dish away before heading straight to the shower. He usually went for a run after work, but today, his muscles were screaming. He knew not to push himself too hard. Not when his strength was his livelihood.

As he stood under the steaming water, Evan put a hand to the tiled wall at his left. The wall he shared with Ruth.

Sometimes, in the middle of the night, he heard the pipes on her side of the wall flare to life. The wall was so fucking thin. It was worse in his bedroom; he could hear the creak of her bed every time she lay down. They'd barely spoken, but Evan knew that she slept restlessly, that her bed must be poorly made, and that she showered at odd hours. It made him feel weirdly connected to her in a way neither of them had earned.

Evan's mother had always said that things happened for a reason. He'd believed her, until she'd died.

He was wondering, though, if *this* had happened for a reason—he and Ruth being neighbours. She rarely left the house, she never had any visitors, and if Daniel Burne, the town's darling, treated her like shit... other people probably did too.

And she didn't have an oven. Evan shuddered at the thought of her surviving on Supernoodles. He wasn't sure why, exactly, but the thought disturbed him more than it should.

Maybe because he liked her so much. He'd always liked prickly people. In fact, Evan suspected that he and Ruth could be great friends one day.

If she'd allow it.

He reached for some body wash as he pondered the Ruth conundrum further. She'd eaten the pie—which suggested she'd enjoyed it, right? If she was *really* happy with ready meals, she would've thrown out the whole thing and returned his dish the next day. Right?

So, he should make her something else. It's not like he'd be going out of his way; he was still cooking for Zach and Shirley. He was cooking for himself. And Ruth was just next door.

It was the neighbourly thing to do.

~

AN HOUR LATER, Evan was standing on Ruth's doorstep, waiting for her to answer, being bombarded by second thoughts.

He hadn't expected his odd neighbour to be a young woman living alone, but—well, she was. He knew that now. And it had suddenly occurred to him that his mother's friendly neighbour routine might not be quite so effective coming from a fairly large man.

What if Ruth had been so eager to get rid of him a few days ago because she was... scared?

Just as his mind landed on that worrying conclusion, the door to 1A swung open.

Hands on her hips, Ruth somehow seemed tall despite being quite the opposite. Her halo of dark, crinkly hair created the illusion of height, but her vaguely threatening aura multiplied that by five.

"What do you want?" she demanded.

Evan decided with some relief that, whatever else she was, she wasn't scared.

"I brought you a lasagne." He held out the dish.

She rolled her eyes heavenward. "How very... unnecessary."

Then, before he could think of a retort, she turned and walked away.

Leaving the front door open.

After a moment's hesitation, Evan stepped inside and shut the door behind him.

Her narrow hallway was plain and nondescript—except for the enormous stack of magazines piled against the far wall. That stack was about chest-height to Evan. It probably reached Ruth's shoulders.

His brow furrowed, he stepped forward to take a closer look. He managed to discern that the magazines were actually comic books before Ruth's voice called, "Kitchen."

Right. She'd just invited him in; he could examine her comic book tower another time.

1A and 1B were mirrors of each other in layout, with the same bland magnolia walls and plain, thin carpet. Since Evan hadn't had time to decorate, and Ruth hadn't decorated at all, the two flats seemed eerily similar as he headed toward the kitchen.

Except for the fact that Evan's flat didn't feature dangerously high stacks of comic books scattered around at regular intervals.

He stepped into the kitchen to find Ruth standing by a kettle, its orange light shining. "I assume you want tea," she said.

"I didn't mean to intrude," Evan began. "I just thought—"

"Thought you'd bring me more food." she said the words without inflection, her face impassive.

Impassive, but pretty, he realised with a jolt. Glowing

skin, doe eyes that were magnetic even when she glared. Her mouth was always slightly open, maybe because her front teeth were too big. He wanted to stare at her until he figured out the exact configuration of her every facial feature, but he wouldn't.

She was already uncomfortable; he could tell. Her gaze fluttered around him like a butterfly, hovering but never settling. Then again, from what he remembered, she always looked like that. Maybe she was just a nervous person.

Shifting his weight, Evan tried to look less... huge. It probably didn't work—there was no hiding 6 foot 3—but he tried anyway. "I really don't want to bother you," he said, putting the lasagne on her little kitchen table. "I can go."

She ignored that statement completely. "How long are you going to play personal chef?"

Something in her tone was different. Slightly lighter than usual. Evan looked up to find the hint of a smile on her lips.

That almost-smile triggered an odd sort of warmth in his chest, soft and gentle. He smiled back. "I don't know. Until I'm satisfied that you're not developing rickets over here."

"Are you always so meddlesome?"

He didn't even have to think about it. "Yes."

The kettle hissed, and she turned to open a nearby cupboard. It was mounted on the wall, and Ruth was so small, she had to rise up on her toes to grab the mugs.

When she turned back to face him, she rolled her eyes. Clearly, she did that a lot. "What are you smirking about?" she demanded.

"Nothing."

"Liar."

Like a fool, he blurted out, "You're little."

She snorted. "You're disgracefully tall. What's your point?"

"Disgracefully?"

"It's indecent," she said. "You can't possibly need all that height. One sugar or two?"

"Three."

She wrinkled her nose and repeated, "Indecent. Sit down."

Apparently, Ruth Kabbah did not make requests; she gave orders.

Evan was okay with that.

He sat and watched as she poured the tea, retrieved milk from the fridge and sugar from its container. She wasn't graceful. She was, in fact, the opposite of graceful. He worried for her safety once every five seconds at least. When she poured half of the hot water onto the counter, he was only surprised that she didn't scald herself in the process.

"You okay?" he asked as she snatched up a cloth.

She grumbled in response.

When the tea was finally ready, she brought it over to the table and sat across from him. Because the kitchen was tiny, and the table a little semi-circle, they were close. Close enough for him to feel the presence of her legs beneath the table—even though they weren't touching—with that odd, sixth sense people sometimes developed.

His mug was modelled to look like Spider Man's face. Hers looked like a face too, only it was jet-black—bar a few strategic silver lines.

Evan pointed at the cup. "Is that Black Panther?"

She squinted up at him. "What do you know about Black Panther?"

"I saw the film."

She shrugged. He wasn't sure what that meant.

"I liked it," he added, because for some odd reason, he wanted her to talk.

She said, "Good." Then she sipped her tea. Which had to be fucking scalding. Evan winced.

"You like comic books?" he said. Then he wanted to wince again, this time at himself. *You like comic books?* He'd already seen a hundred of them lying around the flat. She drank tea from superhero mugs. She was wearing pyjamas with the Hulk's face on them. *Yes,* she liked comic books.

The look she gave him was narrow and suspicious. "Why do you ask?"

"Just making conversation."

"If you're planning on reporting back to Daniel, don't bother. He already knows what I like."

That sentence seemed oddly phrased. Then again, most of her sentences seemed oddly phrased. Evan didn't understand this woman, not even a little bit—but something about her made him want to.

"You two don't get on," Evan said. He was full of scintillating conversation today.

"I suppose not," Ruth replied, her tone hollow.

"Is that why he called you slow?" It had bothered him, that word. *Slow.* Plenty of teachers had called him slow, because he wasn't particularly academic. It stuck in his teeth like grit.

Ruth set down her mug. "He called me slow because he thinks there's something wrong with my brain."

There was a pause. To save it from becoming awkward, Evan drank some tea. The liquid nearly burned his tongue, but she'd managed it, so he would too.

"Before you ask," she said, "there's nothing *wrong* with my brain."

Evan swallowed. "I wasn't going to—"

"I'm autistic."

He put his mug on the table. "Cool. I mean, you know—got it. Okay. Yeah."

Ruth took another gulp of tea, then got up to put the mug in the sink. She'd... finished it. She'd finished the tea. In less than two minutes. *Okay, then.*

She turned, folded her arms, and pinned him with a hard look. "Are you a serial killer?"

"Has it only just occurred to you that I might be?"

"Sadly, yes. I suppose it's too late for me now."

He laughed. Ruth didn't.

Instead, she continued, "You have to stop bringing me food."

Evan leaned back in his seat. The wooden chair creaked dangerously beneath his weight, but he didn't worry; he was used to that sort of thing. Sliding his hands behind his head, he met her gaze head on.

She looked away.

"Why?" he asked. "Does it make you uncomfortable?"

"No," she said firmly. Almost defiantly, her pointed chin lifting. He was struck again by how pretty she was. Which was strange. He didn't usually notice that sort of thing.

Clearing his throat, he asked, "Why, then?"

"I'm not a charity case or a child. I know how to feed myself."

Evan raised his brows. "So you can cook?'

He hadn't thought a person could glare so hard. If looks could kill, Ruth would be a weapon of mass destruction.

"No," she clipped out. "I can't."

"Is that why they took your oven?"

"*I* removed my oven," she corrected, "because I knocked some comics onto the hob and nearly burned down the flat. Plus, I lost twelve vintage *X-Men* issues." This last was muttered with bitter regret.

"So what do you eat, then? Aside from Supernoodles?"

"Toast," she said. "Scrambled eggs. Carrot sticks."

Evan stared. "It's like you're encouraging me."

"I beg your pardon?"

With a sigh, he stood. "Listen. I get what you're saying—I really do. But I already make food for... other people. So it's no trouble, especially when you're right next door. Also, I enjoy helping. And I really am worried about you."

She put a hand against her stomach and said, "Do I look malnourished?"

Evan shrugged. "I'm not a doctor. But, aside from anything else, the idea of you eating carrot sticks for dinner is frankly depressing."

She spluttered. "You can't—I don't—we don't even know each other!"

"Sure we do." Evan gave her his best smile. The one he usually saved for crotchety old ladies. Why he was using it to convince his neighbour that he should be allowed to bring her food on a regular basis, he had no fucking clue.

What am I doing right now?

Just go with it.

"That wall's so damned thin," he continued, "we might as well be best friends."

There was a pause, during which she seemed flummoxed. But then, with obvious reluctance, she said, "That's funny."

"Uh… thank you?"

"You're a good cook."

Evan's uncertainty faded with that clear compliment. He winked. "Wait 'til you try the lasagne."

She looked at the foil-covered dish on the table. He wasn't sure if she seemed eager, horrified, or perhaps some odd mixture of both.

Then she looked back at him and said, "You liked *Black Panther*?"

Evan blinked. That conversational boomerang had come around so suddenly, he felt slightly whiplashed. But still, he managed to gather his wits fairly quickly. "Yeah. I did."

"You into comics?"

"I read some when I was a kid," he said slowly. "But as I got older, things got…" He hesitated, unsure of how to explain his sudden transition from cheerful teenager to hardened adult. "Complicated," he finally managed. "Things got complicated. I guess I stopped."

She cocked her head, her eyes bright and dark. "We could make a deal, if you want."

"A deal?"

"You give me more of that shepherd's pie. I give you comic books."

Evan stilled. Something inside him celebrated, popping champagne as if she'd offered him the keys to the town.

He'd liked comics once upon a time, but the prospect of reading them again didn't really excite him.

What excited him was the fact that she appeared to be relenting.

Since when are you so eager to cook for random women?

He wanted to help, he reminded himself. She seemed lonely. He just wanted to help.

"Okay," he nodded. "That sounds like a deal."

"You can't keep them, though," she added hurriedly. "I'd just lend them to you. So you can read them. But you have to bring them back."

Evan held up his hands, unable to hide his grin. "Don't worry, little one. I won't steal your comics."

She shot him a glare. "Don't call me that."

"What about short stuff?"

"No."

"Sprite?"

"Fuck off."

He laughed, and her lips twitched slightly. She did this odd thing where the corners of her mouth lifted a millimetre, and her eyes sparkled, and her lips pursed, and she wasn't *technically* smiling—but she was.

Then the technically-not-a-smile disappeared. She said, "Stay there," with the sort of serious inflection he'd use to instruct a child.

Evan raised his brows. She ignored him, striding out of the kitchen—brushing so close to him as she passed, he caught her scent. It must've been hers. Chocolate and coconut. He had no idea why a woman who didn't cook would smell like dessert, but his nose was rarely wrong.

Maybe he should ask her.

Hey, I noticed you smell like chocolate. Mind telling me why?

Yeah, that would go down well. She wouldn't think he was a complete creep, or anything.

As suddenly as she'd left, Ruth returned. She thrust two slim, hard-backed books in his hands before saying flatly, "You can go."

Bemused, Evan looked down at the books. "These are—?"

"*Black Panther.* For the lasagne," she cut in. Her eyes were flat, her full lips pursed. Not in an almost-smiling way, though. She looked firm, severe. Her hands were clasped in front of her, so tight that her dark skin paled slightly.

She was nervous again.

"Alright," Evan said, trying his best to sound soothing. "I'm going now. Goodbye."

Ruth nodded, making no move to follow as he left the kitchen.

But, just as he opened her front door, he heard her voice.

"Thanks," she called. If he hadn't been listening, hoping she'd say something—*anything*—he might've missed the word.

"No problem," he called back.

Silence.

He left.

CHAPTER SEVEN

THREE DAYS after the Disastrous Lasagne Deal—as Ruth had christened it—she found herself standing on Evan Miller's doorstep.

She had no idea what she was doing.

Well, that wasn't entirely true. His enormous Pyrex dish was in her hands, its delicious contents having been finished earlier that day. Stacked beneath the dish were a few more comics for him to read.

But Ruth felt suddenly unsure of herself, despite the fact that this was the bargain they'd made. He probably didn't even like comics. He'd probably agreed to the deal because he just wanted to keep cooking for her.

And why *did* he want to keep cooking for her? So far, she had a few theories, none of which made her very happy.

The first was that, having heard of her reputation, he was on a mission to try the town bicycle for himself. The second option, that he was acting as some kind of spy for Daniel, trying to sniff out her weaknesses for a future,

54

unknown torture, wasn't much better. Her third suspicion was that Evan was actually a murderer and planned to slowly poison her under the guise of neighbourly good deeds.

Running through that list again made Ruth want to run back into her own flat. But it was too late for that; she'd already knocked. And since these flats only had two homes per floor, if she disappeared before he answered the door, he'd almost certainly come looking for her anyway.

With a sigh, Ruth awaited his arrival. A full minute passed in silence.

Perhaps, like her, he didn't always answer the door—but that seemed unlikely. Evan Miller was the sort of do-gooding, neighbour-of-the-year type that *always* answered the door, even if they were in the middle of something important. Like sex. For example.

Not that Evan was in there having sex. She'd already know if he was; she'd have heard him. Through the wall.

Unless he was really quiet.

Why in God's name was she thinking about this?

Without warning, the door finally opened. Ruth immediately remembered why her mind leapt to sex whenever it thought of Evan.

Dear Lord.

He'd been in the shower. It didn't take a genius to work that out. He wore nothing but a towel wrapped around his slim hips, one that fell to his knees—which was a shame. She'd have liked to see his thighs. Ruth loved thighs.

But she'd satisfy herself with what she could see, which was plenty. His golden skin glistened with tiny drops of water. They decorated his broad shoulders, his thick arms and solid torso, sliding over his tattoos. She rather liked those tattoos.

She'd thought about getting one herself, only the sound of the machine made her eyes blur. Clearly, Evan had no such problem, because the ink covering his arms adorned his chest, too—and those little drops of water gleamed over it all. Ruth imagined chasing the trails of moisture with her tongue.

Then Evan cleared his throat, and she snatched her gaze away.

For the first time, she focused on his face. Oh, dear. He was watching her with an expression she couldn't decipher, his brows raised.

"You done?" he asked, his voice low.

"Quite," she clipped out, absolutely mortified. She thrust the dish and comics forward, and promptly hit him in the stomach.

He didn't even wince. "Are you okay?"

"I'm fine." *I'm dying of embarrassment.*

Laughter laced his voice as he asked, "Is there something on my chest?"

Ruth ground her teeth. "Actually, there is *nothing* on your chest."

"Oh, I see. Is that why you're blushing?"

"I am *not* blushing," she gritted out. She was, but he had no way of knowing. Did he? "If you want to answer your door half-naked, that's fine by me. Town Jezebel, remember?"

"Yeah, I don't know about that." He folded his arms, leaning lazily against the doorframe. His posture was always so perfect that this new position seemed dangerously calculated. "Are you retired?" he asked. "Reformed, perhaps? It's just, you never seem to leave the house. So how are you—"

"I *do* leave the house," she snapped. "I leave the house every Sunday."

"Church?" he enquired mildly.

She glowered. "Sunday dinner. At my mother's."

"Ah," he said. "Sunday dinner with your mother. How scandalous."

"Will you take your bloody dish?"

He looked down at her—or rather, at the Pyrex dish she was waving. He seemed bigger than he had before, maybe because there were no clothes to hide the raw power of all that muscle. Ruth wasn't sure; she just knew the sight of him was making her mouth weirdly dry and her knees worryingly weak.

Beneath that thick, dirty-blonde beard, his lips curled into a slow smile. "Did you like the lasagne?"

"Yes," she ground out.

"And you're bringing me more comics, I see."

"*Yes.*"

"Do you want to know what I thought of the first ones?"

That brought her up short. *Did* she want to know?

Maybe. It hadn't occurred to her that he'd have any opinion to offer—which was ridiculous. Of course he'd have an opinion. Everyone had opinions.

But no-one ever seemed to have an opinion on the things *she* cared about—aside from, *"That's stupid"*. The only people in this town who wanted to debate comics were the kids at the local library, and Ruth hadn't volunteered there since... well. Since before.

But there was no use thinking about that now.

She studied Evan's soft smile, the clear, bright blue of his eyes. He was basically an overgrown Cub Scout with unreasonable muscle definition. He wouldn't be cruel to her, would he?

Probably, her mind said.

She ignored it. "Okay."

He stepped back, opening the door completely, and said, "Come in."

Oh. *Oh.* She hadn't expected that.

Ruth couldn't back down, and she couldn't show weakness. Especially not *her* weakness, the sort that other people didn't understand. If she said, *Oh, I thought you were suggesting that we talk in the future, and I planned to prepare for that interaction in advance because I have to plan most conversations very carefully so that I don't freak other people out...* Well, he'd probably be freaked out.

So she walked into his flat and tried not to jump as he shut the door behind them.

Evan led her into a living room that was the mirror image of her own—but much tidier and better decorated. He said, "Hang on; I'll be back in a second." Then he disappeared down the hall, hopefully to get dressed.

Because as much as she enjoyed staring at his near-nudity, it wouldn't help her a bit when it came to decent conversation.

Ruth put the dish and the comics down on his low, glass coffee table, staring at the flat screen TV mounted on the wall. She didn't have a TV. She only ever watched Netflix on her laptop.

For the first time in a while, she realised how strange she must seem.

This was one of the many, many reasons she didn't talk to other people. Why she stayed in the house and only called her sister or her mother. Being around people who were supposedly 'normal' made her feel *abnormal*.

She'd never had that problem before. Her life was split in two like that: before versus after.

"You're my sweet little weirdo, aren't you Ruthie? God, I love you."

"You hungry?"

Her heart almost leapt out of her chest. She came back to the present, staring blankly at the man in the doorway. Evan. He was, tragically, completely clothed.

"No," she said. "I'm not."

"You sure?"

Ruth stared. "Are you a feeder?"

Evan wandered over to her with a slight frown marring his pretty face. He sat down beside her, and even though the sofa was big enough for three, she felt slightly panicked.

Too close. She wouldn't mind, if she didn't know she'd end up embarrassing herself somehow.

"What's a feeder?" he asked.

"Someone who has a fetish involving... you know, feeding people. Feeding fat people."

He looked down at her, his eyes running over her body, achingly slow. Ruth swallowed.

Then he looked up at her face again and said, "I'm not a feeder. Are you wearing pyjamas?"

"I always wear pyjamas."

"Why?"

Ruth felt her cheeks heat. "I just do," she muttered.

"What if you went out somewhere? Say, on a date. Would you wear pyjamas?"

"I don't go on dates," Ruth said.

He smiled again. "You're not good at this 'Jezebel' thing."

"Ask your friends how good I am."

Evan cocked his head. "Are you trying to put me off?"

"Put you off what?"

He studied her for a moment, his eyes boring into her face. His gaze was a living, breathing thing, and she was suffocating beneath it.

Not necessarily in a bad way.

Eventually he said, "Don't worry about it."

She had no idea what he meant, but she was used to that. He probably wasn't making fun of her. In fact, she was almost sure he wasn't.

Which was odd. Ruth was rarely sure, when it came to that kind of thing.

He produced the comics she'd given him the last time they spoke, holding one in each hand.

"These were good," he said. "I mean, a good place to start, for someone as ignorant as me. They seemed to follow on from the film."

"Kind of," she nodded, "but the MCU often differs from the comic books in multiple ways, for commercial reasons."

"MCU?" He arched one thick, blond brow. She liked it when he did that, which was a disturbing realisation.

Looking down at her hands, Ruth explained, "MCU: Marvel Cinematic Universe. There are lots of different timelines and realities when it comes to this sort of thing, and it's good to know and separate them. Otherwise you open a book expected T'Challa and Storm to be estranged, only to find they actually have a son."

"Huh." Evan blinked down at the comic books. "Sounds like some soap opera shit."

"Of course. Comics are very dramatic."

"They're kind of... very *everything*, aren't they?" he asked.

"There's drama, comedy, tragedy—"

"Everything!" Ruth echoed. Her voice was louder, more excited than she'd meant it to be. *Oops.* Toning it down slightly, she went on. "That's exactly it. That's why I love them so much."

He grinned. "I get it."

And it quickly became apparent that he really, truly did. They spoke for ages about the comics he'd read, and then he spent even longer trying to trick spoilers out of her. He failed, of course. Ruth Kabbah was no fool.

At least, she didn't like to think she was.

Eventually, when the window showed the orange glow of streetlights instead of the afternoon sun, Ruth pulled herself back into the real world.

"I should go," she said, cutting off Evan's speech about the upcoming *Avengers* film. She'd pulled up the trailer on her phone—and now, of course, he was full of opinions and questions.

But she couldn't stay to hear them.

He frowned. "You're leaving? Already?"

Ruth checked the time. "I've been here for over three hours."

He looked astonished. *"Three hours?"*

"Yes. I should go."

"Wait—" As she stood, he reached out to grab her wrist.

His long fingers pressed firmly against her skin, hot as a brand. Ruth choked down a gasp at the sudden, unfamiliar sensation.

He heard. Instantly, he let go. "I'm sorry. I didn't mean to—"

"It's fine," she said quickly. It took all of her willpower not to look down at her wrist, not to cradle it against her chest as though he'd hurt her. He hadn't hurt her.

He'd scared her. Because, with just a touch, he'd set her alight. That had happened once before, and it had been bad news.

Evan stood too, towering over her. For the first time, his expression betrayed something other than confidence. He seemed uncertain, confused.

"Well," he said, his voice gentle. "I'll... see you tomorrow?"

She shook her head. "It's Sunday. I'm going to my mother's."

"Oh." He nodded slightly. "But I'll see you soon. Right?"

"I don't know."

"Ruth." He didn't touch her again, but he did move slightly in front of her. Not enough to block her way; just enough to make her look at him, whether she wanted to or not. "I like talking to you," he said. "I'd like to keep doing this. Like... a book club. Would you like that?"

Ruth swallowed, hard, under the force of his gaze. It was so gentle, and yet it seemed so intense. It was strange; she'd always expected his beauty to be the most dangerous thing about him, but it wasn't his handsome face or strong body that compelled her to nod.

It was his kindness.

"Good," he said softly. He smiled, as if he were actually, truly happy about the prospect of doing this again. Sitting around talking comics with a neighbour he barely knew.

Maybe there was something wrong with him.

That would probably make him perfect for her.

"I'm leaving," she said, and left. Instead of stopping her, or trying to tease out a proper goodbye, he simply followed her to the front door. He unlocked it for her, held it open. Stood in the doorway and watched as she opened her own.

"I'll see you," he said.

She shrugged and went inside.

Then she hovered in the front hall, her hand against the paper-thin wall that connected them. After a few, long minutes, she heard his door shut too.

Ruth decided that the next time she saw Evan Miller, she would wear her best pyjamas.

CHAPTER EIGHT

IT WAS Zach who invited Evan over on Sunday—but Evan spent most of his time talking to Shirley.

He perched on a stool by the older woman's bed, where she lay propped against a mountain of pillows.

Zach leant in the doorway of her bedroom, his arms folded, a teasing smile on his face.

"You got designs on my mother, Miller?"

Evan gave Shirley a wink. "Maybe. But I doubt she'd have me."

Zach barked out a laugh. Shirley chuckled along too, clutching at her chest as though it was the funniest thing she'd heard all week.

Her amusement was real. Zach's was hollow. There was too much worry beneath his smile, too much force behind his joviality. While Shirley laughed, Zach looked at his mother with so much hopeless love in his eyes, Evan felt his own heart twist.

He met Zach's gaze. Hoped the message was clear. *Go somewhere. Do something. Try to breathe.*

Zach nodded slightly. "Tea, Mum?"

"Oh, yes, please, my darling."

"Evan?"

"Cheers."

Zach left, and Evan hoped he'd take a minute, or even a second, to calm down. To occupy his mind with something other than concern and heavy dread. He knew from experience, though, that it wasn't easy.

"So," Shirley said, flicking the tail of her silk scarf over her shoulder. "How have you been, sweetheart?"

Her crooked smile was a feminine twin of Zach's. Evan returned it with ease. Shirley, as he'd discovered the previous week, was a fun time.

"I'm good, Shirl. What about you? Any luck with the nurse?"

Shirley winked. "She's playing hard to get."

"Don't give up."

She leaned forward slightly, her arm outstretched. He realised with a start that she was reaching for him, for the hand resting against his thigh. So he gave it to her, and was surprised when her thin, pale fingers clutched his firmly.

"I hope you're doing well," she said, with a gravity that he didn't quite understand. "Zach was telling me about you the other day. He said you met a couple of weeks ago."

"That's right," Evan said slowly. "I moved to Ravenswood at the end of February."

"I've known the people in this town for years," she said. "Zach's had the same friends since he was at school. And since my diagnosis, we've heard nothing from any of them."

Evan swallowed. He remembered that part well. Remembered people who were a backdrop in his life disappearing one by one, just as he needed them most, proving how alone he and his mother really were. At the worst possible time.

Then Shirley patted his hand. "But here you are—a man he's known five minutes—bringing me lasagne and letting me talk rubbish in your ear." She eyed him closely. "You're a good person, Evan Miller."

"I'm nothing special," he said. "I just... I treat people how I'd want to be treated. And Zach's a good guy."

"He is. I'm very proud of him." A slight smile curved her lips, her eyes hovering toward the door. Then she turned their watery blue back to Evan. "And I'm pleased that he's made a friend like you. Zach has been playing a certain role for far too long. He needs someone to help him get out of it."

Evan shifted. "I'm not sure what you mean."

"You'll see." She smiled. "You're very caring. Caring people are observant." Then, as suddenly as she'd taken it, Shirley released his hand. "Now, then," she said brightly. "Never mind my nurse troubles. Have you found anyone interesting in our little corner of the world?"

"Aside from you, you mean?" Evan winked.

"Oh, stop it. I'm immune to your charms, Mr. Miller. You get yourself a nice young thing to run around with."

Evan's mind flew to Ruth without hesitation. He wondered how she'd feel about the fact that, in his head, she was apparently a *nice young thing*.

She'd probably push him in front of lorry.

The thought, perversely, made him smile.

~

EVAN HADN'T COME over on Monday.

Which was *fine*. Microwaved Chicago Town pizzas had fed Ruth well, and they'd do the same tonight.

She was trying her best to convince herself of this utter falsehood when she heard the familiar heave of 1B's front door. It had already opened and shut once this evening, making her jump out of her skin, but Evan had not appeared.

Now she held her breath and fiddled with her pizza box and tried to pretend that she wasn't waiting for him to knock.

He knocked.

She, of course, dropped the pizza.

When Ruth finally made it to the door, she found Evan waiting with two huge, steaming bowls instead of his trusty Pyrex dish.

"Hi," he said.

She ignored his greeting and got to the point, nodding toward one of the bowls. "Is that for me?"

"It is." He smiled, and she ignored that too. Or rather, she ignored the hysterical flip it triggered in her tummy. How embarrassing.

"What is it?" she asked.

"Just Bolognese. If you hadn't noticed, I'm not a very exciting cook."

Ruth didn't bother to explain that she could not stand exciting food. "Is that one for you?"

He looked over at the second bowl of pasta, his smile

fading. "Yeah. Huh. I don't know why I dragged it over here."

"What rubbish. You're trying to worm your way back into my house."

He grinned. "Okay, I suppose I am."

"Well, come on." Ruth knew very well that her voice was flat and that her face, according to most people, was blank.

But internally, her nerves were a mess, like multiple pairs of earbuds shoved into the same coat pocket. She didn't know where one feeling ended and the other began, or how to disentangle them; all she knew was that anxiety and hesitant pleasure and anticipation coiled around each other in her gut, and altogether, they made her feel slightly sick.

In a good way. Kind of. She wasn't sure.

They sat down at her tiny kitchen table wordlessly, and she provided both cutlery and glasses of water. If he wanted anything else, he was shit out of luck. She didn't *have* anything else.

Except tea. She'd forgotten to offer him tea. Was it too late to mention? She wasn't entirely sure. Once she managed to knock herself off the socially acceptable path, Ruth could never figure out how to climb back on again.

"So," Evan asked. "What do you do?"

Was it worrying that she'd been hoping he'd seek her out? That he'd come over, and they'd spend time together again, as soon as humanly possible?

Probably.

"Ruth?" he said again.

This time, the words penetrated, soaking into her brain like oil into muslin.

"I... I produce a web comic," she said, twisting pasta around her fork. She usually avoided this topic, but the words came out before she could think to control them.

"A web comic?" A slow smile spread across his face. "I can't say I'm surprised."

This should be a safe conversation. It was one of the topics on her list of Acceptable Things to Say: *What do you do?* Along with, *Where are you from?* and, *How's the family?* If they'd met in the ordinary way, she'd have asked those things immediately instead of blathering on about nonsense.

For some reason, with Evan, she didn't feel as much pressure to use her list. She didn't feel a need to waste energy on trying to seem acceptable—but she didn't do her best to seem outrageous, either. On Saturday, their conversation had meandered from the ridiculous to the impossible and back again.

She didn't want to think about what that meant.

Instead of chasing his comment about her work, she said, "What do you do?"

He scooped up some Bolognese. "I'm a blacksmith. I work for Burne & Co."

Ruth almost choked on her pasta.

Evan noticed, too. Of course he noticed. He'd already figured out that she was, in a word, clumsy, and now he watched her like a hawk. It had all started when she told him about burning her comic books. Or, as everyone else called it, setting the kitchen on fire.

Now he pushed a glass of water toward her, clearly concerned. Ruth glared as she took a sip, the cool fluid soothing her raw throat. Glares were her most common expression of thanks.

"You okay?" he asked.

"Burne & Co., hm?" she shot back. She hadn't meant to sound quite so bitter, quite so accusatory, but her tone was searing.

She took another sip of water. *Oops.*

Evan frowned. "Um... yeah. Why?"

She ignored the question and studied his face, searching for the clues she must have missed. The sly judgement, the hidden disdain.

She didn't find anything incriminating, because she was rubbish at that sort of thing. Evan stared back at her, and all she gained from the uncomfortable eye contact was unwelcome arousal. He really was gorgeous. It was quite inconvenient.

"That explains why you were with Daniel Burne," she finally said. Clearly, she'd have to rely on words here.

"Well, yeah," he replied. "It's not like I spend time with him voluntarily."

Ruth took a moment to digest that. "Hmph," she grunted, aware that she sounded like a grumpy old woman. To move the conversation on, she added, "So you're a blacksmith. Is that what you did in the army?"

His brows flew up. Mission accomplished. "How'd you know I was in the army?" he asked.

The truth was that she'd stalked his social media through her friend Marjaana's account—since Ruth didn't have Facebook. But that would sound incredibly odd, so she lied. "It was your speech about Captain America on Saturday. You're a complete fanboy."

Evan smirked. "That doesn't mean I was in the army."

"There's honestly no other reason for anyone to like Captain America." Which was true. "Unless you think he's hot."

"Well, I don't think he's hot."

"He kind of looks like you."

Evan's eyes lit up. "Do *you* think he's hot?"

Ruth froze, her fork halfway on its journey to her mouth. "I..." Her mind rushed to process what, exactly, had just happened. It failed, probably because it was trying so hard. So she blurted out, "Yes. I do."

For a moment, Evan's eyes seemed to darken. He leaned forward, and Ruth licked her lips. She was suddenly hyper-conscious of her breathing—or rather, the rise and fall of her own chest.

Which was a bad sign.

But then, just as quickly, the crackling tension in Evan's eyes seemed to fade. He sat back in his chair and said, "Well, you're right. I was in the army. But that's not why I like Captain America."

Relief flooding her, Ruth stuffed a mouthful of pasta into her gob and mumbled, "Why then?"

Evan put down his fork, looking thoughtful. "I don't know. He seems very... noble. Is that the right word?"

"He's an annoying do-gooder."

"You're a very harsh woman." He said it almost... fondly. A smile tilted his lips.

Ruth reminded herself that harsh women were not to anyone's taste and took another bite of pasta.

CHAPTER NINE

WHEN THEY WERE DONE, Ruth grabbed the plates and took them both to the sink. She turned the taps on as high as they'd go, and watched the water rise over the dirty dishes, and tried to convince herself that she could not feel Evan staring at her.

That would be ridiculous.

To prove it, she took a peek over her shoulder at him. Just a little one, she told herself, to quiet her rambling mind. To prove to herself that, just because he was awfully attractive and funny and sweet, and he seemed to like spending time with her, didn't mean this was a... *thing*.

She found him lounging in her tiny kitchen chair, watching her with almost painful intensity.

Oh.

When he arched a brow, his lips curving slowly into a smile, Ruth realised that her little peek had become a very long look. Her cheeks heating, she turned back to the sink.

Step one of washing dishes: water. What was step two,

again? She couldn't remember. Every time she tried to get her mind in order, she was assaulted with images of Evan. Evan's long legs spread wide, his thighs straining beneath his jeans, tattooed arms folded over his chest. Right behind her. Shit.

"The way you look at me sometimes," he said. His voice was low. She shouldn't have heard him over the running taps, and yet the deep rumble seemed to vibrate in her belly.

And between her legs.

"I'm not sure what you mean," she said, turning off the stream of water.

"Really?" There was something in his voice that might've been humour if it hadn't been so heavy. "The day we met, you looked at me like you'd never seen a man before."

Because I'd never seen a man like you. "That was shock, actually. You know, because I fell." She was impressed with the steadiness of her own voice. Her own lying voice.

"And Saturday?"

Ruth swallowed. "I don't know why you're fishing for compliments. You must know that, objectively speaking, you're very attractive."

She heard the scrape of chair legs against lino, heard his familiar tread as he crossed the narrow space. "Maybe. But I'm trying to figure out your opinion on the matter."

She knew, somehow, that he would touch her.

When he did, it was better than she'd expected.

His chest pressed firmly against her back, the heat of his body surrounding her. He put his hands against the counter in front of them, bracketing Ruth with hard, warm muscle. "You see," he said, his tone conversational, "sometimes I think I can read you. Then something happens, and I realise I can't. Not completely. Not yet."

Ruth shivered.

He leaned in even closer, bending down until his mouth brushed her ear. "So why don't you tell me, Ruth? Tell me what's going on inside your head."

She couldn't speak. She also couldn't help herself. Ruth raised a hand, reached back until her fingers slid into his hair, felt the curve of his skull, pulled him closer, and wondered what the fuck she was doing.

Then she let her head fall to the side, exposing the line of her neck. A moment later, she felt his breath whisper over the sensitive skin of her throat.

Ah. *That's* what she was doing.

Oh, dear.

Evan kissed her neck, his mouth soft and hot and everything she'd ever needed. Ruth's knees might have buckled if she hadn't been ready, completely ready, to feel this level of ecstasy at his touch.

"I'm sorry," he murmured. "I'm usually much better than this." His hands came to rest on her hips, sliding under the hem of her pyjama top.

"Better?" she echoed faintly. His fingers traced circles over the sensitive skin of her belly, and she moaned. Heat flooded her pussy, zipping up to her nipples.

"Better at controlling myself." His tongue slid over her pulse, and then, lightly, he bit. "I don't know what I'm doing. We barely know each other."

Ruth arched against him, pressure building deep inside her core. "You've never slept with someone you barely know?"

"No. I couldn't sleep with you yet. It wouldn't be gentlemanly."

Of all those nonsensical words, *yet* was the one that caught her attention.

It had never occurred to her, while she was drooling over his unreasonable hotness, that he might somehow find her attractive. Why had that never occurred to her?

"They all think you're ugly. But I know you're beautiful, Ruth."

She pushed the memory away. It wasn't even hard. Not when one of Evan's hands slid away from her hips, down toward the apex of her thighs. His palm flattened against her cotton-covered mound and he pushed her more firmly against him. The thick column of his erection pressed into her lower back.

"Jesus, Evan," she breathed. At the feel of that insistent length, a pulse of energy rocketed to her clit. Her stomach tightened. She hadn't felt like this in so long. She hadn't deserved it. She wasn't sure if she deserved it now.

He laughed, but it wasn't a laugh she recognised. It was low and dark and sent a thrill up her spine. "Do you like this, love?" He pressed the heel of his palm against her clit, the pressure delicious even through her clothes. "Tell me."

Ah.

Just like that, the blazing purity of pleasure drained away. The reality of who Ruth was—*how* Ruth was— crushed her the way pianos crush cartoon characters: she was still breathing, somehow, but she shouldn't have been.

Ruth absolutely could not *tell him* anything. Anything at all.

Swallowing down her sudden panic, she said, "We should stop."

In a breath, he went from surrounding her to disappearing. She felt suddenly cold, suddenly alone, without his arms around her.

But that, she reminded herself, was the safest way to feel.

"Are you okay?" Evan asked softly.

Hesitant, she turned to face him. His cheeks were flushed, his eyes heavy-lidded, his lips parted. Beautiful. Still, she saw apology written over his face. He folded his hands in front of his waist, and she wondered if he meant to hide the bulge straining against his jeans or draw attention to it.

"I'm fine," she said.

"You don't seem fine."

Ruth didn't know what to say to that.

After a pause, he said, "I'm... I'm sorry, Ruth."

"You don't need to be sorry—"

"But I am. I shouldn't have done that." He cleared his throat. His posture was perfect as ever, almost painfully stiff.

Almost, her mind thought feverishly, as stiff as his—

"I didn't come over here to... to harass you," he said. "I just wanted to see you. I hope you believe that."

She licked her lips and nodded. She had no idea what, exactly, was happening here, but it seemed polite to let him finish.

"I very much enjoy spending time with you," he said. "I hope you might consider me a friend."

"I do."

That, at least, drew the ghost of a smile from his lips.

"Good," he said, almost to himself. "Good. I... I'd understand if you didn't want me to come over anymore."

"But I do," she said firmly. "I *do* want you to come over."

She should be grateful, really. He was saying all the things that should be coming out of her mouth, as if following a script. So why was she arguing?

His gaze was intense. "Are you sure?"

"Yes," she practically cried. "I'm sure."

"Okay." He gave her a short nod. "Well... I'll be going, then."

"Alright."

"Alright."

For a second, they stared at each other across the kitchen. She could still feel the rasp of his fingertips against her belly, could still feel the pressure of his palm against her clit. She tried to make herself forget—she was good at forgetting—but found that she could not.

When he finally walked out of the kitchen, she sagged against the counter in relief.

And when he came over the next day, and the next, she told herself that talking and joking and never, ever touching was absolutely fine.

CHAPTER TEN

"Evan! You going out?"

Yes. To avoid you.

Evan pulled his face into something that wasn't quite a smile, but at least didn't feel like a scowl. Then he turned to Daniel Burne and said, "Yep."

"I'll join you." Daniel fell into step with Evan as they pushed out of the forge's double doors. "Need to pick up some fags."

Great. So they'd head to the newsagents together and make stiff, forced conversation that made Evan want to stab himself in the gut.

Usually, he liked to talk. Just not with Daniel Burne.

"So," Daniel began.

That short, sharp word was all it took to set Evan on his guard. He shot a glance over at Daniel and found the other man a picture of calm, looking straight ahead, nodding politely to passers-by.

"So," Evan echoed.

"You meet your neighbour?"

Evan clenched his jaw. He remembered the way Ruth had felt against him three days ago and said, "Yeah. I met my neighbour."

Daniel was quiet for a moment. Then he said, "Nice guy?"

Evan sighed. "Do you think you're being subtle?"

"I beg your pardon?"

"You want to know if Ruth is my neighbour. Just ask."

Daniel gave a rueful smile. "I suppose that right there is my answer."

"I suppose it is."

There was a brief, blessed pause. During that pause, Evan allowed himself to hope that the conversation would now be over.

He was, of course, disappointed.

"I hope you didn't judge me too harshly, the other day," Daniel said. "It's just, I've known her a long time, and we… we don't get along."

Evan failed to see how anyone could not get along with Ruth. Yes; she was prickly and awkward and blunt to a fault. She was also adorably excitable, unapologetically passionate, and secretly, achingly, shy. But then, a man like Daniel would respond poorly to a woman like Ruth. He seemed to expect instant adoration, and Ruth wasn't capable of that.

Evan liked her wariness. It made every inch of her trust a reward.

And you almost ruined that by throwing yourself at her. As if you've never known a beautiful woman before.

He pushed that thought away, because it was woefully incomplete. Ruth was not just a beautiful woman. She was the woman who'd made him want so badly, and with so little effort, that he'd completely lost control.

"You'll find out eventually," Daniel said. Apparently, he took Evan's silence as a cue to continue.

"Find out what?" Evan asked. He wasn't remotely interested in anything Daniel had to say, and yet, his upbringing would only allow so much rudeness. He was closely reaching his personal threshold.

"How she is." Daniel paused to greet a pair of older men in flat caps, his smile wide and genuine. He introduced Evan with grace and charm, and Evan wondered how the man who had been so cruel to Ruth could seem so thoroughly... decent.

They went on, the newsagent in view now, but their pace so meandering that it might take another five minutes to reach.

"We were at school together," Daniel continued, as if the conversation had never stopped. For someone who didn't like Ruth, he really liked to talk about Ruth. "I'm older than her, but... she lost all her friends, you know." Daniel paused. "She destroys relationships."

Evan pushed down his rising temper. "I don't think that's any of my business. Or yours."

"I'm just warning you. If you want a girl in this town, you won't get one with Ruth sniffing around. All the women in Ravenswood know what she is."

"Good thing I don't want a girl."

Daniel gave him a sideways, knowing look. "Because you want Ruth, right? I get it. She's kind of cute, in her own little way. But I don't want to see you get hurt."

It was funny, because Evan had been thinking that, too.

Not about himself, but about Ruth. He didn't want to see her get hurt. He'd touched her because he wanted to, in the way his body *wanted* to draw breath. And then something had changed. Some odd tension had fallen over the room, and she'd stopped him, and he'd been struck with dread at the thought that he might've done something wrong. He did not want to see Ruth get hurt.

"You don't need to worry about me," he said.

Daniel nodded sympathetically, falling into a silence that lasted until they reached the newsagent. If Evan was watching this interaction from afar, he might think that Daniel really meant well.

He was like a seller at the market, Evan decided, turning bad fruit over so shoppers couldn't see the mould.

Mrs. Needham, proprietor of Needham's Newsagent, was one of those who didn't see the mould. She cooed like a demented dove when Daniel stepped through her door, and Evan's presence only seemed to magnify her excitement.

The woman bustled out from behind the counter, throwing her hands in the air as if she'd found a long-lost son. "Daniel!" she trilled, reaching up to pat his cheeks. "How *are* you?"

"I'm very well, thank you, Beverly. Have you met my friend Evan?"

"Oh, yes!" Mrs. Needham turned her watery, blue eyes to Evan. "Our newcomer! I'd never forget a face so handsome!"

Of course, the few times Evan had come in here alone, Mrs. Needham had barely said a word—except to warn him about the shop's 360 CCTV. But Evan dredged up a smile anyway, as if they really were friendly. He'd never embarrass a lady.

He'd love to embarrass Daniel, though. Every time he saw such an awful man treated like royalty, the injustice of it gnawed at Evan's gut.

Another old woman appeared in the doorway behind the counter, apparently emerging from the shop's backroom. She had an armful of Kit Kat boxes, but she set them aside as soon as she set eyes on Daniel.

"Well, good afternoon, darling!" she cried, pulling off her silver spectacles. Brushing her hands on the front of her linen trousers, she shuffled out from behind the counter, too.

Resigned to a long and effusive visit, Evan floated off toward the magazine rack.

There were kids' magazines lining the bottom shelves; they screamed about Disney Princesses or Charlie and Lola. One featured the face of a disturbing cartoon pig. Evan skimmed past those to the next shelf, which was filled with what appeared to be American gossip magazines.

He stared for a moment, frowning at the incongruous row of paper rags, their front pages splashed with headlines and images more audacious than anything he'd ever seen.

"Oh, you've found our imported stock."

He jumped slightly and turned to find Mrs. Needham standing beside him. Apparently, he was more than worthy of attention now. Or perhaps she was just making sure he didn't intend to steal anything.

"These are from the U.S., right?" he asked.

Mrs. Needham nodded. "Strange, I know. Daniel's wife, Laura, started requesting a few, and next thing we knew, all the town's girls were buying them! We have a regular shipment, now." She looked proud as punch. "It's expensive sometimes, but Laura's always happy to buy up any extra. The Burnes are such a help to this town."

Ah. That explained Daniel's warm welcome.

"I'm sure that's not what you want, though." She peered up at him, and Evan realised that she was right. He'd come over to the magazine stand looking for something specific.

He wanted to see if they had any comics. For Ruth.

Before he could open his mouth to say as much, Mrs. Needham plucked a magazine from the middle rack. "This is very popular with our menfolk," she said conspiratorially. The glossy magazine read, CLASSIC CARS. "I think we even had one of those, around here," Mrs. Needham murmured, tapping the little green car on the front cover. A frown creased her wrinkled brow.

"I'm not much of a car guy," Evan admitted.

She shook her head, as if to displace a buzzing fly. "Nonsense. Here, Daniel, darling." Waving the magazine over at the counter, where Daniel stood, she said, "Didn't you have a car like this?"

Daniel squinted at the image. "Not exactly," he said, his voice slow. "That's a Lancia Flaminia GT."

"Oh." Mrs. Needham pouted. It was an... interesting look, on a woman her age. "But you know the one I mean, don't you?"

"Oh, yes," Daniel said. And his gaze settled firmly, strangely, on Evan.

"The green one," Mrs. Needham prompted, as if he hadn't said yes.

"That's it." Daniel's green eyes seemed to burn into Evan's skin.

Mrs. Needham added, "The one that Kabbah girl smashed to pieces."

Evan turned and walked out of the shop.

"Sir?" he heard the other woman call after him. "Sir? Are you alright?"

He ignored them.

Evan had a rule when it came to other people's business. He tried not to pick it up anywhere but the horse's mouth. Of course, in a town like this, people fell over themselves to pour gossip into the ears of strangers.

Which Daniel clearly fucking loved.

Evan walked fast, his heart pounding. He didn't know why, but he was certain that if Daniel came after him right now, he'd lose it.

In fact, he did know why. He knew exactly why. He thought about the hours he'd spent with Ruth the other day, about how simply and passionately she'd answered all his questions, about how eager she was to talk about comics, of all things. She was a sweetheart, even with all her grumbling and awkwardness and short, sharp words.

He'd wanted to befriend her, but that wasn't all he wanted. Not anymore. Not at all.

Evan wasn't exactly surprised to realise that his feet were taking him to the town's car park. He watched the slab of tarmac draw closer as he walked, almost dreamlike. It was the one place in town guaranteed to be busy; the council hadn't added more spaces as Ravenswood grew, so finding a bay was always a battle. Nevertheless, Evan reached the place where he and Ruth had first met without any difficulty.

Apparently, even the cars circling like slow vultures,

looking for spaces, didn't want to mess with Evan Miller just then.

He looked down at the hard ground where Ruth had fallen. He wasn't sure he was in precisely the right space, but it seemed right; a few feet from the leafy central reservoir, in line with the town's library across the street. Evan stared at the innocuous space, that mundane piece of the world whose significance only he knew.

There was no-one else who would look at that spot and think about hypnotic, angry eyes; no-one else who would see a hard-won smile or a perilous stack of comic books. Even Daniel fucking Burne wouldn't see that.

Or would he?

I'm the town Jezebel.

Evan shook his head, dislodging the thought. It didn't matter. What mattered was that standing here, thinking about Ruth, sent a familiar warmth surging through his blood.

He had no idea what had happened the other day. Well, that wasn't true; he knew very well that he'd lost control, moved too fast, and generally fucked up. When he thought about the way she'd looked, the way she'd touched him, the silk of her skin beneath his lips...

Jesus.

But that part didn't matter to anyone but Evan and his cock. The thing that mattered was the fact she'd pulled away.

He'd been trying to figure out, these past few days, if she'd meant *Not now* or *Not like this* or *Not ever*. If she wasn't so fucking... *Ruth*, he'd just ask her. But he had a feeling, if he did anything so blunt, she'd avoid him for the rest of their lives.

She didn't trust him. Not entirely. But something inside him was desperate to prove that she could.

With a sigh, Evan ran a hand over his face and turned away. If he wanted a chance to eat lunch, he needed to go back to work.

He jammed his hands into his pockets as his mind ran through possibilities, memories, fantasies. The fantasies were the worst part. He'd imagine Ruth smiling as she opened the door to him, not just because she wanted to eat or to talk, but because she wanted *him*. He imagined her touching him, not the way she had a few days ago, but the way a partner would. Casually, pointlessly, simply because she couldn't stop herself.

Something about her made him hunger and thirst like an unnatural creature, as if she were more than addictive—as if she were vital. And yet, she was so fragile. The friendship they'd built would be so easy to shatter, if he pushed. He knew it.

So he wouldn't push. He'd make his own position clear—not with words, because she'd hate that, but in any way he could. And then he'd let her do the rest. If she wanted him, eventually, she'd show it.

It wasn't a solution, but then, Ruth wasn't a problem.

Plus, it helped to have his feelings clearly labelled in his mind. He wanted her. He'd take her any way he could, and if that meant waiting a thousand years for her to trust him, he'd do it. And if he was mistaken and she didn't want him at all, well, he'd think about that some other time.

He headed back to Burne & Co. and found Daniel hovering by the doors.

"Hey," Daniel began. He moved forward with an apologetic look on his handsome, shitty face. "I'm sorry if—"

"It's fine," Evan said, walking past him.

"It's just, I know it must be a shock." Daniel hurried after him, voice painfully earnest. "And I know you like her."

"Daniel." Evan turned, looking the other man in the face, keeping his own carefully blank. "I said, it's fine."

Daniel studied him for a moment, green gaze clashing with blue. Then he shrugged and said, "Alright, mate." From the sympathetic look on his face, he clearly assumed that Evan's eyes had been opened. That he'd seen Ravenswood's collective light and decided to avoid 'that Kabbah girl'.

Nothing could be more wrong.

CHAPTER ELEVEN

"You can go now." Ruth said the words because, if she didn't, she might do something foolish.

But Evan looked up at her with a smile that seemed to encourage foolishness. It was too sexy, too sharp, too pointedly knowing, to be accidental.

Wasn't it?

She didn't know. She'd been asking herself those sorts of questions all evening, ever since he'd come over with dinner, and she still wasn't sure of the answer.

"If you want," he said.

She shrugged and held out the comic they'd been discussing. "This is for you."

"You know," he said, "it's Friday night. Not that late, either. Maybe we could go somewhere."

Go somewhere? What the hell did that mean?

Carefully, she said, "I don't go out on Fridays."

"That's usually the day people *do* go out."

"Exactly." She waved the comic at him, and he finally reached out to take it.

Except, instead of taking the end held out to him, he reached higher. His fingers closed around the plastic sleeve protecting the cover, perilously close to hers. So close that his thumb brushed over her knuckles.

Accidentally, she told herself, even as her mouth dried and her breasts tingled and the steady ache between her legs sharpened. It had been an accident.

Dragging her gaze away from the sight of their touching hands, she said, "Goodnight."

He gave her an unreadable look. "Goodnight, love."

When he was gone, Ruth grabbed her phone and fell into bed. As usual, the bed frame creaked ominously. As usual, she ignored it.

She'd been mid-conversation with Marjaana when Evan had arrived and, because she was an awful person, she'd kind of abandoned her best friend in the whole world to talk comics with her next-door-neighbour.

In all fairness, Marjaana lived a thousand miles away— or however far it was to Finland—and they were each used to the other disappearing mid-chat. Such was the nature of internet friendship.

Marjaana: Where'd you go? Do you have deadlines n shit?

Ruth: Yeah

Marjaana: ...

Marjaana: I'm gonna call you

Ruth: Please don't call me

Marjaana: AHA! You are hiding something

Ruth: Suck a toe

Marjaana: Tell me.

Ruth stared at the phone. Surely one of the upsides of being an anti-social shut-in was *not* having people interrogate her about things?

And yet, if it wasn't her sister, it was Marjaana. If it wasn't Marjaana, it was...

Evan. Her *friend*. Her friend who had come over for dinner every day that week and kept his hands completely to himself.

The snot.

Ruth knew that she would regret it, but still, she typed out the words.

Ruth: Maybe you *should* call me.

It took all of five seconds for the video call to come through.

"Jesus," Marjaana said, blinking rapidly. As always, she was flawlessly made up, and her false lashes waved like exotic, charcoal fans. "Have you done your hair?"

Ruth patted her single braid. "No. I've just been remembering to wrap it at night. You know, so it doesn't frizz."

Marjaana stared. "Why?"

"I... I'm trying to... grow it?"

"But it's already long."

Ruth gave what she hoped was a rueful smile and shrugged. Shrugging was her favourite nonverbal weapon. People usually interpreted it to mean whatever they wanted, which was always convenient.

But Marjaana's eyes narrowed. "Are you wearing lip gloss?"

"No," Ruth said with complete honesty, because it was tinted lip balm. Gloss, after all, would get in the way of kissing.

Which was irrelevant, since no kissing had occurred that evening, and clearly never would.

"Are you alright?" Marjaana asked innocently, wrapping a wave of turquoise hair around her tattooed finger. "You're behaving *so* strangely. I just can't *think* what's gotten into you, Ruth." Her eyes widened.

Ruth tried to imagine how that speech would look written down. Where the emphasis would be, what images or emojis or GIFs might accompany it. She decided, after completing the English-to-Internet translation, that Marjaana was being sarcastic.

"Fuck off."

Marjaana grinned. "Tell me, since I cannot possibly guess. What's keeping you offline lately? Making you *request* a phone call?"

People always seemed to do this—be painfully direct. Get to the meat of an issue quickly. Ruth preferred a good half hour to mull things over, to prepare her speech precisely and predict every avenue the conversation might take. To be ready.

But then, Marjaana didn't judge by weird, unspoken standards that Ruth had no access to. Marjaana took people as they were. So maybe preparation time wasn't needed.

Ruth said, "My neighbour keeps making me dinner and he's very attractive and I think that we're friends."

Marjaana blinked. "You say that like it's a problem."

"He, um..." It would be so much simpler if she could say, *He kissed me.* But Evan had somehow done both less and more than that. "Earlier this week he... came onto me, I suppose?"

Marjaana's little nose wrinkled. "And you didn't want him to?"

"I *did* want him to. I really fucking did."

"Ohhhh." Marjaana grinned wide. "Still not seeing the problem. Unless you threw up in his mouth. Guys hate that."

Ruth blinked. "Pardon?"

"Never mind." Marjaana flapped a be-ringed hand. "Continue."

"Well…" Ruth slid her braid over her shoulder and coiled the end around her finger. "It was good, but then I panicked a little bit, and I said we should stop, and he stopped. And then he said sorry. And now he's being all normal and friendly and nice and whatever."

Marjaana nodded. "Which is a problem, because *you* want him to be—"

"Normal and friendly and nice, and also on top of me."

"Then why did you stop him?"

Ruth shrugged helplessly. "Because I remembered what a fucking terrible idea it was, and then I felt like I was choking."

"Why is it a terrible idea?"

Ruth bit her lower lip, tasted the lip balm, and stopped. "You know why."

Marjaana really was her best friend, after all. She knew everything.

But she didn't nod or make some hum of understanding. Instead, blonde eyebrows arched, she said, "I know you had a bad experience in the past, but I don't think that should affect *this*. And I don't think it is. I think it's something else."

Ruth frowned. "Something else like what?"

"Tell me," Marjaana sighed. "What is this neighbour like?"

Well. There was a dangerous question.

"He's... he's lovely. I mean, he's kind, and thoughtful, and he lets me think, and he always has something funny to say. I don't know. I just like talking to him."

"So he's nothing like—"

"No," Ruth said quickly. "No."

"Hmm," Marjaana murmured. "So you think a lot of him. Maybe more than you think of yourself."

Ruth stared blankly. Marjaana stared back, but Ruth could do this all day, and would if necessary.

Apparently realising that fact, Marjaana sighed. "If he's a friend, and you trust him, why don't you tell him how you feel? What you're thinking? Talk it through?"

The mere idea of discussing emotions and issues and all that shit made Ruth feel like she was suffocating. "I can't. I just—I can't." She swallowed. "These past two years—I thought I'd figured things out. I thought I was okay. But now this is happening, and my head is all over the place, and I'm starting to wonder if I ever really dealt with things at all."

"Well, let me help you out with that," Marjaana said dryly. "You didn't."

"I tried."

Marjaana gave her a hard look. "You *didn't*. You accepted a hell of a lot of shit and told yourself that you deserved it. That's not dealing."

"Oh, stop. Less counselling, more seduction tips."

Marjaana snorted. "Tell me something else: how long have you been into this guy?"

Ruth wanted to say *Since the day we met*, but that wasn't strictly true. There was a difference between the desire she'd felt when she'd first laid eyes on Evan Miller and the way she felt now.

A big difference.

"I don't know. Barely any time at all, really."

"But how often do you see him?"

"Every day."

Marjaana paused, her perfect brows flying up towards her hairline. "Seriously?"

Ruth shifted, suddenly uncomfortable. Her gaze crept away from the phone towards a particularly interesting pencil, lying on the floor. "Yeah. Except Sundays."

"And you're not sick of him?"

Sick of him? If it was up to her, he'd stay all night. He'd never leave. She had to force herself to give him the option —and thanked God that he always took it.

"No," she admitted. "I'm not sick of him."

"Then, honestly, I think you're overthinking this."

Shocker. Ruth Kabbah, overthinking.

"It sounds like you really like him," Marjaana said. "And I think he must like you. Only, he's not going to do anything after you told him to stop. Maybe you should give him a signal."

Ruth shrugged, feeling suddenly tired. She had no idea how to *give him a signal*. She didn't know if she even wanted to. The thought of touching Evan was fantastic, but the thought of what she'd have to do to get to that point...

It was just too hard. Too risky. Too stressful. Too much.

"Maybe," she hedged. "I mean, you're probably right. I'm thinking too much. Let's change the subject."

Marjaana arched a brow. "Okay. Are you gonna tell me what the hell you're doing with this *Blazing Glory* arc?"

Ruth managed a smile as she thought of the latest plot-twist in her space opera web comic. If even Marjaana was unsure, she was doing something right.

"You can't guess what happens next?" she teased. "You always guess."

"My first thought was that Lita and Rose might get together during the mission. But then I thought, if that happened, you'd kill B-9 off within a couple episodes, and I *know* you wouldn't do that to me..." Marjaana squinted at the screen. "Would you? Would you do that to me?"

"I'm not telling. You have to guess."

"But I never know when I've guessed right! Your poker face is unbeatable."

It wasn't a poker face. But if the lack of expression that made people so bloody uncomfortable helped protect *Blazing Glory* plotlines—well, good.

"Just guess," Ruth prodded. "You always get it right."

"But I never know until you release the next episode!"

"That's the point!"

"You're a torturer. Lita and Matthias?"

Ruth shrugged, giving her most enigmatic smirk. She'd practiced it in the mirror. Hannah said it looked like she had gas, but Hannah was probably jealous of Ruth's mystery.

"Oh, honey," Marjaana winced. "Are you okay?"

Ruth blinked. "Yeah. Why?"

"You looked like you were in pain for a sec there."

With a huff, Ruth turned the phone's camera to the ceiling and flopped over onto her back.

CHAPTER TWELVE

OVER JUST A FEW WEEKS, Ruth and Evan had managed to establish a routine.

He'd come home from work, and she'd hear his front door slam. Most days, he went for a run, and when he came back she'd hear the pipes of his shower clunk. Soon after, he'd turn up with dinner. She'd let him in with faux reluctance, and they'd talk shit for the next two hours. Or three. Or however long it took her to regain her senses and kick him out.

Ruth was aware that, as they said in American films, she had a good thing going. She *rarely* had a good thing going. She would not derail it by introducing complications such as kissing and touching and talking about serious things, even if she felt a painful need to engage in the first two and a strange, tentative desire for the last.

She bore that fact in mind on Saturday, when she heard Evan's familiar knock. He'd come over early because it was a weekend, she told herself firmly. He had no work, and time to kill. It didn't mean he was eager to see her. She shouldn't be eager to see him.

Ruth forced herself to walk to the door, stifling the urge to skip through the house like a kid hyped up on E numbers. She took a deep breath before she opened up, hoping that the anticipation bursting in her chest wouldn't show.

"Hey," he said. "Since when do you wear glasses?"

Crap. Ruth yanked off the round, baby-pink frames, as if he hadn't already gotten a good look. "I only wear them when I'm working." And then, to explain their frivolous appearance: "I got them years ago."

Back when she'd been someone else.

He followed her inside, toward the kitchen, as was their habit. "Don't you need them all the time?"

She shrugged and took today's steaming dishes off his hands, hoping he wouldn't notice her lack of response.

But Evan noticed everything. "You know," he said, arching a brow, "I'm kind of glad you don't go out much. I'm surprised you haven't been hit by a bus."

"I don't like having things on my face." She sat down and dug into what appeared to be steak and kidney pie.

"Even if those *things* allow you to see?"

"Eat your food."

"As my lady wishes."

"Shut up."

He smirked. It wasn't an unusual exchange for the two of them, but something in the way he looked at her, something smouldering beneath the calm depths of his ocean eyes, made Ruth suddenly and uncomfortably... aware. Aware of him, aware of herself, aware of the memory of his hands against her skin. *Painfully* aware.

She hoped to God that she wasn't making it obvious. Only, knowing her, she absolutely was. Somehow. Ruth went over their every interaction as she ate, running through memories of the previous days, making sure she hadn't messed up.

"You finished?"

She jolted at the sound of his voice. His plate was empty, and so was hers, though she didn't remember eating. She did that sometimes: disappeared.

He was looking at her expectantly, with his usual gentle smile—and was she imagining something else there? Something satisfied and hungry all at once?

Maybe she was projecting. That was another thing she did sometimes.

"Yes," Ruth said, jumping up from her seat. "Of course. Let me take your plate."

"I can—"

"Let me!" Her voice sounded squeakier than it should. She cleared her throat. "Um... Can I get you some..."

"Tea? Yes, please."

She set the plates aside and went through the familiar motions of preparing their drinks. Typically, this was what she did toward the end of the evening. If she hurried up their unofficial routine, he would leave earlier. Right?

But you don't want him to leave.

Yes, I do.

No, you don't. He doesn't want to leave, either.

"Ruth?"

"Quiet!" she snapped. It was automatic. Any interruption

to the voices in her head, especially when she felt on the verge of an Important Discovery, was to be avoided.

But then she remembered that telling guests to shut up was extremely ill-mannered, and *then* she remembered that Evan was one of the few people in the world who deserved all of her time and all of her kindness. Clapping a hand over her mouth, she turned to face him. "I'm sorry! I didn't mean that."

He didn't look offended. In fact, he was sitting casually in her little kitchen chair with an easy smile on his handsome face. "I know. It's just your artistic temperament."

Ruth pursed her lips. "I do not have an artistic temperament." She turned back to the counter and grabbed a couple of tea bags, plopping them into the mugs before pouring the hot water.

"Sure you do. It's why you won't let me see your web comic."

"No-one sees my web comic."

"How do you make money from it if no-one sees it?"

The familiar back-and-forth eased her tightly coiled nerves. Feeling a little more like herself, Ruth rolled her eyes. "No-one I *know* sees it." Except Marjaana, of course. "Strangers see plenty." One sugar for her. Three, disturbingly, for him. Though she supposed his excessive taste could be justified by his ridiculous size.

"See?" He nodded sagely. "Artistic temperament. It also explains why you're so moody."

Ruth gasped. She turned, either to get the milk or argue with him. He already had the milk, was somehow standing before her, holding it out like bait. And she could tell from the gleam in his eyes that he *wanted* her to argue.

He arched a brow. Just one. It was something he did often, and it made her stomach flip every time. "Why do you look so outraged? Aren't you the woman who threw me out for preferring Ayo over Okoye?"

"I didn't throw you out," she muttered.

"Okay." His massive shoulders lifted. "Let's say *firmly invited me to leave.*"

She bit her lip to hide a smile. "Whatever. Dinner was over anyway."

He laughed, shaking his head. "If you say so."

She rolled her eyes and picked up the mugs. He deftly took them from her and carried them into the living room, as if she wasn't capable of handling it herself.

True, she usually spilled tea everywhere. But her balance would never get better if she didn't practice.

Evan lowered the mugs onto her coffee table with irritating grace before sitting on the loveseat. Not for the first time, she wished she owned properly sized furniture. But when she'd bought these things, she hadn't expected visitors.

He lounged against the plush, purple loveseat, his arm slung over the back, one ankle resting on his knee. Usually, he didn't take up this much space. Or maybe she was just imagining things.

Wetting her lower lip slightly, Ruth sat.

"I enjoyed starting *X-Men*," he said, and she relaxed. This was normal; this was their routine. It was just Evan, after all. She knew him, as much as you could know anyone after... how long had it been? Three weeks? Four? It felt like more than that. Could it be more than that?

She shook her head and focused on the conversation.

Time didn't matter, and neither did her rather inappropriate attraction. As long as she focused on *X-Men*, everything would be simple.

Everything was not simple.

Ruth didn't know exactly when she transformed from a normal human being into an embarrassing jelly of desire. Maybe it started when he reached out, mid-conversation, to pull on a tuft of hair that had somehow escaped her braid.

He pretended not to notice the fact that she stumbled over her words, that she licked her lips a thousand times in the space of a minute. And she refrained from asking him what the fuck he was doing, because whatever it was, it sent a delicious streak of excitement through her, and she liked it.

Then he touched her again, casually, bumping his knee into hers. He'd never done that before. How many times had they sat together, just like this, and he'd never done that before? Enough, she thought.

And yet, tonight, his knee brushed hers repeatedly. And, as if something drew her toward him, Ruth did the same. She forgot to be careful about avoiding him, forgot to hold herself stiff and apart. And when she let go of that tightly-wound control, they came together like magnets. Until she regained her senses and pulled back.

Only, she kept forgetting to pull back.

By the time he swallowed the last sip of his tea, she was almost frantic. Could he see her tightening nipples through her clothes? It was times like this she wished she could wear a bra without wanting to be sick.

What if he noticed the stutter in her voice, the way her

gaze lingered on his big hands, on the ink winding over his forearms?

What would he do if she knew that she was sitting next to him, barely listening to word he said, underwear soaking wet?

"I'll get you some more tea," she blurted out.

He looked surprised. "I don't—"

"It's fine. I want more too." She stood quickly, practically leaping away from the warmth of his body. Then, with a tight smile, she reached down to take his mug. He stared up at her, a bemused expression on his face. But something heavy and molten burned in his eyes. It was something she'd only caught flashes of before, something that made her heart pound.

She wasn't afraid of him. She should be, but she wasn't. Strangely, it was her own fearlessness that scared the shit out of her.

As he passed her the mug, his fingers brushed over hers. A surge of electricity shot through her, dancing along her nerve endings, stoking the flames between her legs.

She whimpered.

His eyes flew to hers. "Ruth."

She ignored him. As if nothing had happened, she picked up her own mug and turned to leave the room.

"If you don't come back here, I'm coming to get you."

She didn't reply, because she couldn't trust her voice. Instead she marched to the kitchen, as if movement could erase the mortification of what had just happened.

She'd *whimpered*. Jesus fucking Christ. She would never live this down.

CHAPTER THIRTEEN

"Ruth."

She sucked in a breath at the sound of his voice, a smoky caress. Evan filled the kitchen doorway, his face shadowed for a moment. Then he stepped into the light and stole the air from her lungs.

He was so fucking gorgeous.

He moved toward her, so slow and deliberate that she should have panicked. She should have felt clumsy or awkward or uncomfortable. Instead, she looked at him and remembered comfort and laughter and contentment, and somehow those memories short-circuited all her defences.

Ruth turned to the sink and dropped their mugs into the waiting water. She was suddenly and unreasonably outraged, because this wasn't supposed to happen. It didn't make sense. There were friends, and then there were men you'd shag senseless. He couldn't be both, and yet somehow, he was, and if she blew up from the pressure of wanting him it would be all his fault.

She certainly wasn't making him any more tea, the inconvenient bastard. He could survive on fresh air for the rest of his life, for all she cared. What the bloody hell did he think he was doing, *looking* at her like that? Being all gorgeous and smouldering and... *ugh.*

While she scowled at the sink, he moved closer. So close that she could feel his presence, even as she refused to look up. His face—his beautiful bloody face—would only make things worse.

"You do realise," he said, "that you're talking to yourself."

She blinked. Finally, foolishly, looked up at him. "I beg your pardon?"

He was closer than she'd thought. His eyes were almost electric, heavy-lidded, his lips parted. This was how he looked when he wanted.

"You're talking to yourself," he repeated, his voice a gentle rasp. "And I heard every word you just said."

Ruth swallowed, forcing moisture into her suddenly dry throat. "You can go now."

"No thank you." His voice was low, husky, raw enough to make her stomach flip and her heart rate spike. "I think I'll stay here."

Every night, there came a point when she gave him the option to leave. Every night, he took it. And now, all of a sudden, he was not.

Oh, dear.

"You don't like the way I look at you, Ruth?"

"I don't know what you mean." She stared down at the bubbles in the sink and licked her lips.

"That's what you said. I heard you. Do you *want* me to leave? Because if that's what you want—"

"It's not," she blurted out. Who the fuck said that? It couldn't have been her. Except, it definitely was.

"I didn't think so." His strong fingers reached out to cage her wrist, and sensation soared through her. His skin was warm against hers, the heat of his body pushing into her like a tidal wave. He was right there. She couldn't ignore him.

He wouldn't allow it.

"You ran away," he said, his voice softer now. "Why?"

She swallowed, forcing herself to look up at him. "I... I don't know."

His lips quirked, full and soft beneath that thick, sandy beard. She'd spent too many nights this week wondering how that beard might feel against her skin.

"I do," he murmured.

Desire bloomed between her legs—not like a flower, but like the mushroom cloud of an explosion. She knew what Marjaana would say right now. *Talk.*

Meeting his gaze, she asked, "What are you doing?"

His thumb skated over the inside of her wrist. "This is called flirting."

"This is *not* flirting."

He smiled. "Too much?" His hand slid from her wrist to her palm, their fingers locking together. Beneath the heat in his gaze, she saw that ever-present concern. "Tell me to stop, and I'll stop. You know that, don't you?"

Silently, her pulse thundering in her ears, Ruth nodded. His hand tightened around hers.

"There's something I've been wanting to do," he said. "And I know you don't take hints well."

Ruth bit down on a smile. Somehow, in the middle of all this shimmering tension, he managed to make her smile.

"So I've decided to ask you outright," he murmured.

His hands moved to her waist, tightening before she could process the sudden touch. He lifted her, just slightly— enough for her to perch on the edge of the sink. Then he let go. But she still felt the ghost of that unexpected pressure, the heat of his palms burning through her clothes. Bubbles soaked into the seat of her pyjamas, and she didn't even mind. Her underwear was already wet.

"Ask me what?" Ruth whispered. Now they were face-to-face. She allowed herself, for a moment, to float into the sky of his eyes.

He leaned in, his hands resting on the counter either side of her. She held her breath as he lowered his head to her throat, his nose grazing her racing pulse. "You always smell like chocolate," he said. His beard tickled, and so did his whisper. "Chocolate and coconut. Why is that?"

"Is that what you want to ask me?"

"No. I'm just curious." He shifted closer, and she opened her thighs, and he slid between them like it was home.

Ruth swallowed. "It's cocoa butter. And coconut oil."

"What does that mean?"

"Evan," she repeated, her hands gripping the edge of the sink. "Ask me *what*?"

He relented, a smile teasing his lips. "I wanted to ask if I could kiss you."

She didn't reply. It seemed both difficult and unnecessary. Instead, Ruth raised her hands to his face, sliding her fingers into that rugged, blonde beard. Holding him in place. She didn't want to fuck this up, because this was Evan, and somehow, Evan was everything.

She leaned forward, inch by inch, until she could see the silver-gold of his eyelashes. He was so still that, if she hadn't felt his gentle breath against her lips, she might've thought he'd stopped breathing at all.

And then, because he was Evan, he spoke.

"I think," he murmured, "you're supposed to close your eyes."

She whispered, "You first."

"Would that make you feel better?"

"Yes."

He closed his eyes. "Can I touch you?"

Fuck. Why did he have to ask that? Why did he have to be the kind of man who needed an answer, who needed to know what she wanted?

Because he was Evan, and he cared, and that was why she liked him in the first place. Ruth knew that. But it didn't stop the panic clawing at her chest, and suddenly she realised with startling clarity that the panic never really left, and she was absolutely fucking sick of it.

He was right there, and he was beautiful, and he wanted her, and *she* wanted—

A bell rang.

Ruth yelped and fell into the sink.

"Shit," Evan laughed. His eyes were open now. His face was calm and lovely and barely intimidatingly sexy at all. Except for all the ways in which it was.

But Ruth didn't have time to think about that, because she was dying of embarrassment.

"What the fuck was that?" she gasped, clapping a hand over her heaving chest.

He gave her a strange look, even as he pulled her gently from the sink. Just the firm grasp of his hands around her biceps made her breath hitch. How embarrassing.

"It was your doorbell," he said when she was safely on two feet, her backside dripping.

Oh. Right. The doorbell. Ruth had kind of forgotten how that sounded.

"Um..." She looked down, as if a code of conduct was written on the kitchen lino.

Evan pushed her chin up gently, until she looked at him. She shouldn't be as aroused by the sweetness of his smile as she had been by his touch, but somehow she was. "Want me to get it?"

"Oh, would you?"

He went without another word, and Ruth sagged in relief. It was silly. She knew it was silly. After all, she hadn't always been so... anxious. She'd grown up confident. With a mother and sister like hers, how could she not be?

Then again, all it had taken to destroy that confidence was one hard knock. So maybe she'd been faking all along.

With a sigh, Ruth hurried off to her room. If she was quick, she could change her pyjamas.

CHAPTER FOURTEEN

T<small>HE</small> <small>MAN</small> at Ruth's door wore a deep green uniform with gold lettering that read: W<small>ESTON</small> F<small>LORAL</small>.

But the enormous bouquet in his arms spelled out his purpose clear enough.

"Ruth Ka..." the man squinted at the clipboard balanced in his hand. "Ruth Kab..."

"Ruth Kabbah," Evan snapped.

The man shrugged, then dumped the crystal vase of red roses and tiny white flowers into Evan's arms. "There you are mate," he said, ticking something off on his clipboard. "Ta-ta."

Evan kicked the door shut with his foot. Then he stood in Ruth's hallway and stared at the flowers.

Her flowers.

Who the hell was sending Ruth flowers?

The flare of bitterness in his chest was unnerving. He'd never been jealous before.

Surely, if she was seeing someone, Ruth wouldn't have

had dinner with him every night for weeks. Then again, they hadn't been *dates* exactly. And he'd given her that ridiculous speech about being friends, or whatever the fuck he'd said.

So maybe she'd taken him at his word and moved on to someone else.

Was that why she'd hesitated to kiss him? Was that why she seemed so jumpy? He'd thought she was shy. He'd thought she was... fragile.

Maybe she was just guilty.

Ah, shit. He was jumping to conclusions.

Evan frowned down at the flowers, catching sight of a little white card tucked between the green stems. He didn't mean to look, exactly, but the word *childish* leapt out at him. Confused, he squinted at the golden, printed script

Don't be childish, baby.

He shouldn't have read that.

But he hadn't *meant* to read it. It had just been there. His eyes had just...

"Evan?"

Her voice made him jump, as if he'd been doing something illicit. Which he had, really. Guilt flooded him as if he'd thrown the flowers out the damned window instead of just reading the card.

But Christ, he really shouldn't have read the card.

Ruth came padding down the hall in a new set of pyjamas. The T-shirt was as oversized and high-necked as ever, the bottoms as long as loose as always.

He had no idea why people thought of her as a seductress. She was the least seductive person he'd ever met.

And you still want her desperately. So what does that tell you?

The same thing as the roses, he supposed.

Forcing a smile, Evan hefted the crystal vase—like she could miss it. "You got flowers," he said.

Her face fell. His heart headed in the same direction.

This was the part where she broke down and confessed to having a boyfriend who was InterRailing around Europe.

Except she didn't. Instead, she said, "For me?" Her voice was quiet, hesitant. She looked suddenly horrified, seeming to shrink in on herself, collapsing like a disturbed soufflé.

Evan's gut twisted. The suspicions crowding his mind couldn't change the fact that an upset Ruth was *not* something he wanted. "Yeah." He searched for the right thing to say and came up blank. "They're... I bet they're from your dad, or something."

Ruth laughed, but the sound was hollow. "I don't have a dad. I mean—my dad's in Sierra Leone. With his wife."

Wow. Somehow, he'd managed to say exactly the wrong thing.

Nice one, Miller. Fucking fantastic.

All at once, Ruth strode forward. She pulled the vase from his arms with a grunt, taking the weight before Evan realised what she was doing.

"Hey, let me carry that. It's heavy."

"No," she said flatly, heaving it down the hall.

"You'll drop it." He rushed after her, back toward the kitchen, holding out his arms in preparation for some tragic, Ruth-like disaster.

"Calm down." She reached the table and put the vase in the centre with a heavy *thud*. Then she reached into the blood-red blooms and plucked out that fucking card.

Evan hovered beside her, holding his breath, watching

her face as she read. How had this happened? Ten minutes ago, she'd been ready to kiss him. Now he was trying to figure out if she was seeing someone else.

She sighed heavily and put the card on the table.

"Who are they from?" The words shot from his mouth without permission. He hadn't meant to ask something that sounded so damned desperate. "I'm sorry. You don't have to answer that."

She looked over at him, a little furrow between her dark brows. "It's... an apology."

An apology? *Don't be childish, baby?*

She was lying. Except, he knew what Ruth did when she was being less than truthful, and she wasn't doing any of those things now. Her face wasn't carefully blank, her eyes weren't dead, and she wasn't pushing him away.

Like a robot jerking into motion, she straightened up and grabbed a fistful of roses from the vase. Ruby petals peeped out from between her knuckles, the stems dripping. She turned toward the dustbin.

"Uh..." Evan frowned. "What are you doing?"

Ruth shoved the flowers in the bin and looked up at him. "You want them?"

"No," he said slowly.

"Well, neither do I." As if that settled the matter, she grabbed some more roses.

"Ruth." He stepped forward, reaching out to still her hand. She sucked in a sharp breath as his fingers caged hers, bringing her movements to a stop.

Her eyes flew to his, and for a moment their gazes met. With Ruth, that was so rare, it felt momentous.

Just as quickly, she looked away again. But he didn't

mind. It would be ungrateful to taste a drop of heaven and ask for more.

"You can go now," she said, her voice flat.

She always said that. Suddenly, abruptly, at the end of a night filled with laughter and effortless intimacy, she would always, always say that. And Evan would leave.

But he wasn't leaving her like this.

He tightened his grip on her hand, pulling her closer. She stumbled, but he'd expected that; she stumbled more than she walked. So he wrapped an arm around her waist to hold her upright, and he watched as her eyes widened.

"What if I don't want to go?" he asked softly. "Would you let me stay?"

She tilted her chin. "Because you want to—"

"No." That was her defensive voice, the same voice she used to tell him what an awful slut she was. He knew what she was about to ask, and he didn't care for it. "I'm saying I don't want to go yet."

She continued as if he hadn't spoken. "Because you want to sleep with me."

Evan looked over at the decimated bouquet. "Who sent you the flowers, Ruth?"

She stepped back, away from him. He let go and thought his reluctance must colour the air around them, stronger than the roses. She didn't seem to notice.

"Mind your business," she said.

"You aren't my business?"

"Nope. I'm your neighbour. Now fuck off."

He'd expected nothing less, so he was prepared for the sting of rejection. Didn't make it any easier to swallow.

"If you have a boyfriend," he said, "you should've just told me."

"I don't have a boyfriend. I've never had a boyfriend in my life."

"Bullshit."

She grinned at him. The expression was almost manic. "You go and ask somebody. Anybody. Say, 'Has Ruth Kabbah ever been in a relationship?' They'll tell you."

"I don't want someone else's version of your life, Ruth," he gritted out. "I just want you to trust me." *I want to know why you don't go anywhere or see anyone, why people say your name like it's a scandal in itself.*

I want to know why you destroyed Daniel's car.

She sighed. "I'm not the kind of girl who just trusts people, Evan."

He swallowed down his bitterness. Maybe she was right. He barely knew her, and he'd come barging into her life, expecting to unlock all her secrets like she was some kind of puzzle. His conscious, reasonable thoughts didn't help, though. They didn't put out the searing flames of childish anger edged in hurt.

"Fine," he clipped out. "I get it. We'll just leave it at that."

She stared at him, eyes sharp. "What do you mean? What does that mean?"

He shook his head and said, "Don't worry about it."

CHAPTER FIFTEEN

"WHAT'S GOING on with you today?"

Ruth shot her sister a glare as they cleared the table. "In a minute," she whispered.

Hannah rolled her eyes. "Mum's got *Deal or No Deal* on. She's not listening."

As one, the girls turned to look across the dining-cum-living room. A few metres away, their mother stared, transfixed, at Noel Edmonds's silver bouffant.

Patience Kabbah had a serious crush.

Still, Ruth wouldn't run the risk. She said again, her voice hushed, "Wait." Then she piled the last of the dishes into her arms.

"Woah," Hannah laughed, swooping in to take most of the load. "Give me those. We don't need to spend the rest of the afternoon sweeping up china." She headed to the kitchen, plates balanced expertly in her practiced hands, without a backward glance.

Ruth allowed herself a millisecond of childish resentment. She was perfectly capable of carrying plates to the kitchen, even if no-one in the world seemed to think so.

Then she remembered why Hannah was such an expert at carrying dirty dishes and wiped her mind clean of disloyal thoughts. Let Hannah be the overbearing older sister. She'd earned it.

With a sigh, Ruth collected a few glasses from the table and followed.

The Kabbah women cooked Sunday dinner together, even though Ruth was a known disaster area. She prepared cassava and sliced yam. Sometimes she peeled breadfruit, if Hannah had picked any up from the market in the city. The heavy-duty cooking was mostly left to Mum—but both daughters insisted that she sit out when it was time to clean up.

So as soon as Ruth stepped into the kitchen, her sister shut the door. Hot water was already filling the sink, and plastic Tupperware was on the counter, ready to hold leftovers.

Hannah paid no mind to anything but Ruth. She leant against the room's narrow island, her arms folded. "Go on, then," she said. "Tell me."

Ruth walked carefully to the sink, sliding the glasses beneath the water, focusing on the iridescent bubbles gilding its surface.

How could something as basic as dish soap and tap water create something as wonderful as bubbles?

"Tell me," Hannah said again, her voice firm. "You're being super weird lately."

"I'm always weird," Ruth said. It was automatic. An in-joke dating back decades.

But Hannah's mouth twisted. "Don't say that. You're not."

"Yes I am." Ruth slid on a pair of her mother's pink rubber gloves. "And so are you. We're the weirdos, remember?"

"Oh. Right." Hannah laughed tightly.

She didn't find it funny; Ruth could tell. Her sense of humour had changed. Everything about her was sterner and tougher than it had been before, and that was saying something.

With a sigh, Ruth turned off the running taps. "I'm fine, Han. I just have some things on my mind."

"You've barely spoken all day." Hannah grabbed a plate and started scraping soggy cassava into the bin. "You didn't even notice when Mum mentioned her date."

Ruth jolted, dropping a cup into the sink with a splash. "Her date?"

"Exactly. You weren't listening."

"Stop having a go and tell me about this date." Ruth turned her most intimidating stare on her sister.

Hannah matched it with an equally unsettling glare of her own. "I'll tell you about the date when you tell me what's draining your brainpower."

Sometimes, Ruth forgot who she'd learned her defence mechanisms from. The student would never outdo the master; at least, not when it came to Kabbah Bitch Face.

"Fine," Ruth huffed, turning back to the sink. "I made a friend and then I fucked it up."

"Okay..." Hannah sounded mildly confused. "So apologise. Check their Amazon wish list or something."

"I don't think I can fix it with presents. Also, it's a real-life friend, so I—"

The sound of cutlery scraping against dishes came to an abrupt halt. "Like, a real person?"

Because, to Hannah, Marjaana and all of Ruth's other friends weren't 'real people'. She rolled her eyes and clipped out, "That is what I said, yes."

There was a pause. Then Hannah asked, sounding almost casual, "How did you meet?"

"He's my neighbour."

"So how did you meet?"

Ruth bit back a smile. "He came over to give me a shepherd's pie." She omitted their actual first meeting. She couldn't mention Daniel Burne in front of her sister. Not ever.

"A shepherd's pie?" Hannah echoed. Her voice was slightly shrill, as if shepherd's pie was threatening rather than delicious. "When was this?"

"I don't know... a few weeks ago?"

"And you're just now telling me?" Hannah's worried face filled Ruth's peripheral vision. The older sister was crowding the younger, using her extra inch of height to command authority. "Look at me," she demanded.

With a sigh, Ruth dropped the glass she was washing and turned. "What?"

Hannah pressed a hand to Ruth's cheek. Her palms were rough. They hadn't always been. "You have tons of friends," Hannah said. Which was rich, since she was the one who insisted that online friends didn't count. "And you fall out all the time because you're snippy. It's never made you come over all empty-headed."

"I'm not empty-headed," Ruth snorted.

"You didn't even finish your yam. You are the definition of empty-headed-Ruth. Now you tell me some man has brought you shepherd's pie. Did you eat it?"

"Yes," Ruth grumbled.

"You didn't tell him to fuck off and throw it back in his face?"

"No," Ruth admitted. *I saved that until last night.* Pushing away her morose thoughts, she added, "If I'd done that, we wouldn't be friends, would we?" Then, because she was feeling vulnerable: "He made me a lasagne too. He made me a lot of things. He cooks for me."

Hannah threw up her hands. "So you are half-in love with him already."

Ruth wondered why her first instinct wasn't to vehemently deny those words. Disturbing. But she'd worry about it later.

For now, she focused on managing her sister. "I certainly am not. I just... I was quite rude to him yesterday, and I feel bad about it, and I'm not sure how to apologise."

Hannah huffed, turning back to the leftovers. "Well, it's reassuring to know that I'm not the only one you're rude to."

"How helpful. Thank you for that wise, sisterly guidance." Ruth scrubbed the glass in her hands, watching light flash off of its gleaming surface.

"You don't need guidance," Hannah said. "You need *me* to tell *you* to apologise, because you can't bear to do it on your own. Because you want to fix things, but you don't think you deserve it."

Ruth considered that for a moment, biting back the instinct to deny it. Eventually, she was forced to say, "True."

There was a moment of disturbing tension, when the cat's cradle of unsaid words and pent up frustrations between them seemed dangerously close to coming loose. Ruth had no idea what it would mean, if that did happen; she understood very little about the distance between she and Hannah.

She only knew that she disliked it and was too cowardly to face it.

But then Hannah sighed. "Just put on your big girl knickers and tell this *friend* that you're sorry. I can't stand it when you're distracted. You're like a robot."

And everything was okay. For now.

Ruth snorted. "You do realise that you're just as rude as me?"

"I'm your elder, and I keep it in the family." Hannah slid another plate into the sink with a wicked smile. "Maybe if you did the same, you wouldn't have to apologise so often."

"Bugger off."

"I love you, too."

CHAPTER SIXTEEN

RUTH HAD BEEN CARRYING a certain amount of guilt for quite some time, and she'd become used to it. Too used to it, clearly, because the extra guilt created by the way she'd treated Evan was unbalancing her quite horribly. She felt too big for her own skin.

She had come home from her mother's yesterday determined to knock at 1B and apologise profusely. She'd managed step one just fine: knocking. Step two had been thwarted by the fact that Evan had not answered, because he was not in.

The man was bloody inconvenient sometimes.

But she found herself grateful for his absence. If he'd been there, what would she have said?

Sometimes my mind gets overwhelmed and all I can do to cut through the confusion is lash out.

Sometimes I think about one thing and remember another and see another and hear another, and that's just too many things, and I don't handle it well.

You shouldn't want to kiss me, because I clearly don't deserve you.

There. That one worked. That one worked just fine.

Her determination faded overnight, and so did the bravery it had provided. Ruth wasted most of Monday trying to work, failing utterly, and talking to herself about why she should or should not apologise.

When she heard Evan unlock his front door that evening, she abandoned the pretence of work completely and lay down on the floor in her hallway, staring up at the ceiling.

The carpet was thin and scratchy. The floorboards beneath it were hard. She didn't mind, because the blankness of it all helped her to think, and she wasn't fit to do anything else.

It wasn't even that bad. You tell him to fuck off all the time.

But you never meant it, and it never hurt him, so it didn't matter. This is different.

The worst part was that he hadn't *seemed* upset at all. He'd remained composed, had barely even flinched, while she pushed him away with careless, reckless words.

So why was she so sure that he'd actually been devastated?

"I just am," she mumbled.

And what if she went over there, and apologised—and therefore admitted that she actually gave a shit about what he thought—and it turned out that he wasn't even bothered?

"Of course he's bothered," Ruth sighed. "He wanted to kiss me. He... he caught me off-guard."

No; the flowers had caught her off-guard. And she'd taken it out on Evan.

You crazy bitch.

"Fuck off," she muttered. Sometimes her mind spit out recycled epithets instead of actual thoughts. Sometimes her mind was someone else's weapon.

And sometimes Ruth reacted badly under pressure and made very poor decisions and pushed away people she kind of sort of needed desperately.

Things happened, sometimes.

"So fix it." She let those words dissolve into the air. Usually, telling herself what to do elicited more efficient results.

It didn't work. She remained on the floor for at least another hour, or possibly ten minutes. She wasn't sure. Her phone was in her room. Evan had her number, but she hadn't heard it beep. She *had* heard him shower, which meant he should be coming over soon, except he wouldn't because she'd effectively told him to fuck off.

Actually, you literally *told him to fuck off.*

Oh, yes.

She got up off the floor.

But wait—she couldn't go over there. If he was avoiding her, she had to give him... space. Right? That was what you did, after a fight. Was it a fight? That word seemed to belong exclusively to couples, to people with actual relationships.

Well, whatever. They weren't a couple, but they'd had a fight anyway. And in Ruth's experience, trying to make up after a fight was... horrible. It involved many cruel words and lots of grovelling and, eventually, mildly painful sex.

The sex part probably wouldn't happen, at least.

What about the cruelty? The grovelling? Suddenly, she wasn't sure. Because Evan... Evan simply wasn't cruel. She didn't think he was physically capable; like an AI with morality parameters, his mouth wouldn't open to emit unkind words. She couldn't see it.

Okay. So she'd be an adult and go over there and apologise. And then she'd see what happened next.

She had a feeling that he'd surprise her.

～

RUTH HAD NEVER FELT self-conscious about her pyjamas until she found herself standing on Evan's doorstep, expecting him to open it and tell her to go away.

It was one thing giving herself pep talks from the safety of her flat, but it was another hearing his footsteps come down the hall. Knowing they were about to come face to face. Realising she was about to admit... that she missed him after a day apart? Desperately needed him not to hate her? Something along those lines.

Before she could psych herself out further, he opened the door.

He looked like shit. There were dark circles under his eyes. His handsome face seemed tight around razor-sharp bones. His thick, blonde hair stuck out at all angles, and when he looked at her, his expression betrayed nothing. Not even a hint of recognition. She might as well have been made of smoke.

"Evan?" She raised a hand to touch him, hesitated, and the moment—the few seconds when it would have been a reflex, and thus justifiable—passed. Her hand fell. "Are you okay?"

He blinked, then rubbed a hand over his face. Just like

that, he became more human than hollowed out husk—but his eyes were still dull, his face still hopeless.

"Ruth," he said. "Fuck. I forgot to make you dinner." His head fell back, and he sighed like a teenager who'd forgotten his homework.

She stared at the column of his throat for a second, the bob of his Adam's apple just beneath his beard, then gave herself a mental slap on the wrist. This really was not the time to ogle his neck.

"You don't need to apologise," she said. "Actually, I should—"

"Quiet," he instructed firmly.

"Um... what?"

"You're going to say sorry. I'm going to say sorry. Everyone will be sorry. I can't take it." This odd little speech was delivered with enough bone-deep weariness to spark Ruth's concern. He looked down at her and said, "Can we just be okay?"

Well. This was a pleasant, if worrying, surprise.

"Ooo-kay," she said slowly. "Um. Are you alright?"

He shrugged. That was the final straw. Evan never shrugged.

Ignoring the rampaging butterflies in her chest, Ruth manoeuvred her way into the flat—which was difficult, considering Evan's size and the narrow doorway. But she managed it, easing into his hallway and saying, "Come on."

He stared at her for a second, blinking slowly. Then his lips tilted in a ghost of his usual smile. "You're voluntarily seeking out my company? I don't have to force it on you?"

"Oh, don't be so dramatic." She rolled her eyes and

stalked off to the living room. After a long, heavy moment, she heard him shut the front door and follow.

She'd only been in his flat once, but she remembered it well. She'd replayed that evening in her mind countless times, going over every word and look and almost-touch between them, trying to decipher their meaning. And the moment he'd *actually* touched her, the moment he'd reached out to stop her leaving...

Ruth came to stand by his living room window, staring out at the Elm block's car park with unseeing eyes. Piecing together the snatches of memory, the rasp of his rough palm against her skin.

She heard him enter the room, and turned to find him watching her, quiet and intent as always.

"Why do you look at me like that?" she blurted out.

His lips tipped into a sharp, unfamiliar smile. "Don't act like you don't know."

Ruth raised her chin. "If we're okay," she said, with ice in her voice, "let's be okay. If we're not, say so and I will leave."

With a sigh, Evan sagged. His broad shoulders slumped, his face darkened. "I'm sorry," he said. "I'm really fucking sorry. Sit down. Let me get you something."

Ruth shook her head. "*You* sit down. You look terrible."

For a minute, she was certain he'd argue. But then, with a shrug, he came to sit on the sofa, just a few feet away from her.

"Stay there," she said, walking past him. She had a plan. It was heavily based on the sort of thing her sister might do in this situation. In fact, as she walked, her mind asked on a loop: *What Would Hannah Do?*

As she passed the sofa, Evan reached out for her. Ruth

stopped dead, feeling as if he'd punched her in the stomach, stolen her air and shocked the shit out of her, when all he'd done was wrap an arm around her waist.

She looked down. His head was bowed, resting against her hip. He took breaths so deep that she could see his shoulders rise. Then, his voice slightly muffled, he asked, "What are you doing?"

Really, she should be the one asking him that. Instead, she said lightly, "I'm looking after you."

He swallowed. "I don't need looking after."

"Why? Because you're the world's saviour?" Ruth smiled as he looked up sharply, surprise all over his face. "Everyone needs looking after, Evan. And you have stolen my apology, so you can let me do this instead."

He gave a weak imitation of his usual laugh. But it still counted. Ruth allowed her hand to settle on his head, just for a second. Her fingers sank into his soft, sandy hair, and she watched as his eyes widened.

Then she pulled away and walked briskly to the kitchen. Her hand tingled.

She wasn't surprised to find his cupboards fully stocked. Ruth chose some bread and three tins of chicken soup. Then she figured out the microwave, because setting his kitchen on fire wouldn't make him feel any better.

Ignoring her still-tingling palm, she heated up the meal.

It was what Hannah would do.

CHAPTER SEVENTEEN

THE SIGHT of Ruth approaching with food should've shocked Evan half to death. But he wasn't exactly himself, so he only felt a muffled sort of surprise as she pushed the tray into his hands. A tray containing buttered bread and a steaming bowl of chicken soup.

He looked up at her, slightly worried. "Did you slice the bread yourself?"

She held up her hands. "I still have all my fingers. See?"

That was true. He stared at her outstretched hands for a moment, at the fine, brown lines etching her palms. Probably for too long. Only, he'd like to trace the lines.

She dropped her hands and said, "Eat."

"Are you going to loom over me until I do?" Huh. Ten minutes with Ruth and he was able to make bad jokes.

She didn't laugh, of course. After a shrug and a wary look at the space beside him, she sat on the far end of the sofa. She crossed her legs, her fluffy, spotted socks peeking out from beneath her knees, her hands folded in her lap. Then she said again, "Eat."

He ate. The hot soup seemed to fill the icy chasm in his chest with something warm and soothing.

Or maybe that was Ruth's glowering presence.

When he was nearly done with the enormous bowl of soup, and feeling halfway human, she spoke again.

"Are you sick?

"No," he said.

"But you're not okay."

Evan felt himself smile. "I'm flattered that you noticed."

"I was just hungry," she shrugged. "Usually, when I'm hungry, you arrive. So I decided to investigate."

"Bollocks. You were worried about me and you wanted to see me."

"Your head is the size of a hot air balloon. What's wrong?"

Those last words were forceful enough to make Evan look up from the dregs of his soup. He frowned over at Ruth, guilt breaking through his foul mood as he realised that she was actually worried.

Did he really look that terrible?

"I had some… bad news," he began.

She nodded, her hands twisting in her lap. It was a movement she made a lot, apparently absent-mindedly; slowly rolling her hands around each other, wringing them gently.

He had no idea how to explain what had happened to him today. He barely understood it himself. But he had the oddest feeling that if he told Ruth everything, she'd see it from a perspective he hadn't considered and say something that would make it all better. So he told her. Everything.

"When I was 15, my dad died in active duty."

Ruth didn't make any exclamations of shock or horror. She didn't apologise. She just nodded, which was good, because if anything interrupted the story he might never finish telling it.

"We got some money. My mum hadn't worked for a while, but she'd been a librarian. So we moved to some town in the south, and she started working at a library again. After a year or so, I started to feel better. You know; happy. Like there wasn't a gaping hole in the family. We were doing okay. But then she got cancer."

He heard Ruth swallow. He watched her bite her lip.

"Are you hungry?" he asked, suddenly concerned. "You haven't eaten."

She looked at him, her eyes gentle for once. "Keep going."

Right. She wouldn't let him stop now. He nodded. "So, she got cancer. Breast cancer. Had chemo, had surgery. Was in remission for a little while, but I feel like she knew..." He shrugged. "I don't know. It ended up in her spine, and I feel like even when they said she was better, she knew she wasn't. But my mum was very cheerful. She was always smiling and focusing on everyone else, on helping people. She didn't think about herself much."

"Like you," Ruth said. Not as if it were a compliment, exactly; more like she was clarifying, verbalising her understanding. *So Paris is the capital of France, and your mother was like you.*

He shrugged, feeling suddenly awkward. "I don't know. I'd like to be like her. She was a good person."

Ruth nodded.

"But when she died I signed up to the army. So I suppose I'm more like my dad. I mean, he was an officer, but I like making things, so I became a metalsmith. That's what it's called." Most people had no idea what he meant, when he told them what he'd done. Ruth just nodded. She was doing a lot of nodding right now. He didn't mind. "I served for eleven years, and I felt like it made me... better. I felt like I got over it."

She gave a sad smile. "There are some things you don't get over. You just accept them and keep breathing. That's enough."

He huffed out a humourless laugh. She didn't know how right she was. Eleven years in the army, while everyone else forged friendships that would last a lifetime, and all he had was friendly acquaintances and fuck buddies.

He hadn't been capable of much else, not for years, no matter how hard he tried. He hadn't been over the loss of his family. He'd just been trying to accept it.

"I wish I'd had someone to tell me that," he admitted. "My mum would've told me that. But..." He shrugged. Because he was better now and had been for a while. "I met a guy here in Ravenswood. At work. I like him. Turns out, his mother's sick too."

"Zachary Davis," Ruth said.

Evan stared. "How'd you know?"

"Hannah told me. Hannah knows everything about everyone."

Hannah, her mysterious older sister. The way Ruth

talked, Hannah just might be God Herself. Evan shook his head, a smile creeping past his sadness. "Right. Well, I've been visiting Zach's mother. She's a great woman. But they..."

Now that Ruth knew who he was talking about, giving her details felt like a betrayal of trust. He wanted to. Desperately. But sharing the Davis's business was not something a friend would do, so he tempered his words.

"They got some bad news about Mrs. Davis's condition," he finished. "Nothing is certain; it could be a mistake. They're running tests. And I don't know why it upset me so much—I mean, it's bad, but I feel like..." Like his heart had been torn out of his chest. Like an invisible hand had plunged into his body, grabbed his guts, and twisted.

Ruth said, "Like your mother's dying again?"

His mouth fell open. His throat was dry, his eyes stinging, his pulse thick and sluggish. "I... Yes. Shit. Yes."

She ran her tongue over her teeth. She was thinking. And since when did he know her every subtle expression? Since when had he learned to read an unreadable woman?

He'd been expecting her to spring into action, but he still jumped a little as she rose. With one of those almost-smiles he'd grown to love, she plucked the tray from his lap and said, "Want to go for a walk?"

Evan stared. "With you?"

Her smile flickered, disappeared. "I... Um... Not necessarily—"

"I just meant—you want to go outside?"

She raised her brows. "You *have* seen me outside before. It happens. You know that, right?"

Evan squinted, pretended to think about it.

"Oh, behave yourself," she huffed. "Do you want to, or not?"

"I do," he said. "I really fucking do."

～

EVAN DIDN'T KNOW what he'd expected when Ruth disappeared to change clothes, but it wasn't this.

They wandered into town, their arms swinging close enough for him to fantasise about holding her hand. He wouldn't, though. She might push him into the road. Instead, he took furtive glances down at her. At this strange, pyjama-less Ruth.

It had genuinely never occurred to him that she might have real clothes. He'd seen her in the car park, after all, the first day they'd met, and she'd been wearing pyjamas even then.

But, as she'd crisply informed him ten minutes ago, that had been a 'period emergency'. He wasn't entirely sure what that meant, but it sounded grim.

Apparently, when she deigned to leave the house, Ruth actually wore leggings and oversized T-shirts. The T-shirt was barely distinguishable from her pyjamas, but the leggings...

Dear God, the leggings.

"I know you're always running and shit," she said. The word *running* sounded like an epithet, coming from her lips.

Evan tore his gaze off of her legging-clad calves just in time. She was looking up at him, waiting for an answer while his mind scrambled.

"You should come with me," he finally managed.

133

She barked out a laugh. "I don't think so."

"It's good for your heart."

"Fanfic is good for my heart. Running is a disaster waiting to happen, and you know it."

Evan snorted. "We should take more walks, then. It's bad for you, staying inside all the time."

"You're such a dad."

He grinned. "That's me."

Ruth smiled back. Not her usual purse of the lips, a smile that was more in the eyes than anything else—no. Her cheeks plumped and her mouth widened and her adorable teeth came into view, and Evan thought he might do something ill-advised. Like kiss her in the middle of town.

Instead, he forced himself to look away. "Speaking of substitute parenting," he said, "have you eaten?"

She snorted. "You know I haven't."

"Do you want to?" Evan's gaze slid back to her legs of its own accord. He focused on her ankles this time, on the snatch of brown skin between her socks and the hem of her leggings. "We could go to the Unicorn," he said, naming the local pub—he hoped. It was hard to think clearly when he could see the shift of her muscles beneath tight, grey fabric. Her thighs shook as she walked. If that T-shirt weren't so fucking huge he'd be able to see her arse.

"I don't know," Ruth said. Her voice was tight. He dragged his eyes up to her face and found her looking tense, distant. She was gazing across the town square at the pub in question, and he had no idea what she was thinking. Probably because he'd been distracted by her legs.

Evan didn't think he'd ever stared at a woman so much in his life. What the hell was he doing? Knowing Ruth, she wouldn't notice for a while—but then she would. And even though they were okay now—supposedly—he had no idea where they stood on the whole... *I'd like to keep you in my bed for a week and feed you grapes but I don't even know if you're single,* issue.

He probably should've asked her earlier, when she'd been ready to apologise. Ah, well.

Forcing himself to stare straight ahead, at the shops lining the street, at the cars circling the square—at anything other than Ruth—Evan spoke. "You don't go to the pub much, I take it?"

It was a ridiculous question, because he knew very well that she didn't. He had the vague idea that it was down to her reputation, as archaic as that sounded. Ruth acted like she was some kind of social pariah.

Then again, so did everybody else.

Evan turned his gaze back to Ruth—her face, this time. She hadn't answered. That didn't necessarily mean something was wrong; she often fell silent for no reason that he could discern. *Thinking,* she'd say.

But she didn't always stare into the middle distance with despondent eyes as she did so.

"Are you okay?" he asked. The urge to touch her swelled within him like a river breaking its banks. He shoved his hands in his pockets.

"Yep," she said shortly.

"Because *that* sounded believable."

"Oh, piss off," she muttered, but her lips tilted into a little smile. Then, after a few more silent steps, she said, "I don't think the pub is a good idea. I'm supposed to be cheering you up."

He frowned. "You are cheering me up. You made me soup."

She didn't laugh.

Evan stopped. And then, finally, he touched her. Wrapped a hand around her arm, above her elbow, because then a layer of cotton would be between them, and she might not react so strongly.

She choked back a gasp, then bit her lip.

He let go. "Does it scare you? When I touch you?"

She met his gaze. "You know it doesn't."

That sparked a flame in his chest, one that felt part hopeful, part hungry. "I don't mean to do it," he said. "I suppose I'm just touchy." He was not touchy. He helped old people carry their shopping; he picked up stray children and gave them back to their parents. That was the extent of his casual touching.

Unless he was around Ruth.

Ploughing on, he said, "If something's bothering you—"

"Shut up," she said. Not in her usual, subtly teasing way, the way that dared him to ignore her. No; her voice was flat, her body rigid, her eyes pinned to something in front of them.

Evan followed her gaze to a group of women about Ruth's age, walking down the street toward them, dressed to the nines. He had no idea where they could be going on a Monday night, dressed like that, but they seemed happy enough. The women chatted and laughed together, looking carefree and perhaps slightly tipsy.

Then one broke off from the others, her smile fading, her stride becoming purposeful. And her eyes were on Ruth.

Evan's internal alarm rang shrilly. Which was ridiculous.

The sight of a skinny woman in a pair of high-heels shouldn't rattle him, even if her biceps were impressively defined.

But then, Ruth *didn't* have defined biceps, and she was staring at the woman as if ready for battle. The woman's face betrayed a similar expression, determination edged with the promise of violence.

And, since he couldn't let Ruth lose a fight, he might have to do something she'd hate, like pick her up and carry her home.

For now, he grabbed her arm and tugged gently. "Come on," he said. "I'll make you something at mine."

"No," she gritted out, her voice mutinous. "You wanted to go to the pub. We're going to the pub." With that, she began walking again, heading inexorably toward the group of women.

What else could he do but follow?

Evan wasn't at all surprised when the women fell silent, one by one, as they noticed Ruth. As if by mutual agreement, when they came within a metre of each other, everybody stopped. About ten women on one side, he and Ruth on the other. The standoff held all the tension of a Wild West shootout.

But, he hoped, with fewer guns.

The woman leading the pack flicked grey eyes up and down Ruth's body as if a gnat had crossed her path. She tossed her long, chestnut hair and drawled, "Ruth, honey. They let you out the whorehouse?"

Evan ground his teeth.

Ruth smiled a wicked little smile and said, "I'm doing a town tour, since you left your men unattended."

This elicited a chorus of scoffs and disgusted sighs from the women. All except one, whose blonde hair fell well past her waist in an improbable riot of curls. "Ruth," she said softly, her voice chastising.

Ruth turned to the girl and folded her arms. "Yes, Maria?"

After a pause, Maria looked away.

"Alright," Evan said loudly. His patience for this—for the sharp, judgemental looks spearing a woman he respected— had worn thin surprisingly quickly. He hadn't meant to force himself into whatever was going on here. But his temper was rising, and he could see that Ruth's was too.

Now was not the time to find out if she did reckless shit when she was angry.

Slinging an arm around Ruth's shoulders he said, "We'll just be on our way. If you ladies wouldn't mind."

For the first time, the women's attention turned to him.

The leader, the brunette, arched a brow. And then she smiled. It was a pretty smile; she was a pretty woman. "You're Evan Miller, aren't you?" she said.

Evan set his jaw. "Yep." He wouldn't ask how she knew. It seemed like everyone did.

But she told him anyway. "I'm Hayley Albright. Daniel Burne is married to my sister. You know, he's told us all *so* much about you." She stepped forward and held out a hand for him to shake.

Since that would require him to remove his arm from Ruth's shoulders, Evan simply gave the hand a blank look. After a moment, the woman's cheeks coloured, and she stepped back.

"Well," she went on. "I know you're new in town, but you should know that—"

The blonde, Maria, cut in sharply. "Hayley," she said, her voice low and warning. "Leave it. Let's go."

Hayley rolled her eyes. It was an eloquent gesture that reminded him, strangely, of Ruth. "Fine," she eventually clipped out. "We can't let a little trash ruin our night, after all."

The group of women, now silent as a funeral procession, made their way past Ruth and Evan. They moved threateningly close, employing expert intimidation tactics.

When they were finally gone, Evan looked down at Ruth. "If we circle past the Unicorn, we can head home and they won't see us."

To his surprise, Ruth nodded without protest. "Please," she said.

Now he was really worried.

CHAPTER EIGHTEEN

EVAN HAD INSISTED that Ruth come back to his flat. She still hadn't eaten, and he wasn't happy about it.

Usually, Ruth wouldn't be either—but that evening's standoff had stolen her appetite. Still, they sat at his narrow kitchen table, and she ate a sandwich, and he watched as if he'd never seen mastication before.

Finally, forcing down a leaden bite of bread and ham, she asked, "What?"

He tapped his fingers rhythmically against the table-top. "You going to tell me what that was about?"

Ruth shrugged. "Figure it out."

"You know, I'd love to. I'd love to figure *you* out. But I need all the pieces before I can assemble the puzzle."

She took another bite of her sandwich.

After a moment, he sighed. "Okay. Keep your secrets."

And, just like that, she felt guilty. It took a few bites of sandwich for the guilt to really get to her, but it was there.

You need to decide if you want him to know you. Don't do things halfway.

Throwing the crust down on her plate, she said, "Me and Hayley and Maria were friends."

He looked up, barely hiding his surprise. "Friends?"

"Yeah." It wasn't really funny, but she still found herself smirking. "I *did* have friends, you know. Before."

"Before what?" he asked immediately.

She shrugged. Deciding to trust him was one thing. Parading her biggest mistakes before a man she really fucking liked was something else entirely.

And shit, she hadn't meant to admit—even to herself—how much she liked Evan. But it was far too late now. Because, all of a sudden, she was thinking about how she *would* tell him.

Eventually.

"Why would your friends treat you like that?" he scowled. "I mean, that Hayley girl—even if you aren't friends *anymore*—"

"I'd do the same," Ruth said, "if I was her. She's loyal."

"To who?"

She looked at him blankly.

"Alright, Miss Mystery." He smiled at her, really smiled. "I won't squeeze everything out of you tonight."

Maybe I wish you would.

Ruth buried her face in her hands and sighed. She was starting to piss herself off.

When she felt the gentle pressure of Evan's hand against the back of her neck, she bit her lip. It was either that or make a highly embarrassing noise.

"What's wrong?" he asked. His fingers kneaded tense muscles, strong and skillful.

She squeezed her eyes shut. "I'm sick of everything being so dramatic. I was trying to make you feel better, and it just…" She didn't even know how to finish that sentence.

Gently, he tugged her hands away from her face. She blinked at the sudden light, then stared at him. His eyes were serious, his fingers still wrapped around each of her wrists. She felt as if she was burning. And enjoying it.

"You did make me feel better," he said firmly. "I very much enjoyed your microwaved soup."

Despite her determination to be dour, she giggled. Then cursed him for it.

He continued, his voice softening. "Just talking to you made me feel better. Also, seeing you in leggings."

Now she didn't know if she should laugh or gasp. She compromised by choking on her own spit.

Evan waited patiently for her eyes to stop watering before he handed her a glass of water.

After a few calming sips, she forced herself to say, "I should go."

He watched her impassively, leaning back in his seat. "Should you?"

For a moment, she wavered. But then she remembered the way Hayley had looked at her. The pity in Maria's eyes.

In Year Eight, Ruth had provided Maria with illicit tampons, because her Irish Catholic mother insisted they were sinful. Tonight, Maria had looked at Ruth and fingered the pearl-studded cross around her neck.

It hurt.

"You should know," Evan said slowly, "that I care about

you. I didn't say that before, but it's important, and I should have."

"It's okay."

"It's not. I asked you to trust me, but I should trust you too. I should trust you to figure out your own boundaries and... you know, all that shit."

Ruth huffed out a laugh. "Yeah. All that shit. But I probably should've told you before now that I'm public enemy number one. And I shouldn't have suggested that walk."

Across the table, Evan cracked a smile. "Because I'm so terrified of the town's avenging angels?"

She snorted. "Keep laughing. They'll eat you alive."

He reached out and caught her hand, placing it palm-up on the table. Casually, his fingers traced the veins in her wrist. "I assume everyone hates you because you're a man-eating succubus."

She tried to suppress a shiver at the languid touch of his fingers and failed miserably. "Pretty much."

"You take advantage of their poor, innocent menfolk."

"Something like that."

He looked up, his gaze heavy. "Would you take advantage of me? If I asked you nicely?"

She smiled. "I think I respect you too much."

"That's funny, because I respect you a lot. But I still want to rip your clothes off."

Ruth's heart stuttered. She bit her lip.

"Tell me no, Ruth." His fingers slid back and forth, over the inside of her wrist. "Or tell me yes. I need to know I'm not losing it."

"I can't do that." She hadn't realised the words were true until they came out of her mouth.

"You can't say yes?" His fingers stopped.

"I can't say yes. I can't say no, either."

He swallowed. Hard. "You're not afraid of me, are you?"

"No." She'd never been less afraid of a man in her life. "I just..." She took a deep, shuddering breath. "I can't give you permission to fuck me over."

He smiled slightly. "That's not exactly what I want to do."

"But you will," she said sharply. Was this really what she thought?

Yes.

"You will, and when you do, at least I'll know I never gave you permission."

He stared. She'd really fucked things up now, she realised; all the ways she was damaged had been neatly exposed in the space of five seconds, and he'd wish he'd never made her that bloody shepherd's pie.

Then he said, "I can't tell you I'll never hurt you. I don't make promises I can't keep."

Even though she'd known it was coming, it hurt. It hurt like the time she'd sketched her favourite teacher and the teacher had crumpled the paper and thrown it in the bin because she was supposed to be doing fractions, except this time the paper was possibly, *maybe* her heart. Or something.

Evan grasped her hand firmly in his, drawing her attention back to him. "But I *can* promise," he continued, "that I will always treat you as you deserve to be treated. That I will always respect you. That I won't lie to you or betray your trust. I try not to say never, but I will say this: hurting you is something I would never choose to do. I swear."

She felt unwelcome prickles beneath her eyelids, threatening tears. How embarrassing. She hadn't cried in years, and she certainly wouldn't now.

"I also know," he said, "that I can't make you believe me. I have to show you. I'm okay with that. But Ruth, *you* need to know that I won't take this any further until you tell me what you want."

"You're impossible," she muttered.

"No," he said. "It's just, I want to do things with you. Not *to* you. There's a difference."

"Believe me," she muttered, "I know." And then, from the flash of concern in his eyes, she realised she'd said too much again.

His voice carefully calm—maybe *too* calm—he asked, "What do you mean by that?"

Ruth shrugged, her tongue feeling thick in her mouth. But he waited patiently for her to find the right words, and she didn't feel the pressure to speak that so often kept her silent.

Finally, she said, "I was with a guy. Kind of. Before. And once I agreed to be with him, I suppose that meant, in his mind, that I always agreed."

Evan's jaw tightened. "You mean—"

"I mean, he didn't really care if I said yes. Most people don't care about yes. A few more people care about no." She shrugged. "So I have this new thing where, if I want someone to leave me alone, I bite their dick off."

It was a joke. Evan didn't laugh. She didn't laugh either.

If she'd ever felt like she could actually do that—like she could fight someone off—maybe it would've been funny. Lighthearted. Even empowering. But she hadn't.

She hadn't even felt like she could scream, because,

145

really, wouldn't that be so dramatic? Wouldn't she be atten-
tion-seeking, or causing problems? People said it all the
time; if you're in bed with a man, you've already said yes.

But she knew that Evan didn't think like that. Evan
didn't think like that, and honestly, neither did she.

After a tense second, he spoke. "If I killed this guy you
were... *kind of* with, would you come and visit me in
prison?"

She bit down on her smile, but it spread anyway. "That's
funny."

"I'm not joking, love."

Ruth forced herself to roll her eyes, because it was easy
and familiar and something other than crying. Why on
earth was she so close to crying?

Pulling her hand from his, she said, "I should go."

And he said again, "Should you?"

Ruth took a breath. "Um... yes. Definitely yes."

This time, he didn't stop her. But he did say, steady as
always, "I'll see you tomorrow."

Was she grateful or terrified?

CHAPTER NINETEEN

THE NEXT DAY was painfully boring. Evan ploughed through his workload with the dull determination of a farm animal, only pausing to thank God that Daniel Burne was mysteriously absent.

As soon as the clock struck five, he was gone. Evan didn't drive to work, because he never used a car when his legs would do—but today, he wished he had. It would be so much faster to drive home.

When he finally reached his little block of flats, he was sweaty from work, dog-tired, and all he wanted to do was see Ruth.

He should've gone to his own door, let himself in, and calmed down. Showered.

Instead, he went straight to 1A and knocked. Twice slow, three times fast. He couldn't remember when he'd developed his own weird knock especially for Ruth. He just knew that she felt better about answering when she knew exactly who was there.

As evidenced by the speed with which her front door opened.

He smiled automatically—but then he faltered. Because the girl standing in the doorway wasn't Ruth.

She had Ruth's dark skin and diminutive height, but her curves were clad in denim jeans and a perfectly respectable, form-fitting blouse. She had Ruth's dense, crinkled hair, but it was held back with cute golden barrettes.

Ruth would rather die than use barrettes.

He looked down at the stranger with Ruth's face and scowled when he noticed her front teeth. Even they were the same; too big for her mouth, slightly too prominent.

His mind thought, almost feverishly, that no-one else should look like Ruth.

"Who are you?" he demanded, as if it wasn't obvious.

The girl looked him up and down, slowly. Her dark eyes lingered critically over his sweaty brow and worn-out clothes, the tattoos on his arms. Then she met his gaze and said, "I'm Hannah Kabbah. And you're Evan Miller. Elm block, 1B. Blacksmith at Burne & Co. Making my little sister act weird as fuck. We need to talk."

When she spoke, her resemblance to Ruth disappeared. Her voice, the subtle expression in her every movement, the sharp focus in her eyes—it was all wrong. She didn't smell like Ruth either; no chocolate and coconut here. She turned on that dead-eyed look like Ruth, but she wasn't quite as good at it. Beneath her glower he could see concern, apprehension, things he hadn't seen in Ruth until he'd gotten to know her.

Evan tried his best to sound patient and friendly. It was difficult, since he'd been waiting all day to set eyes on one woman, and this near-imitation felt like some kind of cosmic joke. "I'm happy to talk to you. But I came to see your sister."

"I'm sure you did," said Hannah Kabbah. "But she's unavailable at present."

Worry spiked. "Is she okay? Did she hurt herself?" Truthfully, it was only a matter of time before an enormous stack of comics collapsed on top of her.

Hannah's flinty gaze softened slightly. "She's—"

Then Ruth's voice interrupted, grumpy as fuck and almost angelic to Evan's ears. "Hannah! Is it the plumber?"

Hannah's jaw set. He knew why. If she said no, Ruth would want to know who it was. If she said yes, Ruth would expect said plumber to appear.

"Need a hand?" he asked.

She rolled her eyes and shrugged. It was such a *Ruth* sort of gesture that he found himself feeling fond of a woman he didn't know.

"I can take a look," he said. "If you let me in."

"What do *you* know about plumbing?"

"A fair bit." It wasn't exactly a lie, because it wasn't a very specific answer.

Before Hannah could respond, Ruth appeared. As soon as she saw him, her face lit up.

She hid it, of course, almost instantly—but not fast enough. He saw the beginnings of a smile, saw her eyes dance, for the split-second before she locked her emotions away.

"Evan," she said, her voice carefully neutral.

Even though he'd planned to play it cool, even though

Hannah's eyes were boring into him like twin drills, he grinned. "What the hell are you wearing?"

She smiled back reluctantly, shrugging beneath the enormous, green thing she was swathed in. "A towel. More effectively than you do, I might add."

Between them, Hannah made a strangled sort of choking noise.

Ruth's smile faded. "I'm sorry," she said, her voice suddenly formal, "but whatever you need—"

"I don't need anything."

"Whatever you need," she repeated firmly, "will have to wait a while. I'm all tied up, as you can see." Ruth cast a significant glance at her sister. Evan's heart swelled, because he could tell that Ruth thought she was being extremely subtle. Her weighted tone and speaking looks actually had all the subtlety of a dying hippopotamus. She was, in a word, adorable.

"If you're having plumbing trouble," he said, taking in her damp hair, "I could take a look."

Ruth wavered. She grimaced. Then she said, "The shower spit something vile at me. I really need a wash."

"Use mine," he said automatically.

Hannah made yet another garbled sound and sagged against the doorframe. She appeared to be having some sort of aneurysm. He ignored her.

"Oh, I couldn't," Ruth murmured.

"Yes, you could. Use mine, and I'll look at your shower until the plumber gets here. I might be able to help."

After a long, long pause, and a flurry of hilariously obvious eye contact between the sisters, Ruth said, "Okay."

Hannah said, "Ruth, love—"

And Evan said, "That's settled."

～

HANNAH KABBAH'S constant hovering reminded Evan, strangely, of his mother.

She loomed in the doorway while he took a look at Ruth's shower. Judging by the brown sludge gathering at the plughole, Ruth hadn't been joking when she said it spat something vile. He was glad to know, thanks to the clunking of his own pipes through the wall, that she was having a long, hot shower right now.

Hannah cleared her throat for the third time in the last thirty seconds, and Evan stifled a sigh. He'd done his best, but he simply hadn't been raised to ignore a woman.

Turning to look at Hannah's oddly familiar face, he said, "Everything okay?"

She looked as if she'd been waiting, just *waiting*, for him to ask.

Straightening her spine, glaring down at him as a goddess might glare down on unworthy mortals, she said, "What are your intentions with my sister?"

Evan smiled. "You might want to keep your voice down. These walls are very thin."

Hannah looked horrified. "*How* thin?"

"Don't worry about it."

She crossed her arms over her heaving chest. Evan bit his tongue, fighting back laughter. This was great. It was like watching Ruth get flustered times a thousand. How did such tiny women hold so much emotion?

"You're friends with Daniel Burne," she finally whispered, accusation making the words a hiss.

Evan stiffened, the smile wiped from his face. "I certainly am not."

"Yes, you *are*. You've been seen together multiple times."

He eyed her suspiciously. "What are you, the town spymaster?"

"I know what I need to know," she said primly. "And I *need* to know why a man like you is sniffing around my sister."

Evan sighed as he unscrewed Ruth's showerhead "I am not *sniffing around* your sister. I am spending time with my neighbour, who is also a friend, because it makes me happy."

"And what does Daniel think about that?" she demanded.

"What is he, her husband? I don't give a shit. Why is everyone in this town so obsessed with Daniel Burne?" His mind distantly registered the fact that his pipes had stopped clunking. Ruth was out of the shower. He glared at the wall and muttered, "That wasn't long enough."

"You're telling me," Hannah tutted. "She didn't even take the Dettol."

He frowned. "Dettol?"

And she threw his own words back at him. "Don't worry about it."

Finally stepping fully into the bathroom, she approached him. Her gaze was still wary, her arms still folded. He wondered if all Kabbah women were this skittish, or if it just happened around him.

"Ruth isn't what she seems," Hannah murmured, her voice low. "She is very... fragile."

Evan stared. "She seems fragile."

"Hm. Most people don't tend to notice that."

"Most people," Evan said, "have their heads up their arses. I'm not one of them. I care about Ruth."

Hannah gave him a wry smile. "Lots of people care about Ruth. None of them treat her very well."

"I treat her just fine," he said, his voice mild. "Ask her."

Hannah didn't reply. The silence was deafening, and when he studied her face he found clear uncertainty there.

"You can't ask her?" he prompted. "You know everything about everyone in this town, but you can't ask your sister about me?"

Hannah shrugged, but the look in her eyes was anything but casual. "She'll lie. She's a good liar."

"She's a terrible liar. You just have to know what to look for."

The front door opened and a loud voice carried down the hall, interrupting what had turned out to be a rather illuminating conversation.

"I thought you were Hannah, you know," the strange voice boomed. "You always did look just like twins."

He heard Ruth murmur something in response.

"Yes, well, never mind that. How are you, anyway? I haven't seen you in an age! My Penny's always harping on about missing you at the library—"

With a scoff of disgust, Hannah marched out of the bathroom. Then she cried with exaggerated pleasure, "Mr. Clarke! There you are!"

"Hannah!" the man said. "You're here and all, are you? You know, I always tell the missus, I say, it's so nice how them Kabbah girls stick together. Our lads are always at each other's throats. They—"

An older man with grey, balding hair appeared in the bathroom door. He pulled up short at the sight of Evan, his mouth hanging open mid-monologue. Behind him, both Ruth and Hannah hovered anxiously. Ruth was clean again, wearing fresh pyjamas. Her cheeks were shiny. Evan wanted to kiss them.

Inappropriate thought. Move on.

He rose from his crouch by the plug hole and wiped a hand on his jeans, then held it out to Mr. Clarke—who, it seemed, was the plumber. "Hi," he said. "Evan Miller. I live next door."

"I know who you are, lad," the plumber said, his tone gruff. "My sister's already called me about some strapping blonde feller who stormed out of her shop. Newcomer, she says. She's taken against ye."

Evan wasn't sure what to say to that, so he kept his mouth shut.

The plumber's face broke into a sudden smile. He grasped Evan's hand and shook firmly and said, "Any man who pisses off my sister is a friend of mine. Or any woman, for that matter." He turned back to look at the girls.

Hannah said, her voice a hell of a lot sweeter than it had been with Evan, "We appreciate you coming out yourself, Mr. Clarke."

The man grunted. "Them lads of mine is alright, but thick as pig shit. Don't know who's worth respect. Let's have a look 'ere, then. You checked the valve, have you, my lad?"

Evan looked down at the copper pieces in his hand. "Oh, yeah. Nothing there. I just—"

"No worries. I already know what it is."

"You do?"

He turned a wry look back at the sisters. "Oh, aye. I come out to a Kabbah girl once every six months at least." He winked conspiratorially and lowered his voice, as if Ruth and Hannah weren't standing a metre away. "I don't know how they've got any hair on their heads, the amount that gets down the plug hole."

"Mr. Clarke!" Hannah gasped in clearly feigned outrage. When Evan looked up, she was smiling.

Ruth was gone.

~

WHILE CLARKE SORTED out the shower, Evan was unceremoniously frogmarched to the door by Hannah. He didn't *expect* so much as fervently hope that Ruth might appear out of nowhere and demand that he stay.

Ruth did not appear.

"Thank you very much for your help," Hannah said as she held the front door open, "but we have things in hand now."

He crossed his arms and tried to think of a reasonable excuse to ignore her. "Where's Ruth? I want to make sure she's okay."

Hannah didn't respond; she just gave him A Look. Kabbah women, it turned out, were very good at looking.

"I told you," he said stubbornly, "I care about her. Why'd she disappear?"

"Because too many people talking at once makes her anxious," Hannah said briskly. Then, after a moment's hesitation, she leaned in and whispered, "and because Mr. Clarke is a terrible gossip."

Evan frowned. "He seems like a nice guy."

"He's one of the few people who doesn't treat Ruth like shit. Or me, for that matter. But it doesn't change the fact that he couldn't keep his mouth shut for a mountain of gold —so by this time tomorrow, the whole town will know that she came out of *your* flat like it was nothing, while you fiddled with her shower." She made this sound like an accusation of adultery.

Evan almost rolled his eyes. Ruth was rubbing off on him. "I don't see how that's particularly incriminating."

"Right," Hannah said with icy sweetness. "Because Ruth really needs the town talking about her love life."

"I—pardon?"

Hannah gave a snort of disgust. "*Men.*"

That, apparently, was her version of goodbye. She jerked her head toward the door, and Evan, in a haze of confused worry, went.

She shut it carefully behind him. He supposed, if she slammed it the way she so clearly wanted to, it'd be more fodder for Mr. Clarke's rumour mill.

CHAPTER TWENTY

"I'LL BE LEAVING EARLY AGAIN," Zach said. "But I'm hoping to finish the wall piece. I don't want you doing that."

"You mean I'm not capable of doing that." Zach was the artist. Evan's work was purely functional.

He checked the oxygen valve in his cooling blowtorch before setting it down and pulling off his goggles. If Zach was hovering around, it was time to take a break.

Sure enough, the other man was leaning against the doorframe, his arms folded over his chest. Waiting.

"Don't kill yourself over it," Evan continued. "If you finish, you finish. If you don't, leave it to me."

"I leave everything to you," Zach murmured. Trying to hide the hint of bitterness in his voice. Evan knew that the bitterness wasn't for him.

"You can't do everything. You know, I…" This was the part where Evan explained his own past, where Zach finally understood why Evan cared so fucking much about this.

But the words seemed too big and sharp to push out of his throat. They hurt on the way up.

In the end, it didn't matter. He was saved from confession by an unlikely source.

Daniel Burne shoved his broad shoulders past Zach, jarring the other man without hesitation. He stormed over to Evan as if they were meeting on the battlefield, his pretty face twisted.

"Miller," he spat, jabbing a finger in the air. Evan eyed that finger with annoyance. He had a sudden and strong desire to snap it in two.

Instead he shoved his hands in his pockets and said, "What?"

Daniel blinked—as if a response of any kind was so unexpected that it had thrown off his rant. "I... You..." After a moment's floundering, he refocused. "You don't listen too good, do you?"

"Actually," Evan said, "I listen very well. I am an excellent soldier." *But you are not my superior.*

"You're not any kind of soldier here," Daniel sneered. "You're a subject. And I'm the fucking king."

Evan's brows rose at the sheer teenage immaturity of that statement. Daniel didn't seem even slightly embarrassed by the words that had just come out of his mouth. Fascinating.

"I thought I told you about that girl," Daniel snapped.

Ah. So this was about Ruth. Evan pulled his hands out of his pockets and crossed his arms over his chest. He dug his short nails into his own flesh, out of sight. Call it a preemptive measure. Because he was 100% sure that he was about to lose his fucking temper.

"You did," Evan said. "I ignored you."

He still remembered Daniel's words, the day they'd bumped into Ruth. *"You're really pissed? Over a girl like her?"*

Daniel came forward, green eyes blazing as he invaded Evan's space. All his insistent charm was gone now, as if it had never existed. "I'm warning you," he spat. "Stay away. You don't mess with a girl like her, not while you work for Burne & Co. She's bad fucking news and my father agrees."

Evan felt like he'd been treading water easily, only for an undercurrent to catch him without warning. *My father agrees.* What the hell did that mean? Was Daniel threatening his job? Was *Mr. Burne* threatening his job?

"What the fuck is your problem?" Evan demanded, his patience slipping. In the doorway, he saw Zach, eyes wide and head shaking frantically. The message was clear. *Whatever you're about to do, don't.*

Evan was too pissed off to listen. His rational mind screamed that this job was a dream come true, and positions in his specialism were hard to find, and he couldn't just move somewhere else and start over. He ignored his rational mind the same way he ignored Zach.

"Are you jealous?" he asked Daniel. "Is that what this is?" Because suddenly, that was exactly how it seemed.

Daniel sneered. "Why the fuck would I be jealous of that? Half the town's had her."

"You sent the flowers, didn't you?"

That wiped the smirk off Daniel's face. He stuttered— actually *stuttered*—"I don't... I don't know what you're talking about."

"Yes, you fucking do." Evan stepped closer, crowding Daniel right the fuck back, fury flooding him. Everything was coming together, now. He couldn't believe he hadn't seen it before. "You want her," he said. "You had her, and now you don't, and you want her."

Which meant that Daniel... Daniel was Ruth's ex. The guy she was *kind of* with. The guy who hurt her.

"You're delusional," Daniel choked out. "I wouldn't touch that bitch if you paid me."

Evan barely heard him. He was remembering, with dawning horror, everything Daniel had ever said about Ruth—said *to* Ruth—and the way she hesitated before touching anyone, and the look on her face when she'd seen those fucking flowers.

"I'm just looking out for you, mate," Daniel said. His tone was reasonable now, soothing. He stepped back. "You know you'll catch something, laying down with that."

It was Zach who caught Evan's flying fist, stopping its trajectory toward Daniel's smug face. It was Zach who filled Evan's blurring world, forcing himself between the two warring men.

"You have to calm down," he gritted out, his eyes burning into Evan's. He wrapped a hand around the back of Evan's neck and squeezed, hard. "Listen to me. *Listen to me.* Calm. Down."

Evan became gradually aware of the speed of his laboured breathing and the frantic pound of his heart. He squeezed his eyes shut and forced himself to count to ten. Then he counted back from ten to one.

By the time he'd regained control, Daniel was gone. Thank God.

Zach stepped back, eyeing Evan wearily. "You good?"

"I'm fine." He ran a hand over his face as if that would

hide the lie. "Jesus. I'm sorry. You shouldn't have had to do that."

The other man shook his dark head. "Come with me."

ZACH LED him into the break room and shoved him into a chair, his hand hard on Evan's shoulder. Hard enough to chase away the last dizzying dregs of rage.

"Take a breath," Zach ordered. His voice, the familiar cadence of a command, soothed Evan. "I don't know what that was about," Zach said, "but I do know that beating the shit out of the boss's son is not a good idea. For many, many reasons."

Evan bore those words in mind, tightening his grip on his composure. "I know. I... thank you. For stopping me."

"Stop thanking me. We both know I owe you more than that."

Their gazes met for a moment. Just long enough for Evan to see more gratitude in the other man's eyes than he'd ever expected.

It made Evan uncomfortable, when people thought they 'owed' him. He didn't do the right thing for credit. He did it because he had to.

"You want a cuppa?" Zach asked suddenly.

"Yeah." Evan's shoulders relaxed. "Please."

Zach turned toward the little kitchenette, filling up the kettle. Now that his back was to Evan, that desperate gratitude was invisible. Thank God. Its weight was suffocating.

"So you've got a girl," Zach said. "And Daniel doesn't like it."

Evan let out a sigh. "I don't know what his problem is. He's married, isn't he?"

"Daniel Burne has never let a little thing like marriage stop him from getting what he wants." Zach fiddled with tea bags and grabbed milk from the fridge. "Who's the girl?"

"Her name's Ruth."

Zach paused, every muscle in his broad back frozen. "Ruth Kabbah?" he asked, voice slightly incredulous.

Evan wished he could see the other man's face.

Relaxing back in his seat, he crossed his arms to hide his clenching fists. "You gonna warn me off too?"

"No," Zach said immediately. Like a robot rebooted, he began to move again. "I don't judge," he continued, voice mild. "That family's never done me a wrong. Anyway, my brother's got a criminal record, too, and—" He finally turned around, just in time to see the shock on Evan's face. "Shit," Zach said. "You didn't know. I—"

Evan held up a hand. "Just... don't say anything else."

"I'm sorry, man—"

"Don't. It's fine." His mind was flying in a thousand different directions, but none of those directions were Zach's business.

Well; except one.

"You have a brother?" Evan asked, his voice stirring the cauldron of awkward air.

Zach nodded, looking relieved at the change of subject. "Yeah. You'll meet him soon. He's moving home again, because of..." Zach's voice trailed off, his face darkening. But then he cleared his throat and continued. "It's taking him some time. He's down in London. Got two kids and a business to pack up."

Evan smiled, and managed to mean it. "You're an uncle?"

"Yeah," Zach grinned. "Got a niece and a nephew." He pulled out his phone and produced pictures with a pride that seemed almost parental.

Some of the images contained one child, some both. They shared Zach's jet-black hair and blue eyes. Their father was in a few of the pictures; a man who looked like Zach with longer hair, more tattoos, and a hell of a scowl.

The children didn't seem to mind the scowl, though; they clung to their dad like happy little monkeys. There were no other adults in any of the images.

"Is your brother a single parent?"

"Why? You interested?" Zach wiggled his brows.

Evan rolled his eyes.

"Oh, of course you aren't," Zach grinned. "You've got a Kabbah girl."

"I haven't *got* anyone." Evan gulped down his tea. "And we're wasting a break gossiping like old men. Let's go."

Across the coffee table, the other man straightened his spine and gave a mock salute. "Aye aye, Captain."

"I'm not a captain," Evan muttered.

"Ah, whatever."

CHAPTER TWENTY-ONE

EVAN HAD INSISTED on taking Ruth's number a while back, but he'd never used it.

Not until today.

Ruth stared at the two texts he'd sent in quick succession, trying to figure out if she should be nervous. The first said that he was leaving work and coming straight over. Which was weird. He didn't text her when he left work, and he didn't come straight over after work.

She should definitely be nervous.

Even though the second text said: It's nothing bad, so don't stress.

Hah. As if telling her not to stress could ever stop her from stressing.

Ruth knew very well that she was, as always, overthinking. Expecting the worst. Still, that knowledge didn't stop her from rushing to answer the door when he knocked.

In fact, she was so quick to let Evan in that she didn't even notice the knock wasn't his. So she experienced the shock of her life when she opened to door to find Trevor Burne on her doorstep.

Daniel's father had been a familiar, shitty fixture in her life for years. Before, he'd come to 'visit' a few times a year at least—depending on Daniel's behaviour.

But this was after, not before, and she was supposed to be free. He shouldn't be here.

The burly, greying businessman speared her with a familiar glare and said, "Leave my boy alone."

Ah. Just like old times.

"Mr. Burne," she clipped out. "I won't pretend I'm happy to see you."

With a disgusted huff, he barged into the house. That was his usual tactic, when it came to these clandestine, vaguely threatening visits. Jesus, had she fallen back into 2008?

Following him into her own damned flat, Ruth snapped, "What the hell do you want?"

"You know what I want." He eyed her comic books. "I see you haven't changed a bit."

"Neither have you. Still a bullying prick."

She thought he seemed startled at those bold words, at the vehemence behind them—but he recovered quickly. "Oh, yes," he said, finding his way to the living room. "Ruth Kabbah. Eternal victim. I always do forget." He sank onto the loveseat.

Ruth would rather eat her own vomit than sit next to him, so she perched on the coffee table—after pointedly dragging it far, *far* from Mr. Burne.

"Go on then," she said, crossing her legs. "Get on with the speech."

He glowered at her. Those grass-green eyes shouldn't affect her anymore, but Ruth felt shame creeping over her skin. It was like a Pavlovian response.

And it was pissing her off.

"I don't know why you do this," Burne said in long-suffering tones. Which she found ironic in the extreme. "How many times have we had this conversation, Ruth? You know what I want. You know why I'm here."

"I don't," she said. "I haven't done anything to Daniel." The words came like an abandoned habit: with depressing ease.

"Bullshit," Mr. Burne said succinctly. "Do you know what he did the other day, at dinner? In front of the whole family? He called his wife—his *pregnant* wife—Ruth."

Jesus. The idea made her want to wince, but she couldn't. Her tactic, when it came to topics like this, was icy blankness. Impenetrability. Silence.

But all of a sudden, all she could think was, *Why?*

Everyone else got to say their part. Even if their part was complete and utter bullshit, even if the issue was none of their business, even if they were horrible people.

She wasn't a horrible person. She was just weak.

Or she had been.

"Nothing to say for yourself?" Mr. Burne snapped. "Nothing. Ha! The pair of you disgust me. I can't imagine why he persists in chasing *you*, to the detriment of all else—"

Ruth's temper snapped.

"You know," she said, her voice hard. "If you weren't so stuck on the fact that your son is obsessed with the fat, black daughter of an unmarried immigrant mother, you'd have figured this whole thing out *years* ago."

Burne's mouth hung open. He made a series of incoherent, outraged wheezing sounds before he managed to say, "I don't know what you're trying to insinuate—"

"Then let me be clear." Ruth got up off the coffee table, standing tall. "I think that you're a stuck-up, racist snob, and since you've been harassing me for the last decade, I'm well-placed to judge."

Mr. Burne shot to his feet, towering over her. Just like Daniel used to.

Just like Evan did. And Evan wouldn't hurt her just because he could. She pushed down her automatic panic and remembered that, for all his faults, Mr. Burne had never touched her either. He just hated the *idea* of her. Of his son with her.

Which was not her problem, and never fucking had been.

"If you'd never sunk your claws into my son's gut," Burne snapped, "*I* would never have darkened your door! You should be ashamed—"

"Now let's get one thing straight," Ruth hissed. "I am not ashamed, and I never will be."

Those words hadn't always been true. Two years ago, she'd been nothing but shame—and things had only gotten worse. She'd hidden from the world for shame, and pushed away her friends for shame, and stewed in guilt, which was shame's best friend.

And now she was fucking tired of it.

"I fell in love with your son," she said. "I fell in love with the school's biggest bully, the guy who made fun of my glasses and called me a freak and wanted to kiss me behind the gym, because that's what teenagers do. They fall in love with the wrong people. And yes, I stayed with him, even though he hid me from the world and treated me like shit—even though you appeared every so often to call me a gold-digging whore—because that's what people in love do. They make bad choices."

She broke off, heart pounding, chest heaving, and took in Mr. Burne's slack expression with something close to pride. He'd wanted to know. He'd always, always wanted to know. He'd screamed at her before, demanding answers Daniel wouldn't give—first, *Why is my son always sneaking off with you?* Later, *Who gave you that? Who took you there? Was it Daniel? I know it was.*

And always, always: *Why the hell did it have to be you?*

She wasn't good enough for the Burne family. Even Daniel had told her that.

Seven years, they'd been together. No-one had known 'til it was over.

"It's always fascinated me," Ruth said, "how little you care about Daniel."

Mr. Burne stiffened. "How dare you?"

"Oh, I dare. It's disturbing. Almost unnatural. You're desperate to know why he's obsessed with me, but you're not concerned by the fact that your son is obsessive. Do you know he asked me out for two years straight? That's how long it took him to convince me. And I was a teenager; I thought it was romantic. But now I realise that it was just fucking weird. It was harassment." She flicked a disdainful look at Mr. Burne. "Like father like son, I suppose."

His jaw tightened, but he didn't argue. He dug his fingers

into his own thighs, white knuckles against faded denim, and said, "You're in a talkative mood."

"Yeah," she said harshly. "I am. Because I'm sick of this shit. You want to know the truth? Here's the truth. Daniel knows that you despise him. That you don't think he's good enough. You're the reason he's a manipulative, hateful bully —and you're the reason why we were together."

Mr. Burne's thick, bristly moustache, auburn streaked with grey, twitched. He wanted to argue so badly, but he remained silent. Waiting for her to hurry up, to get to the point. He didn't know his son, so he didn't realise that this *was* the point.

"I despised Daniel Burne," she said. "I really, really did. But he was held back in sixth form, and we wound up in the same classes. Eventually, we were paired together for a project, and I came to your house. I don't think you knew I was there—he wasn't exactly happy about my presence, and he made me keep it a secret." She laughed slightly. "I suppose that was a sign. Anyway, you came home from work, and he tried to talk to you, and you spoke to him like he was worthless."

Even though she'd hated Daniel, her blood had burned. It still burned now, when she remembered the casual way Burne had hurt his only son.

At least the man had the grace to look ashamed. Slightly.

"Daniel came back to his room," she said. "He knew I'd heard. I expected him to lash out at me, but he didn't. He just... broke. It was awful. I hated him, but my heart ached for him. So when he kissed me, I allowed it.

"That was the first time he asked me out. Two years later, I finally said yes. But he told me that we had to be a secret, because of you—and I agreed, because I was a romantic fool. I hoped that eventually Daniel would stop trying to gain your approval. I thought that if I waited until he was older, until he was established in the world, things would change.

"I was wrong. Obviously, I was wrong. But somehow, seven years passed. Can you believe that?" She shrugged. "How does that even happen? You know, he bought me a house."

Burne jolted, his shock a tangible thing, floating in the air between them.

Ruth nodded. "Oh, yes. He bought me a house, and a car. I wouldn't take the house because my sister would ask questions. I took the car. I started writing a web comic, pretended it was my job to explain away all the money I had. My mother didn't understand the concept and my sister wasn't interested, so it worked." Ruth felt herself smile. "It's funny, really. I ended up publishing the comic. Now it *is* my job.

"I loved him the way people do in films. You know, when you're watching and you think, *'That girl's ridiculous. How could she do something so foolish? For love?'* You laugh at her. You think, correctly, that she threw her life away for nothing. Well, I was that girl.

"But Daniel's hard to love. He's not so good at it. I figured that out the day he told me about his engagement to Laura."

For the first time, Burne spoke. He said, his voice wooden, "I don't understand."

"Well, Mr. Burne, it's quite simple." When she'd explained this, years ago, to Hannah, the words had burned her throat. The *shame* had burned her throat.

Now she felt only detachment as she explained.

"On Thursday night he came over. He told me all about your latest transgressions. We watched *Modern Family*, and then he took me to bed. The next morning, he kissed me goodbye and went to work. On his lunch break, he called to say that he wasn't coming home, because it was he and Laura's engagement party that night. But he'd be back Sunday at the latest, he said. He'd see me then, he said."

Ruth almost found the story amusing. It was funny, how unsuspecting she'd been, how sure. How he'd caught her unaware and given her the information so blithely.

She gave Burne a smile. "You know the rest, I suppose. Up until a few weeks ago, when I bumped into Daniel and his new friend. I liked the friend, and Daniel didn't like that. He was very rude, as he always is, and then he felt guilty, as he always does. Usually he saves the flowers for my birthday, saves the gifts for Christmas. But he appears to be throwing some kind of protracted, jealous tantrum."

Burne stood on shaky legs. The usually robust man was pale, almost fragile-seeming. "My son is many things," he said softly, "but he is not... he is not *deranged*. You are missing out crucial parts of the story, I am sure."

Ruth shook her head. "If you think I'd give Daniel the time of day after what he did, you're as delusional as your son. I'm sick of him, I'm sick of you, and I'm sick of every stuck-up gossip in this town who thinks Burne shit doesn't stink. Now get the fuck out of my house."

Mr. Burne stared at her for a moment, his face blank. Something about him seemed vacant, his jaw slightly slack, his eyes unfocused. He looked, for an instant, like a man who'd found hell at the end of a rainbow.

Then he visibly pulled himself together, clearing his throat, straightening his clothes. "I..." His voice was hoarse. "I wish you'd said all this earlier. I wish you'd explained this to me."

"When?" Ruth asked. "When I was eighteen years old and in love with a man who told me you were the devil incarnate? When I was twenty-two and you called me a gold-digging slut? When I was twenty-five and you gave your police statement?"

He winced. "I believed... that is, Daniel led me to believe—"

"I don't care." She really didn't. Ruth looked at Mr. Burne's bewildered face and felt nothing but exhaustion.

He nodded wearily. Despite his still-handsome face, his still-powerful body, he looked like a confused old man. Like the sort of person Evan would swoop in and rescue.

Evan, who was on his way home right now. Christ.

"I really need you to go," Ruth said.

"Of—of course." Her jaw nearly dropped at the hesitance in those words. And then he said, "I'm sorry."

Her jaw *did* drop.

Mr. Burne's did too, as if someone else had said that. His eyes widened. He wandered from the room as if in a dream, and she followed, shock lapping at her like waves against the shore. A tentative triumph coalesced in her chest, not because of those two little words—words he hadn't meant to utter—but because she'd told him. She'd told him her truth, and she'd told him to leave her alone, and nothing terrible had happened.

Because allowing yourself to be manipulated by a man like Daniel wasn't a crime, and you never deserved to be punished.

When she opened the door to let him out, she felt elated. When he looked over his shoulder and said, voice subdued, "I won't bother you again," Ruth felt like she was flying.

But then she heard him say to someone she couldn't see, "Evening, lad. I hear you've been misbehaving."

And then she heard Evan's voice say, tightly controlled, "Mr. Burne."

Oh, shit.

CHAPTER TWENTY-TWO

EVAN STOOD, frozen, as Mr. Burne emerged from Ruth's flat.

The man was eerily similar to his son; they shared the same height and breadth, the same startling colouring. Only Mr. Burne's body was slightly softer, his red hair streaked liberally with grey. A literal silver fox.

The man had interviewed Evan for his position, all those weeks ago; despite being so loaded, he still liked to oversee the minutiae of his business. He was that kind of guy. In fact, for a short while, Evan had liked Mr. Burne.

But getting to know Daniel had soured that somehow.

Their eyes met, and Evan set his jaw. What should be alarming him most, here? Probably the threat of losing his job, whether for attacking the boss's kid earlier, or because he hadn't left Ruth alone.

And yet, the only thing on Evan's mind was what Burne had just said to Ruth. *I won't bother you again.*

So he'd been *bothering* Ruth.

Evan was pissed.

"Evening, lad. I hear you've been misbehaving."

Those words should've made him nervous, coming from the man who controlled his income. Evan was too angry to be nervous. He released his words slowly, because he was in the sort of mindset where he might easily be carried away. "Mr. Burne." He paused, collected his thoughts, continued. "I must apologise for—"

Burne held up a hand. "Never mind that. My son is a grown man. If he had the spine of one, he wouldn't come running to me over every conflict. So let's pretend I don't know, since I shouldn't."

Evan tried to hide the shock on his face, but probably failed.

With a nod, Mr. Burne walked past Evan and down the corridor. In seconds, he'd disappeared into the stairwell.

Leaving Evan to face Ruth.

Suddenly, the things he'd wanted to say—the careful words he'd planned on his way home, about how he knew everything, and he didn't care, and he understood—were nowhere to be found.

Fucking Burnes. A scourge, the lot of them.

To his surprise, Ruth stepped out of her doorway and came toward him. She spoke first, without prompting. He almost collapsed in shock.

"Evan," she said, her voice hesitant. "I—I don't want you to think that—"

"It's okay," he said. She looked so worried, his heart constricted in his chest. In two strides, he closed the gap between them. He wrapped his arms around her and expected her to stiffen at first—even to pull away—but she didn't. Not for a second. Her arms slid round his waist,

175

and her head fell against his chest, and everything was perfect.

For a while, they stood there, breathing in synch, and Evan felt more peaceful than he ever had in his life. Then he felt Ruth's hand slide beneath the hem of his T-shirt. She didn't do anything, really. She just pressed her palm against his back, against his bare skin, and left it there.

But that, apparently, was enough to make Evan hard. Then again, it never did take much around Ruth.

She laughed, a husky chuckle whose vibrations he felt in his chest. Then, tilting her head back, she looked up at him. "I can feel that, you know."

Evan smiled ruefully. "Sorry. Ignore it." Even as he spoke, his fingers trailed over the back of her neck. Her skin was softer than silk.

She exhaled, the kind of long, heavy breath that spoke volumes. Then she said, "I don't want to ignore it."

He looked down at her for a moment, his mind scrambling. Then finally, thankfully, he scraped together enough wits to choke out, "We should go inside."

"Yes," she said. "Let's."

~

RUTH HADN'T FELT powerful in a while. Years, actually. It was exhilarating. It was fantastic. It was also, somehow, arousing.

Or maybe that was just Evan.

She dragged him into her flat by his T-shirt, hoping she wouldn't bang into the door or fall over or something equally embarrassing when she was trying her best to be sexy. She *was* capable of being sexy. As long as she avoided unfortunate incidents.

Clearly, God was on her side, because they made it over the threshold without issue. Maybe He thought she deserved some dick. That was probably it.

Evan slammed the door shut without a backward glance. His eyes never left her. In fact, they devoured her, hungry and insistent, and Ruth realised that the way he usually looked at her was nothing. It was restrained, controlled.

This was something else entirely.

The knowledge that he wanted her, and badly, was enough to send liquid heat pooling between her legs. And she wanted to give him that same feeling, that heady drunkenness of being desired, even if it went against her every instinct.

So Ruth swallowed down her nerves and put her hands on his chest, pushing him back against the door. Even though she wasn't strong enough to move him, he pretended as if she was, falling back against the polished wood with a sharp exhalation.

Licking her lips, Ruth looked down at the growing bulge in his jeans.

"Ruth," he murmured, drawing her eyes back to his face. "I need you to say something."

She nodded. "Something like, I want to suck your cock?"

He blinked. "Um... I... I meant something like, *'This is fine'*. But that's great. That's fantastic. Please, continue."

Despite Ruth's commitment to sexiness, laughter burst from her lips. "Thank you for the invitation."

"Oh, you're welcome. Now, before you get too distracted..." He reached out, catching her hand in his, and tugged her forward. Closer, closer, until she was forced to slide her hands around his neck, until he could wrap an arm around her waist. "We were interrupted," he murmured. "The other day. But—remind me—did you say that I could kiss you?"

Ruth took a breath and rose up onto her toes, sliding her body against his. Everything about him was hard, strong, perfect. He brought up a hand to cup her face, the pad of his thumb rubbing her lower lip.

"Talk," he said gently. "Remember?"

She nodded. "Kiss me."

His eyes darkened. The arm around her waist tightened. He pushed his thumb slightly into her mouth, parting her lips, and she bit down. When he let out a tight little breath, Ruth's confidence grew—or rather, she forgot to think about confidence or nerves or anything at all. She sucked where she'd just bitten, and Evan actually moaned.

It was a quiet sound, deep in the back of his throat, but she heard it and she wanted more. Ruth sucked his thumb harder, and he flashed a dark smile. "You like things in your mouth, kitten?"

She released his thumb with a pop. "Some things more than others."

With a low growl, Evan bent his head and kissed her.

The tip of his still-wet thumb dragged down Ruth's lower lip, nudging her mouth open as he tasted her. He licked at Ruth's tongue, somehow gentle despite the pressure of his hand on her face, the way he held her still and devoured her. His lips were so soft against hers, his beard tickling her cheek, and she felt caution in the way his arm cradled her waist.

But when it came down to it, his mouth was demanding.

He was demanding. Ruth was finding that she very much enjoyed being obviously wanted. It wasn't exactly something she'd experienced before.

When he pulled away, he didn't really pull away at all. He still held her body against his own, still cradled her face with one hand, and let his brow rest against hers. But their lips finally parted, and he dragged in breaths as if he'd been submerged under water. She did too. For a moment, all that existed of the world was the shadowed little space between them, where air was shared and bodies were connected.

"That," Evan finally rasped, "was worth the wait."

And Ruth, who must have been possessed by some sex-crazed demon, murmured, "This will be too." Then she reached between them and tugged at his jeans.

Because he knew her well, Evan gently moved her hands and deftly undid the buttons. Then he put her hands back, as if she needed encouragement.

She yanked the fabric down, and he sucked in a breath and leant back against the door, watching as if hypnotised.

She was impatient, she realised. Had been for a while and hadn't even known it. For a moment, as she hooked her thumbs beneath the waistband of his boxers, she wondered: could she really need him this desperately?

Then she dragged the boxers down his muscular thighs, and saw the thick, dark length of his cock, and decided that yes, she fucking could.

She wrapped a hand around him, hummed a moan at the velvet feel of him, then squeezed. He was iron-hard. She could smell his skin, raw and natural and warm. She felt dizzy.

He slid a hand over her neck and said, almost absently, "You're perfect."

She scowled. "Shut up."

"Make me."

A reluctant smile curving her lips, she leaned up and kissed him again. His cock in her hand, his tongue in her mouth, Ruth kissed and stroked and moaned and *felt*. From the energy pulsing in her clit, in her nipples, to the empty ache between her legs, to the scorching heat of his flesh against her palm.

He was vulnerable because of her. He was standing there with his jeans around his ankles, with his cock in her hand, ready to do whatever she wanted—to *take* whatever she wanted—and the thought tipped Ruth well past patience. She broke the kiss, ignoring his wistful moan, and sank to her knees.

Evan watched with lust in his eyes, his tongue sliding out to wet his lips. She'd expected him to offer token protests, to pretend she couldn't *want* to swallow his cock whole, but of course he didn't. Because he knew this was exactly what she wanted. He'd made sure.

She wondered if he also knew that she was embarrassingly aroused, her nipples tight and her pussy slick, just at the sight of him half-dressed before her.

Probably, she decided. A man couldn't look like him and suffer from a lack of knowing.

She'd wanted to take her time. She'd wanted to trace her thumb over the fine veins mapping his rigid length, play with the pearlescent drop forming at its tip, feel the impossible velvet hardness against her cheek.

But then he pressed a hand to her face. He looked down

at her with something far too soft in his eyes, and held her far too gently, his thumb tracing her cheekbone.

So she had to lean in, had to run the flat of her tongue along his length, from root to tip. And it worked. His hand slid back to her neck, and he groaned. His head fell back, and his eyes screwed shut. "Ruth," he panted, his hips jerking. "Yes. God, yes."

The sound of her name on his lips was easier to handle than the adoration in his eyes. She'd have to get used to the latter, she thought. But she was kind of looking forward to doing so.

I want to take everything you have to give, and I want to think that I deserve it.

She licked him again.

CHAPTER TWENTY-THREE

Evan had intended to come home and have a *talk* with Ruth. A mature, serious talk that culminated in him asking some schoolkid shit like, *Will you be my girlfriend?* and her laughing in his face but saying yes.

What good intentions he'd had. And now here he was, trying not to disgrace himself while she lapped pre-come from the swollen head of his cock.

He couldn't quite feel bad about it.

Evan snatched in a breath as Ruth's lips wrapped around his length, hot and soft and wet. Her tongue slid out to massage the underside of his erection, and then she sucked him slowly into her mouth. He forced his eyes open, even though sheer ecstasy made his lids heavy. She was too beautiful to miss.

Her hands were squeezing his thighs, her short nails digging into him. He didn't mind. He didn't mind at all. Evan watched as his cock disappeared into her mouth, inch by inch, and felt the pull of her lips at the same time, and could have passed out from the pleasure. When he felt the impossible pressure of her throat, he almost choked.

Something drove him to press a hand to her neck, beneath her chin. He felt her muscles relax, expand as she swallowed him.

"Fuck," he gritted out. "Holy shit, Ruth."

She made a sound he couldn't decipher, but when she looked up at him with dancing eyes, he knew she was laughing. Or trying to. She couldn't quite manage it with his cock filling her mouth.

When her nose brushed against his belly, and she sucked in the last inch of him, Evan realised that he was biting his own fist hard enough to leave marks behind. He had to, just to maintain the last scraps of his control. To stop himself from bucking against her, from fucking her mouth.

After a few seconds of perfect, *oh-fuck-yes* pleasure, she pulled back. His length slid from her lips, glistening wet, and she gasped as she caught her breath. Then, before he could ask if she was okay, she took him hungrily back into her mouth.

"Jesus," he growled as she sped up the pace. "Jesus Christ, you're so fucking—ohhh shit." He watched her slide back and forth along his near-painful erection, her eyes fluttering shut, her low moans sending vibrations along his cock and up his spine. He couldn't stop his hands from cradling her face, sinking into the softness of her hair, even as he chastised himself.

He didn't do things like this. He didn't give into his urge to rut against a woman's face, to use her mouth, even if his balls were tightening and his vision was blurring, and his lust was an uncontrollable beast.

But Ruth pressed a hand over his, as if encouraging him. He looked down and realised that she'd slid her other hand beneath her waistband, that she was touching herself. His knees almost buckled. Evan sagged back against the door and pressed a hand to the wall for support.

Christ, he wanted her naked. He wanted to watch as she played with her own pussy for him, as she came with his cock in her mouth. He wanted to see her cunt wet and soft and wanting him.

"You like this," he grunted, his hips jerking as she sucked him deep.

She moaned again, her eyes meeting his, her tongue working him expertly.

"I want you to come," he said. He didn't recognise his own voice. It was harsh, commanding, nothing like him, but it tumbled from his lips anyway and it seemed right. "I want you to come," he repeated, firmer now, "and then I want to fuck you."

She shook her head slightly and pulled back, releasing him. "In my mouth," she breathed.

If he hadn't been desperate before, he was now. The sight of her gleaming, swollen lips, the sound of her breathless murmur—it was all too much. She sucked him again and he gave in. He tightened his grip on her hair and thrust, holding her still as he pumped into her, gritting his teeth as the hand beneath her waistband moved faster.

When she came, squeezing her eyes shut, her throat seemed to tighten around him. He felt the vibration of her long, drawn out moan, and he let go. Sensation danced along his spine as he groaned out his release, holding her tightly against him, burying himself. She clutched his thighs and swallowed everything he gave her.

Completely drained, Evan ran a hand over his face. His skin was hot, sweat gathering at his brow as if he'd run a damned marathon. He found himself grinning from ear to ear, which wasn't really surprising. He might've just had the best orgasm of his life.

Ruth started to rise. In the interests of efficiency, Evan simplified the process and picked her up.

She gave a very un-Ruth-like shriek, followed by a reassuringly Ruth-like scowl. "What are you doing?"

Evan clasped his hands beneath her arse and tried not to look too smug when her legs tightened around his hips. "Nothing."

"Oh, really?" She glared at him, her nose an inch from his. "It's just, looking you in the eye is usually harder than this."

"You never look me in the eye anyway."

"Incorrect. I look you in the eye at least once a day. It's disgracefully intimate." Her lips were pursed, her eyes dancing. She was smiling his favourite kind of smile, the one that didn't seem like a smile at all.

Evan kissed the corner of her mouth softly. He'd thought he loved that mouth before; now he was ready to pay it tithes. "You're in a good mood. I don't suppose—"

"It has nothing to do with you," she cut in primly. "So don't be smug."

"Nothing?" He grinned. She huffed. He leant against the door and readjusted his hold on her, because she didn't seem to mind the fact that he was essentially grabbing her arse.

So he might as well really enjoy it.

"Maybe it has something to do with you," she admitted. "Slightly. Perhaps."

"Perhaps." His smile grew wider.

"Perhaps. By the way," she added, her brow furrowing. "Why did you text me? I mean, did you want something?"

"Aside from this?"

She snorted. "If you're trying to say that you rushed home from work for a blowjob—"

"To see you," he corrected. "I rushed home from work to see you. I wanted to talk."

"About?"

Evan tried to remember the way he'd been going to say things and failed. He'd been aiming for something approaching a romantic declaration, but not romantic enough to make Ruth choke on her own spit. Or hit him and run away. Then again, she seemed unusually receptive to gentleness right now. Apparently, orgasms loosened her up.

"Well," he said slowly, "It's funny, what with Burne being here and all, but I actually wanted to tell you that, well, that I know about Daniel, and I don't care."

She blinked. "I beg your pardon?"

"He, um..." Evan searched for a simple way to explain. "He and I had a disagreement at work today."

Ruth had become very still, very stiff and upright in his arms. "A disagreement about what?"

"You, I suppose."

The last scraps of contentment faded from her expression. "Are you taking the piss?"

"No. I—"

"Put me down."

This was not going well, but then, he hadn't expected it to. "Why?"

"Put me down," she repeated, "and put your bloody dick away."

He sighed. "Whatever you want." Letting go of Ruth felt like throwing away a vital organ, but that was silly. She was still right there in front of him, glaring in a comfortingly familiar manner. Evan yanked his clothes into place but didn't bother to zip up his jeans. "You're upset. Do you want me to keep talking, or do you want to rant?"

"Keep talking," she said, "and I'll rant when you're done."

"Okay. I guess that girl we bumped into—his sister-in-law? Told him that she saw us together. Or maybe it was the plumber. Or maybe it was both. Anyway, he was pissed. And I realised that..." Evan sighed. "He's jealous. Right? He sent the flowers. He's your ex."

Ruth wasn't looking at him anymore. She was looking at the wall, her face as blank as the clean, magnolia paint. "You realised. You just... *realised*."

"Yeah. I don't know why I didn't figure it out before."

She looked at him sharply. "Why would you figure it out before?"

Evan had the feeling that he was heading into dangerous territory, but he couldn't tell if the ground would fall out from under him, or the walls would close in around him, or something else entirely. He didn't know where to look for the threat. "Well... he always told me to stay away from you.

He was so fucking smug when I found out about his car. He—"

"His car?" Ruth looked furious now, but he wasn't sure who she was furious with. "He's still banging on about that *fucking* car?"

"Not exactly. But—"

"He had no right to do that." She jerked back, began to pace. Evan stared. He had never seen Ruth pace. He had seen her wander around a room as she spoke, and he had seen her sit in odd places or in strange positions, and he had seen her wring her hands and tap rhythms out against table-tops. He had never seen her stride from one end of a space to the other with a look on her face that screamed *murder*, and he didn't like it.

"It's okay," he said. "I don't care."

"You don't care about *what?*" she demanded.

He couldn't decipher the look on her face. He should be cautious, he knew—but she was upset. Ruth was upset, and he couldn't stand it, and he thought he could fix it. So he said, "I don't care if you have a criminal record because you smashed up that dick's car."

Ruth stared at him for a moment, her face impassive. Then she said, "I think you should go." Her tone was mild, unreadable. Which meant that she was hiding a hurricane of emotions he'd never have access to.

"Talk to me," he said. "Tell me why you're upset."

She shrugged. "Why don't you go and find whoever's been feeding you this shit and ask them, since they know everything?"

"Ruth. No-one's—"

"You've been sitting around talking about my family,"

she said quietly, "and you want me to act like you've done something good."

"No." He shook his head. If the movement was a little frantic, well—it matched his mind's desperate cries of *Fix it!* "That's not what happened, and that's not what I want."

"So what do you want? Because I'm really starting to wonder. Do you want to do this? Do you want to be with me? Or do you just want to solve a mystery and save a girl?"

"What the fuck?" He had no idea how things had gone so exquisitely wrong. "Ruth. You know it's not like that."

"It's not?" Her jaw was hard, as if she were clenching her teeth. Her dark eyes shimmered like ink. "If it's not like that, why would you fight over me with Daniel?" She thrust a hand into her hair, began pacing again. "Jesus, that's probably why Mr. Burne came over."

"We didn't *fight*," Evan insisted.

She paused to give him a disbelieving look. "I know Daniel. I know you."

"And I *want* to know you!" Evan burst out. Because it had become almost painful, the way everyone knew something except him. The way Daniel or random women in shops or even Zach could drop shit on him about someone he—

Well. About the woman his life revolved around.

But he didn't know how to explain that to Ruth without sounding sickeningly selfish. He realised suddenly that his intentions tonight—his idea that he'd reveal all the knowledge he'd collected and excuse her of all sins like some kind of fucking God—*had* been selfish.

She looked up at him, a heartbreaking little frown on her face, and said, "You *do* know me."

Evan swallowed. "That's not what I meant."

But it was too late. He could see that in her weary, hopeless eyes, in the way she rubbed at her temple.

Then she said, "Just go. Okay? Please?"

Jesus. He didn't want to go. He didn't want to leave things like this, and he didn't want to leave her at all.

But he couldn't refuse. So he went.

CHAPTER TWENTY-FOUR

PATIENCE KABBAH WAS neither observant nor assertive. Those who knew the Kabbahs often wondered how, exactly, she had produced one daughter who was particularly sharp, and another who was especially demanding.

If anyone had thought to ask Patience, she would have told them that it happened quite by accident. But people rarely asked Patience about things.

Her name suited her well, but 'Contentment' would have suited better. She was, by nature, an eternally satisfied woman—and despite the difficulties life had thrown at her, this commitment to satisfaction always carried her through. Of course, she didn't think of it as a commitment to satisfaction. She saw it as God's plan and followed faithfully.

When the love of her life, an older, powerful lawyer, turned out to be married, Patience had not worried. She had simply loved him anyway, and been rewarded with two children, a large house, and a life-long income.

That the house was in England as opposed to Sierra

Leone, and that the love of her life eventually moved on to greener pastures, did not trouble Patience overmuch. She supposed that England would do, since she spoke the language well and it was not *too* foreign. She supposed also that she would eventually find the *next* love of her life, and at least she could take her time looking.

And so, decades after arriving in Ravenswood, Patience was, always had been, and doubtless always would be, blissfully content. Her greatest sorrow was that, somehow, her daughters had ended up quite the opposite. Neither of them were happy to simply float through life, and as far as she could tell, it caused them nothing but trouble.

Take this Sunday, for example. The family had cooked together, as they did every week, but their usual laughter was absent. It was not at all hard to discern why. Within minutes of her daughters' arrival, Patience deduced that Hannah was worried about Ruth, and furiously resentful of the fact. She also deduced that Ruth was oblivious to Hannah's resentment, but was certainly upset over... Something. With Ruth, one never really knew.

Patience spent the rest of the painfully silent afternoon wondering if she should assist her awfully prideful children in resolving their issues—all of which stemmed from caring and doing far too much in a world made for the careless and passive. She decided, after many internal sighs, that she'd better. Her daughters had a knack for running into trouble if left unattended.

"Girls," she said, as they moved to clear the table.

Hannah answered quickly and politely. "Yes, Mummy?"

Ruth, who had always been a strange and disrespectful child, said, "Yeah?"

"Do not come out of the kitchen," Patience said, "until you have solved your problems."

Ruth frowned. The child would certainly wrinkle before her time. "What problems?"

With a weary sigh, Patience said, "Ask your sister." Then she turned and began her search for the TV commander. She was quite exhausted by that tense interaction, and she wanted to watch *Deal or No Deal*.

～

"What was that about?" Ruth crouched by the cupboard under the sink, hunting out a fresh bottle of washing up liquid.

Then she heard the kitchen door shut with a decisive *click*.

Ruth pulled her head from the cupboard and stared. Her sister was standing in front of the door with her arms folded, a familiar, stern set to her mouth.

"You know," Ruth began cautiously, "Just because Mum said—"

"She's right. She's always right. I want to talk to you."

The word *talk* had become Ruth's personal nightmare over the last few days. She'd examined it from every angle, explored its every connotation, remembered every time Evan had asked her to do it, and decided that talking was for the devil.

But she always tried not to upset her sister. So Ruth stood, dusted off her hands on the back of her leggings, and said, "Okay."

Hannah sighed. Ruth knew from experience that this

indicated an extensive lecture on the horizon. Accordingly, she leant back against the counter.

And then she remembered Evan lifting her up to sit on the edge of a sink, asking her—*asking* her—for a kiss.

"I heard that Daniel and Evan had a disagreement," Hannah said.

Ruth sighed. "Seriously? That's what you want to talk about?"

"I thought that was why you're so upset. Apparently, Evan's in a bad way."

Ruth stared. "Evan's fine."

"Really? No black eye?"

"Um… no."

"No dislocated shoulder?"

"Definitely not."

"Hm," Hannah sniffed. "I suppose that rumour came from Daniel, then. But you admit they fought?"

"I really could not care less," Ruth lied.

And Hannah said, "I'm tired of you pushing me away."

For a minute, Ruth's mind stuttered; was this Hannah, or was it Evan? Or was it Maria, two years ago, or Hayley, before her?

Ruth swallowed. "I don't mean to."

"I know," Hannah said. "That makes it worse."

Ruth wanted to turn away. She wanted to avoid her sister's gaze and pour her focus into something else, some mundane task. She wanted to split up her attention so that processing these words wouldn't seem quite so intense. She wanted this conversation to feel like less of a slap in the face. But she was done with being a coward, so she stayed exactly where she was.

"I'm sorry," Hannah said. "I'm really fucking sorry."

Well... *that* was a surprise. Ruth frowned, trying to figure out if she'd missed something.

Finally, she just had to ask. "Sorry for what?"

Hannah gave her a look. "You know what. And I know that this is—God, *years* too late—but if it weren't for me acting like a damn fool you wouldn't be in the position you are now."

The pieces slid together. Ruth stared at her sister with growing horror as she realised what Hannah was trying to say.

"No," Ruth insisted. "No. That's not true. It's not your fault. It's my fault, and his fault, and—"

"Your fault?" Hannah echoed, her face incredulous. "Jesus. Sometimes it occurred to me that you might genuinely think that, but I didn't believe it." She rubbed at her own temple for a moment, her expression melting into weariness. "I should have, though, shouldn't I? That's why you're like this. That's why you're punishing yourself."

Ruth looked down at the kitchen tiles; familiar, cream squares. Following the lines of pale grout between them helped her clear the thoughts crowding her head, helped her pinpoint the most important part. "I'm not punishing myself. I'm not pushing you away."

"Bullshit," Hannah said, her tone incongruously gentle. "I know you adore that man."

Ruth's breath caught in her throat. "Evan?"

"Yes, Evan. And now you can't deny it, because if it wasn't true, his name wouldn't have even occurred to you." Hannah gave a little tilt of the head that brought to mind their childhood, the pointless, circular arguments they'd have that she would always win.

Ruth bit down on the inside of her cheek. "I don't see what Evan has to do with us."

"I suppose he's just a symptom of the issue." Hannah spoke quietly, her voice clipped. "You're so committed to keeping people at arm's length, you can't tell your own sister that you're falling in love. We don't do secrets anymore, Ruth. Remember?"

"Don't," Ruth snapped, her temper flaring. "This is nothing like the last time."

"No, it's not. It's worse. Because he's a decent person, and he's honest, and he's nothing to be ashamed of, and he makes you smile. And I had to find that out on my own, because *you* didn't tell me. You knew I would be worried, you knew I would hear things—"

"Right," Ruth snapped. "Because what you *hear* is so important. Why should I bother saying anything if gossip is all you need?"

"Why do you force people to look for it?" Hannah asked, exasperation in her every word. "I'm your sister. I would *love* to stop relying on strangers to tell me what you're up to, but I *have* to. And if you don't blame me—"

"I don't," Ruth insisted, because she never had and never would.

"If you don't blame me, then why are we so far apart?" Hannah's words were whisper-soft. She gave a rueful twist of the lips that was almost a smile, holding up her hands as if to say, *Answer that.*

"Because I don't deserve you." It felt like a shout, but it came to Ruth's own ears as a whisper. Across the room,

Hannah froze. And Ruth forced herself to say the words again, properly this time. "I love you, and I don't deserve you. Sometimes I can't bear to look at you because I feel so guilty it chokes me."

Hannah's face crumpled. "That's the last thing I ever wanted. You should never feel guilty, Ruth. Not ever."

"I started this whole mess."

"*Daniel* started this whole mess." Hannah came forward, held out a hand. She was hesitant, Ruth could tell, but she was fearless too.

No; not fearless. Rather, she chose to spit in fear's face.

Ruth caught her sister's hand and released a locked-up truth. "I admire you more than anyone in the world."

Hannah choked out a laugh that was perilously close to a sob. "I wish nursery managers around here were so open-minded."

"Fuck that and fuck them." Ruth pulled her sister into a hug. It felt immediately alien, and then, after a breath, wonderful. Like purest childhood reclaimed. She breathed in deep and felt her sister do the same. When they were young, very young, they'd talked about being twins. Imagined, and sometimes pretended, that they were. It had never been hard to convince people.

But, while they looked the same, they'd always been very different. Opposites, even.

Which was fine, Ruth realised. Good, in fact. Because identical puzzle pieces wouldn't fit together like this.

CHAPTER TWENTY-FIVE

THE TEXT CAME FROM ZACH.

Everything okay with you?

Evan stared at the text blankly for a solid few minutes before they sunk into his tired brain.

It wasn't especially late, but it was late enough for him to be lying in bed, wishing for sleep. He should be happy. He *was* happy, in a way. Shirley's tests had returned, and her prognosis wasn't quite as bad as doctors had initially feared.

To celebrate, Evan had attempted to make a fancy dessert from scratch; mille-feuille. Shirley had doubled over laughing at how awfully wrong it had gone, and then they'd all eaten the store-bought apple pie he'd brought along.

And he'd been happy. But, underneath the happiness, he'd still been regretful and hurt and confused and frustrated, and unsurprisingly, Zach had picked up on that. Evan was beginning to realise that Zach watched people more closely than he let on.

After a moment's thought, Evan managed a reply that

wasn't quite false, but also wouldn't worry a man with more than enough problems of his own.

Evan: Can't complain

The phone beeped in reply, its display flashing bright in the dark.

Zach: Any trouble with Daniel?

None. Maybe the prospect of an actual fight had scared some sense into Daniel; he did seem fond of his pretty face. Or maybe Mr. Burne had said something to his son. Mr. Burne, who'd come out of Ruth's flat as if it were nothing.

And truthfully, Evan still didn't know why exactly. Every time he tried to figure it out, he felt both guilty and childishly furious. So he'd given up.

A familiar noise sounded through the thin, stud wall behind his headboard, and he froze in the middle of typing out a negative.

Ruth. Ruth was in her room.

He'd never really minded hearing Ruth bumble about all night; not until Friday. God, Friday. He'd had heaven within his reach, and then it had all gone sour. And now he minded.

He minded recognising the clumsy tread of her footsteps, and he minded that damned creak every time she got into bed. He minded the memory of her mouth on his cock because he couldn't enjoy it when she wasn't even talking to him, and he minded the fact that he was thinking about it now. That he'd thought about it every hour on the hour since the last time he'd seen her, and thought about her pain twice as often.

Swallowing down his feelings before they could choke him, Evan turned his attention back to the phone.

Evan: No more trouble. I'll see you tomorrow.

He propped himself up on one elbow, opened his bedside drawer, and threw the phone in there. Then he settled down to get some sleep.

You should've kept your mouth shut.

That would be lying.

And you told her for honesty's sake? What a joke. You told her to speed up a process that should've been at her pace.

Evan thrust a pillow over his head as if that would silence the warring opinions in his skull. None of it mattered. He would apologise to her—he had to—but it seemed better to give her space first. So that's what he'd do.

Eventually, he almost managed to drift off to sleep. So of course, a booming *thud* sounded through the wall and woke him right up.

His tired brain leapt into wakefulness immediately, because old habits died hard. Evan was out of bed with his ear pressed to the wall in seconds. After that enormous crash, louder than any he'd heard from Ruth's flat, there came nothing but silence.

He held his breath for a moment before giving in to the twist of worry in his gut. "Ruth?" he shouted. "Can you hear me?"

Nothing in the world would ever sound as good as Ruth shouting back. "Of course I can hear you."

Despite his concern, and his confusion, and the fact that words from Ruth were as painful as they were perfect right now, he chuckled. "So you're okay?"

"I'm fine," she called back. And then, after a beat, she added, "Thank you."

Evan raised his brows at the wall.

"How are you?" she continued.

And now he was worried again. "Did you hit your head?"

"You know," she called, "that's not the first time you've asked me that."

"But did you?"

"No. I'm simply making conversation."

"Through a wall in the middle of the night?"

"You started it," she pointed out. And then she said, not exactly *quietly*, since they were shouting, but hesitantly… "If you come over, we could make conversation without the wall."

It was probably pathetic, how his heart leapt at that. It was definitely pathetic how quickly he threw a pair of tracksuit bottoms over his nudity and called, "On my way."

He didn't care.

∽

RUTH OPENED her door just as quickly as he opened his, and that bolstered Evan's resolve. She wanted to see him. He knew it, and yet he wasn't completely sure until they were face to face. She stood in the doorway and he stood on her doormat.

He blurted out, "I'm sorry."

She blinked. "*You're* sorry?"

"Yes. I shouldn't have pushed you. I didn't mean to, and it was selfish, and I shouldn't have done it, and I'm sorry." Huh. He was babbling. He'd never babbled before. But this apology had been trying to burst from his lips for two days, and he found that being at odds with Ruth did not suit him. Not at all.

"Okay," she said, and he relaxed. Because her lips were tilted in that almost-smile, the one he'd worried he might never see again. Then she said, "I'm sorry too."

This was a night full of surprises.

Evan came in, trying not to focus on the door he'd leant against when she'd—well. "You are?"

"Yes. For waking you up."

He bit his lip, felt a smile spread slowly over his face. "You didn't wake me up."

"I didn't?"

"No. You didn't. Still sorry?"

She shut the door behind them and stood there, fiddling with a loose thread at the end of her pyjamas. He saw the moment she steeled herself, saw the moment she straightened her spine and took a fortifying breath. "Yes. I'm still sorry."

"Okay." He studied her, drinking in everything he'd missed. Her wide, brown eyes, her lips and her too-big front teeth. But he kept his voice neutral as he said, "For what?"

"For the other day. I lost my temper and I said some things that just... aren't true. I know you're not a malicious person, and I'm sure you weren't *gossiping* about me, and—and I 'd like to talk. To you. About things."

Evan tried to tamp down his optimism. It felt like trying to fight the dawning sun. "Things?"

Ruth nodded. "Things. I, um... I had decided to tell you, actually. To tell you everything. On Friday."

He squeezed his eyes shut and cursed himself. *I had decided to tell you.* And he'd fucked it up and taken away that choice—or attempted to.

"Really?" he managed.

"Really. And I shouldn't have gotten so angry—"

"There's no *should* or *shouldn't* when it comes to anger." He wanted to touch her, purely because she looked so stiff and alone standing before him. But he rather thought she should make the first move, break the imaginary barrier. "You feel how you feel and that's fine. The important thing is talking through it."

"I know," she said quickly. "I know that. I mean, I'm going to do that. I realise I'm kind of prickly. I'm, um, trying not to be."

Evan smiled slightly. "I don't know about that. I like prickly."

Ruth blinked. She actually looked surprised—not just surprised, but really, truly shocked.

Which bothered Evan beyond reason, because she shouldn't be surprised that he didn't want her to change. Or rather, she shouldn't be surprised that *anyone* wouldn't want her to change. "I like you," he explained. "A lot. And you're prickly, so I like prickly. That's it."

After a moment, Ruth's tentative smile returned. "Well, okay. I suppose I like you too."

Evan rolled his eyes. "You *love* me. I bet you knocked over a mountain of comics just to get my attention."

"I certainly did not! No man is worth that disorganisation."

"Really?" He arched a brow.

She managed to hold back her laughter for a second or two before a rogue giggle escaped. And then she kicked him, very gently, which was almost her version of a hug.

So Evan gave in to the urgings of his heart and pulled her in for an *actual* hug. She made a strangled little noise, but she came, and she wrapped her arms around him and squeezed tight.

"I don't want to argue," Evan murmured, burying his face in her hair. He had to bend at an awkward angle to do it, but it was worth it to breath in that coconut scent. "Ever."

Her voice was muffled against his chest, but he still heard the humour there. "I think arguments are a necessary part of—" Abruptly, she broke off. But then, after a moment, she continued: "A necessary part of any relationship."

Evan pulled back slightly, grasping her shoulders. He looked down at her carefully impassive face and said, "By *relationship*, you mean…"

Ruth shrugged.

With a slow smile, he said, "So what you're saying is, *'Evan, we're in a relationship.'*"

She rolled her eyes. "If you want me to be your girlfriend, you should just ask. Don't be shy." She reached up on her tiptoes and patted his head. Then, eyes dancing, she hurried off down the hall.

He followed. Of course he followed.

～

RUTH COULDN'T QUITE BELIEVE her own daring, but she wasn't complaining about it. Turned out, everything was easier when you opened your mouth and words came out, and you didn't cut them off halfway.

Evan followed her into the bedroom, probably thinking that they were about to have riotous reunion sex or some such nonsense. They weren't, of course. She wasn't quite *that* far gone.

Although... he stood in the doorway, and Ruth eyed the thick outline of his dick against his thigh, visible thanks to the soft, jersey material of his clothes.

Maybe she *was* that far gone.

He squinted over at her bed and said, "What the hell happened?"

Oh, yes. Now she remembered why she'd actually brought him in here.

"My bed collapsed."

He walked over to the pile of wood, dislodged mattress and rumpled bedding, his brows raised. "Yeah. I can see that."

"So why'd you ask?"

He shot her a wry smile, reaching out to tug on her braid. "Quiet, you." Then he crouched down and lifted the mattress with one powerful arm, which should not have made her core tighten or her pulse spike, but did. Maybe because he was shirtless, and she could see every muscle in his back shift as he did it. Maybe because she was quite pathetically in love with him.

What?

Nothing. Look at the muscles.

Ruth obeyed the more sensible of the two voices in her head and moved on. "Can you fix it?"

"Is that what you think?" He threw a grin over her shoulder. "That I can fix it?"

"Are you saying you can't? Because I'd really hoped to sleep in a bed tonight."

For a moment, he was silent. Then he stood, dusting off his hands, and said, "You could sleep in mine."

Ruth gave him a look. "Oh I *could*, could I? How

chivalrous."

"I'm not being chivalrous. Who put that bed together, by the way?"

She said, "Daniel." Then she thought, *Oops.*

But nothing bad happened. Lightning didn't strike, and Evan didn't stop moving toward her. He slid an arm around her waist and said, "Daniel did a very poor job."

"That doesn't surprise me. He's bad at following instructions."

"I bet." His lips quirked, and then he raised a hand to Ruth's face and stroked her cheek. Soft, slow, reverent. He said, "I'd like to sleep with you. And I do mean *sleep.*"

She licked her lips. "Why?"

"Because I want to hold you, and I want to know how you look when you wake up in the morning."

That, Ruth thought, was quite adorable. The sort of simple romance that she'd never experienced and, judging by the butterflies in her stomach, really wanted.

But it wasn't all she wanted.

Ruth held his gaze and murmured, "I don't wear pyjamas all the time, you know."

His brow furrowed. "Uh... you kind of do."

"No. Not when I sleep."

His gaze heated, achingly intense. "I see."

"Shall we go?"

"Yes." As quickly as the word shot from his lips, Evans shook his head. "Wait. Come here." But she didn't have to move, because he grabbed her, pulled her closer, and kissed her. *Oh.*

Ruth couldn't stifle the moan that gathered in her throat as his mouth claimed hers, his tongue tracing the seam of her lower lip. He began with soft, nibbling kisses that mirrored the gentle touch of his hands at her waist—but slowly, bit by bit, the kiss transformed. Heated. Went nuclear.

She slid her palms over his bare chest, feeling every inch of soft, hair-dusted skin and taut muscle, before moving lower. As she neared his waistband, Evan growled against her lips. Then, suddenly, he grabbed her arse with firm hands and hauled her up against his body, kissing her harder. His tongue plunged into her mouth, his lips insistent, devouring, and she took all of his passion and returned it with a fire of her own.

Ruth wrapped her thighs around his waist and felt the growing length of his erection press firmly between her legs. She whispered his name, and he swallowed the sound.

With reluctance, Ruth broke the kiss.

He opened his eyes slowly, pupils blown, and murmured, "What's wrong?"

"Nothing's wrong," she panted. *Nothing's ever been so right.* "Hurry up and take me to bed."

CHAPTER TWENTY-SIX

RUTH TORE off her clothes as soon as she stepped foot in Evan's room. No underwear, because she really *had* been naked when her bed had collapsed beneath her. But she hadn't wanted to apologise with her tits bouncing around between them, because that seemed undignified.

She *had* wanted to apologise, though. Turned out, once you started talking about things, it got way, way easier. And Ruth had discovered there were few people in the world she wanted to talk to as much as Evan.

She was completely naked and tucked under his boring, blue covers before she realised that Evan was still standing in the doorway as if frozen. She propped herself up on one elbow and asked, "Are you coming?"

He swallowed, his Adam's apple bobbing visibly. "You do realise the most I've ever seen of your body is... copious forearm. And some ankle. I'm particularly fond of the dimples above your elbows."

"How scandalous."

Slowly, he came toward the bed. "What's scandalous is you in my bed, naked, and completely hidden from view." He came to stand beside her, staring at the outline of her body beneath the quilt as if he might suddenly develop X-ray vision. "Do you need me to turn the light off?"

"Oh," Ruth said. "You think I'm shy."

He arched a brow.

She smiled, feeling quite smug, and said, "I'm not shy." Then she sat up completely and pushed back the blanket.

Evan sank slowly to his knees beside the bed, his eyes traversing all the hills and valleys of her body—and then repeating the journey again, slower, as if to savour certain parts. She wondered if she should've done this lying down, to minimise the roll situation, but then decided that rolls were fine. If they were going to do anything interesting, rolls would eventually occur. She couldn't lie down constantly whenever they were naked.

Plus, Evan didn't seem to have any complaints.

He bit his lip as he studied her, his eyes moving from the swell of her breasts to the shadowed space between her legs. She could spread her thighs wider, let him see what he wanted to see instead of hiding it away. But that wouldn't be half as much fun.

Because she knew he'd ask, Ruth murmured, "You can touch me."

He looked up, his eyes hungry. "Anywhere?"

"Preferably everywhere."

Slowly, deliberately, he pressed a hand to her hip. Which wasn't exactly what she'd expected—but the slightest touch from him left her breathless.

"I thought about this," he said. His hand slid up, slow and

steady, over her hip and toward her ribs. "I thought about how you'd look naked, and then I felt guilty."

Her breath caught as his hand reached the underside of her breast. "Why guilty?"

He cupped the mound of flesh, no more than a handful for him. "Because I thought about it too much. And every time I heard your shower start or your bed creak, I imagined touching you. Taking off your clothes and kissing every inch of you and then fucking you—and I've never done that. I've never fantasised about... about a friend."

"Because you're too noble," she teased. Then his thumb brushed over her nipple, and her smile became a whimper.

Evan's eyes flew to hers. "You like that."

It wasn't a question, but she bit her lip and nodded anyway.

So he did it again, harder this time, worrying the stiff peak. She could feel her pussy growing wet, the muscles contracting as if searching for something, begging to be filled. Lust riding her, Ruth shoved at his waistband. The fabric slid down easily over his thighs, and his cock bobbed free, beautiful as she remembered, and oh, Jesus, how she'd wanted his.

But before she could touch him, Evan bent his head over her other breast and took the aching nipple into his mouth. She cried out as his tongue flicked the tight peak with impossible delicacy, even as his lips sucked softly at her breast.

"Jesus," she choked out. "Evan. Fuck." He still worked her other nipple with one thumb, and Ruth stared down at the sight. At his big hand against her skin, the knuckles dusted in golden hair; at his head bent over her breast with singular focus, and the muscles in his naked back. She could see the globes of his arse and imagined how they'd look when he thrust into her, how the muscle would shift beneath his skin.

Ruth's own hand ached to move between her legs. But before she could do anything, he released her nipple with a last, hard lick.

Looking up at her with slightly swollen lips, Evan said, "I want to make you come. You look so pretty when you come."

She huffed out a laugh, but the sound was strained. "It's kind of hard for someone else to make me..."

"Show me, then. We've got time."

He said that as if there was no way he'd rather spend that time than trying to get her off. She understood the sentiment, because she'd be willing to spend ages sucking his cock.

Asking for what she wanted in the bedroom wasn't a familiar habit, but Ruth had a feeling that Evan would make it easier.

The words were hard to dredge up, thick and sticky as syrup, but she forced herself to speak because she knew he really meant it. He wanted to know. He was watching her with earnest eyes shot through with thunderous shadow, and his face was so fucking... *dear* to her, even now, with his hand on her breast and his cock straining between them. Her blood burned through her veins at the sight of his body, and her heart squeezed in her chest at the knowledge that he was Evan. Just Evan.

"Well," she managed. "Usually, when someone else makes me come, it's because they, um, used their mouth."

Evan stood, pulling his clothes off completely. It occurred to her that he'd probably been naked too, before her bed collapsed.

God, she was glad her bed had collapsed.

He stood before her, his cock rising proudly against his solid waist, his balls heavy between thick, muscular thighs, and she thought maybe she *would* come tonight. Without the use of her own hand. She had a rather good feeling about this.

"Lying down?" he asked.

She blinked, taking a minute to catch his meaning. "I've only ever done it lying down."

He smirked. "Well, like I said, we've got time." Then he pushed her gently back against the pillows, nudging her into the centre of the bed. For a moment, he slid his body over hers, and a spark of anticipation danced down her spine. His chest grazed the sensitive tips of her breasts, and she felt the weight of his cock between her thighs.

Then he kissed her gently before moving down her body, his lips trailing over her skin. His mouth brushed along the length of her throat, over the swell of her breasts. He lingered there for a moment, flicking his tongue over each stiff peak, and then he said, his voice hoarse, "I love your nipples."

"You do?"

"Mmm." He gave one a firm suck, and she felt the pull between her legs. Then he released her and continued his journey south. Over her ribs, her belly, her hips, went his mouth. His beard tickled everywhere, the sort of tickle that didn't inspire laughter so much as panting, half-hysterical moans.

When his mouth passed her hips, Evan grabbed her thighs. His fingers dug into her flesh just hard enough to make her gasp, and then that gasp turned into a ragged moan when he pushed her legs wider. Ruth felt the slick folds of her pussy spread open, exposed suddenly to the cool air. And then she felt the warmth of his breath against her, the contrast sharp, the anticipation dizzying.

"You tell me what to do," he said, "and what not to do." He pressed a gentle kiss against the inside of her thigh. "Okay?"

She swallowed, nodded, then remembered he couldn't see her. "Okay."

"Good." His hands slid from her thighs to her pussy, and he parted her further, spreading her open with his thumbs. And then she felt that tongue again, big and strong and yet so delicate, tracing her inner folds.

Ruth's breath escaped in a strained gasp, her hips jerking up. And then, because she'd told him she would, she said, "More."

He licked the very centre of her desire, his tongue dipping into her, and she moaned. Arched her back. Felt the last of the blood circulating her brain disappear. Still, she needed something else.

Then his tongue moved up and flicked gently at her clit, and Ruth gave a sharp cry. "Fuck, yes. Evan..."

He licked faster, and then she felt his finger stroke her entrance. For a second, the heat of his mouth disappeared, and Ruth wanted to scream in frustration because *that*— that had been almost perfect, and she needed him to keep going.

Then he pushed the tip of his finger into her, and she felt

herself tighten around him automatically. Desperately. *Christ.*

"Tell me this is okay," he said, his voice low and heavy with a lust that belonged, she realised, to her. He was enjoying this. He didn't just want to make her happy. He was doing it for himself, too.

Her hips jerked against him, pushing his finger deeper as she said, "This is definitely okay. Keep going."

That long, thick finger thrust in all the way, until she could feel his knuckles against her labia. Jesus Christ, it felt good, simultaneously too much and not enough.

"I don't want to hurt you," he said suddenly. "You'd tell me, if I hurt you?"

"Yes. Now, I'm kind of missing your mouth, so if you don't mind…"

He grinned wickedly. "Oh, no. I don't mind at all." Then he buried his head between her thighs again, his tongue massaging her clit more firmly than before. *Perfectly.* So perfectly that she found herself gasping out his name, writhing on the bed with no restraint whatsoever. His finger moved slowly inside her, back and forth, until she softened enough for him to thrust with ease.

He added another finger, and Ruth shuddered at the delicious stretch, and then she rose up on her elbows to look at him and holy shit was he beautiful. So, so beautiful, his handsome face buried between her legs, his eyes closed as if in ecstasy. He stroked her expertly, worked her clit tirelessly, and the twin rhythms had her heart pounding in her chest.

She slid a hand into his hair, pushed him against her as if he could get any closer. "Fuck," she gasped out, the word stretching on a breath. "Oh my God. Please don't stop, you can't stop, please—" because she was suddenly, unreasonably terrified that he might. That he might take away the perfection and the promise of starlight just when she was *almost* there, and nothing would be more unbearable.

He didn't. He kept going, kept up the pace and the pressure until the razor-sharp streaks of pleasure arcing through her reached their peak. Ruth managed to groan out a series of babbled, senseless words—"Oh, my, *fuck* yes, you're so, *Jesus*, Evan, you perfect fucking…"—before her mind gave up completely. She gave a hoarse cry as she twisted up off the bed, but Evan didn't stop then, either. He wrapped an arm around her hips and kept licking, kept stroking, his movements growing slower and gentler as her moans eased.

When she relaxed against the bed, limbs liquid, chest heaving, he finally stopped.

The fact that he'd made her come almost as easily as she did herself should've shocked Ruth. Instead, she felt an odd sort of satisfaction; as if he'd met an expectation she'd secretly already held.

He moved up the bed to lay beside her, his warm body pressed against hers. She rolled onto her side and wrapped her arms around him.

She'd been sated five seconds ago. Now she could feel his hardness pressing into her belly, smell her own arousal on his beard, see the fire burning in his eyes.

She kissed him without a word, sinking into his touch the way she would a warm bath. His hands roamed over her body, sliding down the small of her back, over the curve of her arse. He delved between her legs from behind, stroking her slowly, gently. The way he touched her, as if it were a habit, only made Ruth hungrier.

She reached between their bodies and found his stiff cock, squeezing the firm girth. A flare of pleasure shot through her as Evan sighed against her lips.

Then she slid his erection between her thighs, and he grunted, "Fuck."

CHAPTER TWENTY-SEVEN

WHEN EVAN FELT Ruth orgasm around his fingers, tasted her release on his tongue, he thought he'd never come so close to dying of pleasure.

Of course, he should've realised she'd drive him so much closer before the night was out.

He sucked in a breath as she closed those lush thighs around his cock. So different, the feel of all that flesh, to the wet heat of her cunt. Still sweet enough to make his balls tighten, to call up the ghost of a familiar tingle at the base of his spine.

Evan pushed the sensation away. One day, he'd like to come all over her soft, brown skin. Tonight wasn't the time.

But his hips, pumping of their own accord, didn't seem to agree.

Ruth kissed him as if she'd never stop. He hoped she wouldn't. If they stayed like this forever, or until their air ran out, that would be fine. More than fine. That would be heaven.

He held her close as he thrust against her, silken skin and suffocating pressure conspiring against him until he was ruled more by instinct than sense. His hands grabbed at her roughly, greedily, and his tongue thrust wildly against hers—and Ruth moaned and writhed for him as if she were just as mindless.

She pulled away from his mouth—*bad*—and gasped out, breathless, "You should fuck me now." *Good*. Very, very good.

Evan tore himself away from her because he knew that easing back slowly wouldn't work. He'd never leave the warmth of her skin, the abundant curves of her body. And if he never left, he couldn't grab a condom from his drawer, and then he couldn't finally thrust into her the way he'd wanted to for weeks.

So he took the condom, tore it open, rolled it on, and was lying over her within seconds.

She blinked up at him. Since when had she been on her back? Perhaps he'd put her there.

"That was quick," she said. Something about the tilt of her lips told him, clearly as if she'd actually laughed, that she was mocking him. He liked Ruth mocking him.

"I must be desperate," he said.

"Yes, you mu—*ohh*, fuck," she broke off, squeezing her eyes shut as he slid his cock over her folds.

"What was that?" he prompted. His hips moved in a tight circle, nudging at her clit with each thrust.

"Fuck *off*," she groaned, arching against him.

"You want me to stop?"

"I want you to fuck me," Ruth gritted out. Not icy and controlled, but hoarse and edgy and unravelling. He wanted to make her sound like that every fucking day, for the rest of... for the rest of forever. For as long as was humanly possible.

Evan hooked one of Ruth's legs over his shoulder, opening her up beneath him. So fucking close. Soon they'd be closer.

But the sharp, biting arousal tightening his core was accompanied by softer sensations. By the warmth in his chest that only she elicited.

He touched his forehead to hers for a moment, felt her heavy breaths against his cheek. "Ruth," he murmured. "You're so... I've never felt like this before."

Her eyes fluttered open. "Like what?" she whispered back.

He didn't know. He couldn't say it. He couldn't find the words. But he settled for, "Perfect. I feel like everything is perfect."

And she, always a surprise, flashed him a wicked little smile and shifted her hips. "I wonder how you'll feel when you actually—"

"Shut up," he snorted.

"Isn't that my line?"

He kissed her. Not just because he wanted to distract her —because he had a suspicion that she might need it in a second—but because he simply couldn't not.

Here was Ruth, and she was his, and therefore, he kissed her.

She wound her arms around his neck and sighed. Evan chose that moment to push the aching head of his cock into her, just a little. Just an inch. Her pussy clung to him immediately, the pressure tighter than even her mouth had been.

And her mouth had been fucking good.

He moved his kisses to her cheek, her jaw, and held still. "You okay?"

"Mmhm." The sound was strained, a body that had been fluid around him suddenly rigid.

He looked down at her. "Don't do that. Just tell me what you need, and I'll give it to you."

She exhaled, closing her eyes. "Right. Okay. Just... stay still for a second. Kiss me."

Evan obliged. He was aware of the fact that, because of his size—or specifically, girth—he had to be careful with people, the first time. He didn't care if he had to wait a minute, or five, or ten, for someone to get used to him.

He *did* care about the fact that Ruth seemed suddenly hesitant beneath him, her kisses soft and uncertain, her body stiff.

"Talk to me," Evan whispered against her lips. "We talk now. Remember?"

"Right." He felt her smile. That was a good sign. "Sorry. I just hate being awkward."

"What's awkward?" He reached between their bodies and brushed a finger over her clit. When she clenched around him, he thought he might come on the spot.

She gave a soft moan before answering, her voice slightly breathless, "The fact that you had to stop. Because I—"

"I haven't stopped." He caught her earlobe between his teeth, sucked the soft curve. "I'm right here."

"I think I'm nervous," she blurted out.

"That's okay. I'm definitely nervous."

"What are *you* nervous about?" Her brows were raised,

her lips tilted at the corners. And he felt her relax, just a little bit.

"This is very high-stakes for me," he said gravely. "Since you're the sexiest woman I've ever met, and everything."

She laughed. "If I were in a demonstrative mood, I might say that you're the sexiest man I've ever met."

"I already knew that."

She narrowed her eyes. "You *thought* you knew that."

"Nah, I knew. You stare at my chest a lot."

Ruth gave a gasp of outrage, and Evan muffled it with a kiss, laughing and open-mouthed and clumsy and perfect. She sank her hands into his hair and tugged, and he thought nothing could feel so divine as Ruth pulling him closer, needing him. Then she wrapped a leg around his waist, and he felt her open for him, just a little, and sank deeper.

She gasped against his mouth. It wasn't a pained gasp, but achingly sweet and hungry. Evan reached between them again and found the swollen nub of her clit, massaging with his thumb. And then he waited as she moaned, as she whimpered, as she tilted her hips and pulled him deeper with each languid movement.

Evan maintained his control, reined himself in, until he was completely buried inside her. Silken heat surrounded him, caressing his cock, ratcheting up his lust, but still he kept his head. He kissed her, hard, as he began to move—slowly, so slowly. His tongue slid against hers with all the frenzy that his hips could *not* display. He wouldn't hurt her. He wouldn't hurt her.

Then she sank her nails into his shoulder and moaned, "Harder."

Evan swallowed roughly. "Are you sure—?"

"Fuck, yes, I'm sure." She arched against him, pushing her breasts into his chest. "Please. I need…" She trailed off with a gasp as he twisted his hips, driving into her with more force. "*That*. I need that. Fuck."

He grasped her arse, tilting her hips up, holding her in place. And then he let his control slip.

"Oh my *God*," she hissed, thrusting up to meet him, throwing her head back. Evan grunted as he pounded into her, every movement punctuated by the satisfying smack of flesh against flesh. Sweat dripped down his brow as he gritted his teeth, because Jesus, fuck, he wanted to come, but the look of ecstasy on Ruth's face wasn't something he could bear to take away.

"Evan," she chanted, her voice shaking as he slammed into her. "*Evan*. Fuck, don't stop."

"You feel so fucking good," he panted. "I can't stop. I want you forever." He wasn't making any fucking sense and he knew it. He could barely understand his own ragged speech, and he didn't care.

Ruth didn't care either, because she leaned up and caught his mouth with hers, teeth grazing his lips, tongue thrusting against his. And then she came, so suddenly and so explosively that Evan couldn't have held back if he'd tried. She convulsed beneath him, her cries breathless and throaty, her cunt tightening around his cock, and his vision blurred.

"*Ruth*." He shuddered over her, burying his face against her throat as he came, the sudden release so intense it was almost painful.

They sank back against the mattress as one, and for a moment he simply lay over her and concentrated on breathing. Then he remembered that he was really fucking heavy.

Evan rolled onto his back and dragged Ruth with him. She only came part way, slinging her leg over his body with a drowsy sigh. He stared hazily up at the ceiling as her fingers slid over his chest, toying with the hairs there.

Then, after a moment, he said, "I love you."

There was a pause. A pause in which he thought, *Why the fuck did I just say that?* And then realised that it was because he simply couldn't... *not*.

"Well," she said, before the silence stretched too far. "I had no idea I was that good in bed."

He laughed. "Maybe you're not. Maybe I just love you anyway."

She propped herself up on one elbow and looked down at him. "We haven't talked yet." But there was no wariness in her eyes, or awful blankness. She just looked thoughtful.

"No," he said. "We haven't."

"Maybe... maybe we should talk now."

"If we're talking, I should probably deal with the condom."

"Oh," she said. "Yes. Probably."

He kissed her, light and fast, before disentangling their legs and getting up. As he headed to the bathroom, Evan looked over his shoulder.

There was Ruth Kabbah, lying naked in his bed, staring up at the ceiling.

Smiling to herself.

CHAPTER TWENTY-EIGHT

"I DIDN'T SMASH up Daniel's car," Ruth said.

Evan was back where he belonged—which was, she now realised, under her. On top of her would also do—or behind her, for that matter—but right now he was under her. She laid her head on his chest and felt the steady beat of his heart. It matched the stroke of his hand over her back.

How she loved being naked with him.

I love you.

"So that's just another rumour," he said.

"I don't know. It's not one I've ever heard before," she replied. Hedging. Hesitating. Not because she didn't trust him or because she was scared, but because this part of the story was the worst. The absolute worst. She licked her lips and said, "Who told you? What did they say?"

"I was with Daniel, at the newsagents, and Mrs. Needham was showing me a car. She said it looked like one Daniel had. She said..." He paused as if remembering exactly. "She said, *That Kabbah girl smashed it to pieces. And* then Zach said something too, just a throwaway comment about how he didn't judge because his brother has a record. So I just..."

Ruth nodded, his chest hair tickling her cheek. Then she said, "Hannah did it."

She felt the surge of shock through him. Felt him lift his head to look down at her. "Seriously? *Hannah?*"

"Yes."

"Why?"

Ruth sighed. "Because I told her some things. Things that upset her. *I* was upset. So she calmed me down and put me to bed, and then she apparently went to Daniel's house and smashed the shit out of his car."

Evan released a long, quiet exhale. "Fuck. So Hannah..."

"Hannah was arrested." Ruth could hear her own voice, flat and hollow. "She was charged and convicted with criminal damage and possession of an offensive weapon—"

"An offensive weapon?"

"She used a cricket bat," Ruth said dully. "It was her boyfriend's. She got a suspended sentence, community service, and a fine. She ruined her life because of me."

"Wait—what?" Evan's body shifted beneath her as he raised himself up on his elbows.

She could feel him staring at her, but she couldn't look. It was ridiculous, pathetic, but tears were pricking at the corners of her eyes.

"First of all," he said, "she doesn't seem like her life was *ruined.*"

"Well, it was," Ruth snapped. "She's a nursery nurse. I mean, she *was* a nursery nurse. That's all she ever wanted to do—she got a fucking foundation degree and everything—

and now she's a waitress. She can't work with kids. We used to volunteer at the library together, we did it for years, and now she can't even do that."

Ruth remembered the letter that had come from the council, informing Hannah of her *unsuitability* for the position she'd been filling since they were bloody teenagers. And Hannah had tried to pretend she wasn't upset, but she'd been devastated.

So Ruth had quit, too. What else could she do?

Evan sighed. It was a sad, short sigh that seemed entirely appropriate to Ruth—but then he ruined it by talking unnecessarily. "Okay. I get that. But, love, I don't think you should blame yourself. I'm not saying I don't understand," he added hurriedly when she sucked in a breath. Ruth felt him lay back slowly, felt the soothing stroke of his hand on her hair, and calmed. "I bet Hannah's told you this," he said. "I bet she's told you a thousand times that it's not your fault—"

"And that she's a grown woman who makes her own decisions and blah, blah, blah," Ruth finished. "Whatever. I made bad choices, and it came back to bite me. I brought my shit to her doorstep and—she's my sister. She's my *sister*. Of course she lost it. I was sleeping at hers while she went out and destroyed Daniel's pride and joy in front of half the town."

"Half the town?"

"It was his engagement party."

Evan stiffened. Then he said, "I think you should tell me about Daniel."

So she did. She told him everything she'd told Mr. Burne.

But she told him other things, too. The little things Daniel did, the cruelties she'd barely noticed because they'd been wrapped in silk or laced with diamonds. The way he'd spike every compliment with a put-down, the way he made sure she knew that *he* wanted her—more than anything on earth, too much to leave her alone even when she asked— but no-one else ever would.

"He'd say, you know... '*Ruth, you're the most beautiful woman in the world, to me. It's a shame other people won't see it.*' Or he'd get rid of my pyjamas and buy me a wardrobe full of Gucci."

Evan tensed at that part, which was kind of funny. Even funnier was the outrage in his voice when he said, "That fucker got rid of your pyjamas?"

"Oh, he hated my pyjamas. I was always buying new ones and he was always finding ways to throw them away. He hated my comics, too. I had to keep them at Hannah's."

She could practically hear Evan's teeth grinding. "And you were together for how long?"

"Seven years."

"Seven years," he murmured. "Seven years, and no-one knew."

She shrugged. "Who would suspect? Until that night two years ago, I was no-one. I was Hannah's weird little sister. He was Daniel Burne. It wasn't that hard to hide."

His fingers traced gentle, soothing circles over her skin. Impressive, when she could feel him vibrating with anger.

"And he..." Evan took a breath. "He sends you flowers."

"On a semi-regular basis. He's been jealous, since I met you. He's childish like that. He sends me other things, too, to apologise for the way he behaves every time we meet."

"Why?"

"Because he wants me back, apparently." Ruth snorted, and was surprised to realise that she was actually amused. Not afraid, or silenced, or blaming herself for Daniel's delusions. Just amused, and disgusted, and vaguely pitying. "He's unhappy, and he always will be. Some people are never satisfied. They want endlessly."

"And what do you want?"

She shifted, turning her head to look up at Evan. His face was grave, his blue eyes gentle. "Are you asking if I still care about him?"

"Yeah." There was no judgement in Evan's voice. Even though she'd just told him that she'd spent most of her adult life in a secret relationship with the biggest piece of shit she'd ever met. Even though he now knew that her poor decisions had contributed to the derailing of her sister's dreams.

"He called the police," she said. "He called the police and wrote a statement against my sister over a fucking car he could afford five times over. He ruined her life and he did it to hurt me. And he said—he said I should be grateful that he wasn't suing." Her voice was hard. Her heart, in that moment, was harder. "When I found out about Laura, when I finally realised what he was, that didn't stop me loving him. I left him, but I loved him. When he hurt Hannah, though…" She shook her head. "It was as if I'd never loved him at all."

She didn't think she was imagining the way Evan relaxed, but he hid it well. His fingers never faltered in their slow, soothing circle. He nodded. Then he said, as if making a sudden realisation, "That girl you were friends with; Hayley?"

"Daniel's sister-in-law." Ruth sighed. "That night, he gave Laura some explanation. Some twisted version of what actually happened between us. A version in which I shamelessly seduced Daniel, got jealous when he tried to leave me for Laura... whatever. She told Hayley, Hayley believed her—"

"Why?" Evan demanded.

"Because that's what sisters do. They believe each other. And I didn't exactly help."

Evan sighed. "Let me guess. Someone asked you what was going on, and you very helpfully told them to fuck off."

"Something like that."

Ruth still remembered the raw panic of waking to find Mum pacing the room, biting her nails, looking worried for the first time in her life. Still remembered the words, *"Your sister has been arrested".* Still remembered the acidic fear, the cotton-thick confusion, the regret. The guilt.

"My sisters was arrested and all anyone could ask me about was Daniel," she growled, that memory still sour. "I didn't give a fuck about him or about petty gossip. Then Hayley called and accused me of all this shit so I just... I just said, *'Yeah, sure. That sounds right.'* And I put the phone down."

Evan was quiet for a moment, and she waited, enjoying the way he held her. Casually, thoughtlessly, his fingers still tracing over her back. Like this kind of intimacy was normal.

"So," he said, "that's where all these rumours come from? About you sleeping with half the town?"

"Oh, no," she said. "I actually did that."

"What?!" he spluttered. Then he laughed. "Are you serious?"

"I mean… I *did* tell you upfront."

"I thought you were just being weird!"

She raised her brows at him. "Why would you think that?"

"Well, based on how long it took us to get here…" His smile was rueful.

"It wasn't like this," she admitted. "It was more like, everyone assumed I was easy because of the thing with Daniel, so guys started asking me out. And I…" She sighed. "I'd only ever been with him. And I hadn't enjoyed it, and he made me feel weird and fucked up and kind of gross, so I thought, I'll sleep with someone else and that will fix it, but it didn't, exactly—so I kept going. And by the time I realised nothing would fix it—well. This is a small town."

Evan rose up on his elbows, bent to press a kiss against her hair. "I'm sorry, love."

It was sounding too much like a tragedy for Ruth's liking, so she added, "People do exaggerate, though. It was only, like, fifteen guys."

"That's disappointing," Evan said dryly. "People act like you slept with a Roman legion. *You* act like you slept with a Roman legion."

Ruth sighed. "Okay. You caught me. I have not slept with 5000 men. Yet."

"Shocker."

"Rude!"

"I'm sure you *could*," he said, his voice teasing. "If you really wanted to. Live your dreams, and all that."

"I appreciate the support."

"You're welcome. But, while we're on the subject, I'd actually rather you stuck with me."

She smiled. It was an involuntary smile, an overflowing of the steady warmth that his presence sparked inside her chest. "Oh, you would?"

"Yeah. What do you think about that?"

"I think that sounds just fine." She pressed a kiss to his chest and was momentarily embarrassed by the hint of affection. Then she decided that revelling in mushy feelings was much more fun than being embarrassed and kissed his chest again.

And then, because her orgasm had clearly fried her brain, she murmured, "Does that mean you're my boyfriend, or...?"

He burst out laughing. "Yes, Ruth. Just so we're very, very clear—" He wrapped an arm around her waist, dragging her up his body until they were nose to nose. "I'm your boyfriend." He kissed her gently, and she felt a flicker of warmth in her heart that was as soft as his lips.

"Good," she whispered. She felt slightly conscious of the fact that all her weight was on him now, but when she tried to move, he held her tighter.

Then he said, "Does it upset you?"

He could've been talking about anything, considering the conversation they'd just had. But she knew, because she knew him, that all he really wanted was to make *her* talk. And recently, she'd been feeling the urge to do so more and more.

"Lots of things upset me," she said slowly. "Like the fact that Hannah made a bad decision on my behalf, and she's the one who has to deal with it. The fact that people I grew up with won't even speak to me anymore. Mostly, what upsets me is the fact that... So many people mistreated me, *still* mistreat me, and I didn't feel like it was worth fighting back."

Ruth's words sped up as she spoke, thoughts and feelings she'd been struggling to identify suddenly seeming obvious. It was as if the act of speech cleared the murky waters of her mind, finally allowed her to see herself.

"I felt like I should be punished," she admitted. "For everything. So I stayed inside instead of taking up space. I let people think the worst instead of defending myself. You know, Hayley stopped talking to me so damn fast but Maria —I had to push Maria away. I suppose I pushed a few people away. It seemed easier."

She was remembering, all of a sudden, just how many times people had reached out to her, and how many times she'd turned on them. Like the women who ran the town library Ruth used to volunteer at. She'd left because of Hannah, but she'd cut them off completely—women who used to be her friends.

"I was just tired," she realised. "Tired of hiding things and tired of being talked about. I didn't want to add to the conversation, even if the conversation was about me. I didn't want to convince people that I was worth respect, because I shouldn't have to."

"I understand." He kissed her again, a quick, light touch. But she kissed him back, harder, because she wanted to pour as much affection into this man as possible, and she couldn't do it with words.

But then, as his hands began to roam beyond the planes

of her back, as his kiss heated and his cock hardened beneath her, a thought struck. She pulled back, ignoring his frustrated moan.

"I bet you don't have a satin pillowcase, do you?" she asked.

He frowned. "A what?"

With a laugh, Ruth shook her head. "Don't worry about it."

CHAPTER TWENTY-NINE

EVAN HAD THOUGHT Ruth would be a light sleeper, but she barely stirred when his alarm went off the next morning. When he kissed her cheek, she gave a sleepy grumble and swatted at him. So he kissed her again, on the back of her neck, and then her shoulder.

She mumbled something that sounded like, "Ug uff."

He ignored the fact that he needed to get up and shower within the next ten minutes. Ruth's back was pressed to his chest, her feet tangled with his, and the frown forming above her tightly-closed eyes made his heart swell. Apparently, he even loved the sight of her scowl.

"What was that?" he asked lightly. Then he bit her ear.

She snorted. "Go away, you horrible man."

He laughed. "Alright. I have to get up anyway."

Immediately, she rolled over and slung an arm around his neck. "Why?"

"Oh, now you want to talk?"

"Shut up." She snuggled into his chest and wrapped a leg around him. "Go back to sleep."

"I wish." Gently, Evan disentangled their bodies and got up, checking the time. He could just fit in a shower, if he had a protein shake for breakfast.

When he came back from the bathroom, he found Ruth sitting up in his bed, rubbing her eyes sleepily. Her hair frizzed out around her head like a crown, her braid having lost most of its structural integrity. She offered him a bleary smile. She looked beautiful.

"What are you doing today?" he asked as he grabbed his clothes.

She appeared to consider that for a moment. "I don't know. Um... Do you need me to leave? When you do?"

"Nah." He grabbed the door key from his bedside table and tossed it gently toward her. "You'll be around when I get home, right?"

Silence.

Evan looked up to find that Ruth had, apparently, caught the keys. She was holding them up in the air, staring at her hand as if it were an alien thing. "Huh," he said, a smile curving his lips. "I didn't know you could catch."

Her eyes narrowed. "You are *so* annoying."

"So I hear. From you. Every day."

"Shut up. Are you... are you sure you want to give me these?"

Evan arched a brow. "Why? Are you going to steal all my shit and hide it in your lair? Also known as the flat next door?"

"Maybe," she said lightly. "I mean, I might steal your bed."

"You don't need to steal my bed." After dragging on a shirt, he leant down to kiss her. Her lips were soft and warm, gliding over his with aching gentleness, and when he pulled back, she was smiling.

"Are you saying I can use your bed whenever I want?" she teased.

"Yeah. But also, because I'm gonna fix yours after work."

Ruth's jaw dropped. "Fix it?"

"Yep." He found a jacket and slung it on. "Just need to drill the slats into the frame and cut you a new support beam. There's a lumber yard next to the forge. I can probably grab something there."

"But…" she spluttered. "You said you couldn't fix it!"

"No I didn't. I said you could sleep with me."

"You *prick*!"

He grinned. "I think it was a very charitable offer. It's not like I could've fixed it last night."

"*Charitable*," she repeated, giving him a look. But he heard the laughter in her voice and saw the tilt of her lips that she tried so hard to suppress.

"Yeah. Listen, I have to go," he said, searching for his wallet.

"You walking?"

"At this rate, I'd better drive."

"Great," she said. "You can take me home later."

Evan paused in his search, turning to stare at her. "Home as in…?"

"Home," she repeated. "From town. I'm going in this afternoon to do some things."

He blinked. "You are?"

"Yes." After a moment, when he continued staring, Ruth rolled her eyes. "Aren't you running late?"

Right. He spotted his wallet on the dresser and snatched it up. "Just... be careful." *Don't get into fights with Amazonian women.*

"In case I get chased with pitchforks, you mean?"

"Something like that." He pressed a quick kiss to her forehead. "Text me when you... well, text me on a regular basis."

"Yes, Mother."

He snorted. Said goodbye. Tried not to worry and failed.

~

RUTH TOOK her time getting ready that morning. Which is to say, she dozed for an hour or three after Evan left, helped herself to Earl Grey and English muffins, and, just for the hell of it, used a shit-ton of his lemongrass body wash.

Because she could, because he wouldn't mind, because he'd given her his key.

He loved her. Funny how that knowledge left her both sober and elated all at once.

It was around midday when she finally dragged herself over to her own flat, locking Evan's door carefully. She hung his key up on a coat peg beside her own before heading to her bedroom.

There was a tense moment when she forgot that her bed was a rickety heap, tried to sit down on it, stopped herself halfway, and thought she might go toppling into a stack of comics as she twisted. Luckily, she just landed on her arse instead.

It was, she decided, as good a place as any for this phone call.

Hannah answered the phone with a bright and chirpy, "He-*llo?*" Which told Ruth that she had company.

"Where are you?" Ruth asked.

"You've just caught me on my break," Hannah said. Her voice was still unreasonably perky. She was probably sitting by a manager or something.

Hannah liked to put her best foot forward. Continuously. Even at a minimum-wage waitressing job she desperately wanted to leave.

"Right. You working tomorrow?"

"I am available tomorrow afternoon, from around five o'clock," Hannah said smoothly. "Can I help you with something?" *What do you need?*

Ruth smiled slightly. "I just thought we could go somewhere. Out."

There was a pause. Then Hannah said carefully, "I am only available in the *evening*."

Because Ruth didn't really go out in the evenings. She occasionally went out during the day, when most people were at work. In the evenings, Ravenswood was really busy, and things like—well, things like that nightmare with Hayley occurred.

Ruth forced herself to shrug, even though Hannah couldn't see. She was method acting, or something along those lines. She was doing a Hannah; behaving as if she was already who she wanted to be. "That's okay."

"It is?" Hannah sounded dubious.

"Yeah. I go where I want now. It's this new thing I'm trying."

"Okay," Hannah said finally. "Well, that would be lovely. I approve, actually."

"Cool. I'll call you later."

Because right now, she had plans to attend to.

After fixing her hair, Ruth rifled through her wardrobe for an embarrassingly long amount of time. Usually, her choice in clothes revolved around the way a fabric felt against her skin, whether the cut would make her feel like she was suffocating in strangeness. On the rare occasions when she left the house, she had to take all of that into account, and also try to look…

"What?" she mused out loud. "Try to look *what*? Respectable?" A slight smile curving her lips, she shook her head. That wouldn't do at all.

And just like that, her choice was obvious. She pulled out an old, worn, Captain America tee and a soft pair of leggings. She'd go about her business, as she had a right to, and she'd look like herself while she did it.

~

THE LIBRARY FELL silent as Ruth entered.

Actually, no; she was probably imagining that. *Definitely* imagining that. It was a bloody library. It had been silent in the first place.

She kept her spine straight and her footsteps steady as she approached the front desk. Penny Clarke was there, tapping away at the computer, her gaze occasionally flicking to a handwritten list on the desk beside her. But Ruth knew that, soon enough, Penny's customer service Spidey-senses would kick in.

Sure enough, a moment later, Penny looked up. Her smile was bright and welcoming—an automatic reflex that faltered as soon as she saw Ruth.

Just keep going. One foot in front of the other.

Ruth plastered a polite smile onto her face as she approached. "Hi, Penny," she said quietly.

There was a pause. A pause in which Ruth worried that this arguably reckless decision was going to backfire awfully. She became acutely aware of the pressure of eyes on her, all around her—from the old Hykeham sisters by the audiobook section to Tim Mosely, fluttering his paper loudly by the window.

But Ruth focused on Penny. And so, she saw the exact moment when Penny's shock dissolved into... pleasure?

"Ruth Kabbah!" she cried. Except Penny was more soft-spoken than anyone Ruth had ever met, and so her cry was at the level of the average person's murmur. "Fancy seeing you," Penny continued, her round face splitting into a smile.

She flicked off the brake on her chair and began wheeling around the counter. Ruth, moving as if in a dream, found herself bending to accept her old mentor's hug.

"I haven't seen you in an age," Penny said. She kept a grip on Ruth's arm even after they separated, her grasp firm and motherly. "Where on earth have you been?"

"Nowhere," Ruth said, honestly enough.

"I suppose not! My Norm said he was round just the other day, seeing to your shower. I said, *'Did you tell her?'* I'm always asking after you, I am. He says—"

Penny, like her husband, was a talkative woman. Despite being quiet, she said a lot. She couldn't exactly be called a gossip, because she wasn't ever malicious; rather, her mouth often ran away with her. Ruth let the reported conversation wash over her in soothing waves.

When a lull finally arose, she dredged up the words she'd practiced. "Penny, I wanted to talk to you about…" She cleared her throat. "About volunteering. Again. I don't know if you need anyone—"

"Ooh, yes," Penny beamed. "Of course we do! You know we always need volunteers, especially since you girls, ah, left." Her beaky nose wrinkled. "Nasty business, that."

For a second, Ruth's heart stopped and her sisterly hackles rose, but then Penny added, "The bloody council, so old-fashioned. We could've had a qualified nursery nurse running Toddler Time! But nooo, five minutes behind bars and all of a sudden she's useless."

Ruth didn't bother to correct the *behind bars* comment, or to point out that the council had no control over the law. Truthfully, she couldn't exactly speak. So she hummed agreeably instead.

Penny tutted as she returned to the desk, pulling open a deep drawer. She heaved out a huge file and rifled through its alphabetised sections until she found the correct form. "Here you are, my love. You know how to fill it out."

Ruth stared. She hadn't expected… well, she didn't know what she'd expected. She'd vacillated between envisioning a warm welcome and a complete freeze-out, caught between her knowledge of Penny's character and her soul-deep certainty that no-one would want to oppose the collective opinion of Ravenswood.

She'd begun to suspect, recently, that her certainty in these matters was… well, wrong. And here, she supposed, was the evidence.

As she filled in the application form, Ruth considered the wild possibility that Penny might be utterly oblivious to the town's general attitude. She checked boxes and signed dates and thought that maybe the last two years had simply passed Penny by.

But when she returned to the front desk to hand in the form—which, amongst other things, confirmed her consent to undergo a legal background check—Penny leaned forward.

Her voice even lower than usual, she said, "I'm glad you're back, Ruthie. Me and the girls missed you. Bugger what anyone else has to say."

Ruth blinked back unexpected tears. They had snuck up on her, and now they were close to breaking free in the middle of the town library. Good Lord. How absolutely mortifying.

She shoved them down ruthlessly and murmured, "Thanks."

"Oh, you're welcome, love. You'll hear back about that DBS check."

Ruth nodded, sobering. She'd pass the DBS check, and soon enough, she'd be volunteering again. Introducing the town's kids to comics and fantasy novels the way she'd used to. But Hannah, whose entire life had revolved around working with kids, wouldn't be able to.

Some problems could be fixed. Others couldn't.

CHAPTER THIRTY

RUTH WANDERED AROUND TOWN AIMLESSLY. She could've gone somewhere—the Greengage, maybe—but it had been a while since she'd walked through Ravenswood just for the pleasure of it. And really, if one ignored the large number of irritating inhabitants, it was a beautiful place. She'd missed it.

Plus, she had time to kill.

So she wasted an hour at the park, studying the blooming tulips and following the paths drawn through the thick, verdant copse. By the time 5 p.m. drew near, Ruth had counted seven grey squirrels. No red. She and Hannah had a twelve-year-long bet about who would be the first to see a red squirrel, and apparently, Ruth would not win that bet today.

But the thought of Hannah made Ruth pause to lean against an oak's wide trunk and pull her phone from her waistband—no pockets.

Most people would say that Ruth should call her sister.

And, while Ruth disliked phone calls—it was hard to really *hear* someone's words, when you couldn't see their face— she made them often enough.

Well; not often. But she could, was the point. If she wanted.

Only, she didn't want to now. Hannah was at work anyway, and one phone call per day was quite enough, and—w

ell. Ruth wanted to say something important, and important things were so much easier to write down than to say out loud. So she texted.

What you said on Sunday was right. I'm going to do better.

She paused for a moment, pursing her lips, looking down at those words as she organised the next few in her mind.

I think I've been selfish. I concentrated on feeling guilty about you instead of actually helping you. And I isolated myself without thinking about how that would affect you.

Yeah. That sounded right. Ruth read over the message again and felt pleased; the words actually conveyed what she wanted them to. That didn't happen very often.

She added the most important part.

I'm sorry and I love you.

Then she sent it.

After a last look around the park, Ruth reached down to pluck one of the tulips that had so captured her attention. She felt slightly bad as she snapped the crisp stem, but the things literally carpeted the grass. No-one would miss this single bloom. More importantly, it would grow back. It would recover.

Things usually did.

Hannah rarely used her phone at work, so Ruth wasn't expecting a reply for hours. She got one within ten minutes, though.

Hannah: I love you too. So much.

~

RUTH WOUND her way to the outskirts of the town's industrial estate, following the low wall that circled the Burne & Co. forge. They had a showroom in town, but this was where the blacksmiths worked. She knew because, once upon a time, she'd been forbidden to come here by Daniel.

Well, Daniel could get fucked.

She searched out Evan's crappy old car and perched on the wall beside it, waiting for him to appear. While she waited, Ruth rolled the tulip's bright green stem between her fingers. Its sunshine-yellow bell was streaked with scarlet. The colours reminded her of ripe fruit.

As she trailed a finger over one silken petal, a shadow fell over her. Ruth tensed.

She looked up to find a vaguely familiar man standing before her, his hands in his pockets. She studied his dark hair, his pale skin and piercing eyes, for a long moment before placing him.

"Zachary Davis," she said, speaking the words aloud as they came to her.

He smiled. It was a cute and crooked tilt of the lips that made him look almost boyish, despite his size. Apparently, Burne & Co. only hired enormous people.

"I didn't think you knew my name," he replied.

Oh, she knew his name. She knew his name because he

was the town's male equivalent to Ruth—though, being a man, he was tacitly approved of rather than ostracised. She *remembered* his name because, despite his reputation, he had never tried to get in her pants. Or lied about getting in her pants.

Which made him unusual for a young, single man in Ravenswood.

But instead of admitting any of that, she tilted her chin defiantly and said, "Of course I do. Don't you know mine?"

"Yep." Ah. She'd walked right into that. But then he said, his explanation unexpected: "You're Evan's girlfriend."

She blinked. "Am I?"

"Aren't you?"

She twirled the tulip. He'd taken the words as denial, when really they'd been shock.

You're Evan's girlfriend. He'd said it so casually. Imagine that. She was with Evan, *really* with Evan, and it was not a secret.

"Yes," she said finally, firmly. "I am."

His little, crooked smile became a bigger, crooked smile. "I was in the year below you at school," he said.

Ruth, conscious of the typical escalation of polite conversation, was confused by the subject change. But still, she said, "I know."

He leant against Evan's car. "I always thought you were cool."

Nothing could've possibly shocked her more. Ruth was impressed with herself for not falling off the wall. She maintained her composure and her seat, and said with clear scepticism, "You did?"

"Yeah. You always used to iron Storm patches onto your rucksack. And you had those cool glasses."

Ah, yes; her thick, turquoise, milk-bottle glasses. *She* thought they were cool too. No-one else had.

Except Zachary Davis, apparently.

"My mother ironed on the patches," she said. "I wasn't allowed to use the iron."

His lips quirked, and she realised that she'd given unnecessary personal information. Oops. It was his fault for being so non-threatening. He was kind of like Evan, without the intimidating sex appeal.

Although, she thought wryly, Evan's sex appeal didn't seem so intimidating anymore.

"Hey," a familiar voice called. Zach stepped aside to display Evan himself, coming through the forge's front doors with a wide smile on his face. He reached the car with a speed that belied his easy stride, elbowing Zach in the ribs. "You chatting up my girl?"

"I'm confessing my childhood hero-worship," Zach said. "It was nice to officially meet you, Ruth."

Because in this town, you could know someone without ever actually talking to them.

She smiled. "You too."

Then Zach clapped Evan on the back and said, "See you later, mate."

"Say hi to your mum for me."

Zach nodded and wandered off. He seemed to do everything with an oddly casual air. In fact, she wondered if he knew where he was going, or if he was just… walking.

Then he stopped by a grey Golf and unlocked the door. Apparently, he had indeed known where he was going.

Ruth hopped off the little wall and moved closer to Evan, feeling herself smile. It was a ridiculous and involuntary smile that she wasn't in the mood to stifle. In fact, after her success at the library, she felt more relaxed than she had in a while.

He slid an arm around her waist and kissed the top of her head. "You're cheerful."

"I suppose I am." She held up the flower. "Want this?"

"Is it for me?"

Ruth bit her lip on a smile and shrugged.

Evan's grin widened. "You got me a flower. How romantic."

"Don't get carried away."

"I think I'll press it," he said, a teasing glint in his eyes, "and treasure it forever."

"Behave yourself. Are you busy tomorrow night?"

Evan plucked the flower from her fingers before unlocking the car. "Me and Zach were talking about a drink after work. Why?" He opened her door, waiting for her to get in.

"Well, I wanted to go somewhere with Hannah. Somewhere in Ravenswood. Like the Unicorn."

Evan nodded and shut the door behind her, holding up a finger. He was opening the drivers' door moments later, sliding into his seat. "I see. Did everything go okay today?"

Ruth nodded, watching as he placed the tulip carefully in a cup holder. "I signed up to volunteer at the library."

"You used to do that, right? Before?"

"Yeah, I..." She trailed off as they pulled out of the little staff car park, driving right past the forge doors. Right past Daniel, who stood in the doorway, his eyes wide.

Ruth turned away, looking straight ahead. She wasn't going to spend the rest of her life tiptoeing around, just to avoid him. He didn't bother avoiding her. It was well past time to start living her life.

"He hasn't even looked at me all day," Evan said quietly. Ruth jumped slightly in her seat as the words pulled her out of her defiant thoughts.

"Daniel?" she asked.

"Yeah. He's always in my face, one way or another, but today? Nothing."

She drummed her fingers against her thighs. "Maybe Mr. Burne said something to him."

"He told me I could lose my job if I didn't leave you alone."

Ruth's jaw dropped. "Mr. Burne?"

"Oh, no. Daniel."

Ah. Her growing outrage soothed, and she relaxed back into her seat. "Don't listen to that. He puts his dad's name on his own bullshit. Mr. Burne doesn't even like Daniel. I don't know why they work together."

"Probably because Daniel's so good at his job."

Daniel was good at everything.

Except people, she finally realised. People, and relationships, and happiness and sex.

Speaking of which...

Evan's muscles shifted as he changed gear, pulling into Elm's little car park. She watched the glide of power beneath his golden skin and felt a familiar tightening between her legs.

"So," she said. "Wanna fuck?"

Evan jerked his head round to look at her. Then he burst

out laughing. "I really never know what you're going to say next."

She grinned. "Does that mean no?"

"I need to shower. And I said I'd fix your bed. I got the wood." He yanked up the handbrake and nodded towards the beam laying across the back seat.

But she saw the way his hand tightened on the steering wheel, knuckles whitening. And she saw the way his eyes darkened from summer sky to tempestuous ocean.

So she said again, "Does that mean no?"

He stared at her for a moment. Then he slid a hand behind her neck, pulled her to him and growled, "Nope."

CHAPTER THIRTY-ONE

THEY DIDN'T HAVE sex in Evan's car, because a charge of public indecency wouldn't do anyone any good. But as they entered the building and climbed the stairs, Evan couldn't keep his hands off Ruth. She half-ran to stay ahead of him, pushing him away with a laugh every time he reached for her.

When they got to his door, she slid off her shoe and produced the key he'd given her. Evan arched a brow. "Seriously?"

"This is where I keep keys," she said primly. "When I don't have pockets, I mean."

"Of course it is." He'd already found her phone shoved down her waistband, before she pushed his hands away. Evan shook his head, laughter light in his chest even as lust tightened his core and hardened his cock.

Feelings weren't as straight forward and binary as he'd once assumed; around Ruth, he could feel fifty things at once.

She dragged him into his own flat and slammed the door behind them. Then she pushed him up against it, and he had the most delicious sense of déjà vu.

Ruth grabbed his face, her fingers tight around his jaw. "Come here," she ordered. Her eyes seemed darker than usual, pupils blown into each deep brown iris.

He bent down, just enough to bring his mouth within reach of hers. She rose up, too, and then her lips were slanting over his, soft as the tulip clutched between his fingers.

She caught his lower lip between her teeth and bit gently, and Evan found himself moaning against her mouth. Ruth dragged more noise out of him than anyone he'd ever been with. He didn't mind at all.

With a grunt, Evan picked her up. She released his lip and gave a soft, little laugh. "You can't just pick me up whenever you feel like it."

"Why the hell not?" He carried her through the house, pausing to put his flower on a side table. "Isn't that the point of you being so little?"

"You keep saying that," Ruth muttered, "but I'm exactly average height."

Evan paused, actually surprised. "Are you?"

"I'm 5 foot 3," she sniffed.

"*Are* you?" He considered that for a moment. "You seem smaller."

"You are incredibly ill-mannered."

"That's hilarious, coming from you." He winked. "And, however tall you are, I like carrying you."

"You don't think I'm heavy?"

He felt his lips tip up at the suspicion in her voice. "Evidently not."

"Right. And why are we in the bathroom?"

"Because we're taking a shower." He put her down gently, and then he slid his hands beneath the hem of her T-shirt. "Take this off."

She licked her lips, her eyes trailing over his body. "Yes, Sir."

They undressed each other, in the end, her hands dragging at his clothes with an eagerness he'd longed for. All he'd ever wanted was for her to say yes. And when she tugged his T-shirt over his head with a laugh, when she squeezed his erection through his jeans before unzipping them, that was all he heard. Over and over again, with every hurried touch. *Yes.*

They stepped under the shower's hot spray in a tangle of bodies, Ruth's legs wrapped around his waist, her hands gripping his shoulders like a lifeline. He shoved her against the tiles and she moaned, grabbing his hair and hauling him closer. Kissing him. Giving him everything. *Yes.*

He palmed her breast and she moaned into his mouth. He pinched the nipple and she bit at his lip. He could feel the slick heat of her pussy against his shaft, and he had to remind himself that he couldn't just sink into her. No condom.

Then she reached between their bodies and grasped his cock, wet skin against wet skin, and the burning desire for pressure receded because she, this, whatever she chose to give him, would always be exactly what he needed.

Ruth pulled her lips from his and tipped her head back, water streaming over her face. She looked like a goddess.

She *felt* like a goddess, her hand sliding over his cock faster and faster, eliciting sensations that had to be divine.

"Stop," he rasped out. "I'm trying to last."

She opened her eyes slightly, water collecting on her lashes, a wicked grin on her lips. "For what?"

He kissed her again. And then, because two could play at that game, he reached between them and slid a finger inside her. She released a drawn-out moan, her grip on his cock faltering. When he brushed his thumb over her clit, she swore.

"I'll race you," she panted.

"Race me?"

"I bet I can make you come first."

Evan laughed. "That doesn't seem fair."

"Why not? Don't think you can win?"

He rubbed the pad of his thumb firmly over her swollen clit, and she jerked sharply, her breath catching. With a grin, he pressed her harder against the tiles, using his body to pin her there. "I think I can win," he said. "Even though you've had a head start." *Even though you keep me on the edge constantly, even though a look from you is enough to turn me on.*

She arched her back, water glistening over her brown skin, little droplets clinging to the stiff, dark tips of her nipples. *Fuck.*

"Alright," she breathed, a knowing smile curving her lips. "Let's do it."

Evan lost by a second or two. He enjoyed it thoroughly.

CHAPTER THIRTY-TWO

"So," Zach said. His usually easy-going smile took on a sharp, lascivious edge that Evan had never seen. Raising his brows suggestively, Zach continued, "Is this a double date?"

Hannah Kabbah cast a disdainful look over Zach, from the tips of his messy hair to his workman's boots. Having been on the receiving end of that look, Evan knew how quelling it could be. Then she said, with clipped certainty, "Absolutely not."

Zach blinked rapidly.

Evan bit back laughter.

"I'm here to spend time with my sister," Hannah said, popping open her jewelled little handbag. She produced a tube of lipstick and somehow uncapped the lid with one hand. Then she began applying it perfectly, without a mirror, while talking. "The two of *you* are here to do... whatever it is you do. It's just that apparently, Ruth and Evan can't be more than ten feet apart at any given time."

Evan leant against the busy bar of Ravenswood's only pub and tried not to look as smug as he felt. "There's only one place to drink in this town. Plus, I'm her ride."

"Ruth has a car," Hannah pointed out. "But if you *are* driving her, you'd better not be drinking at all."

Evan raised his hands in compliance, one of which was already wrapped around a Coke.

Still, the gaze she flicked over him was mildly disapproving. He didn't take it personally; disapproval seemed to be her resting state.

Ruth chose that moment to return from the bathroom. She'd insisted on going alone, which had caused her sister to look at her as if she'd grown a second head.

Now, noting the determination in Ruth's set jaw, the way she rubbed her palms against her legging-clad thighs, Evan suspected she'd been giving herself some kind of pep talk.

Ruth talked to herself. A lot.

He reached for her, but she avoided his hand with a wry smile. "We are not here as a couple," she said pertly. "So you can't do couple things."

He grabbed her anyway and pulled her closer, pressing a quick kiss to her cheek. "There," he said. "That wasn't a couple thing."

Hannah rolled her eyes.

But Ruth was fighting a pleased little smile, glaring at him without heat. "We're having a girls' night out. Go away and do whatever it is you wanted to do."

"What if I want to chat up the prettiest girl in the room?" he asked. He heard Zach's groan in the background, heard Hannah's snort, but only cared about Ruth's pursed lips, her dancing eyes.

"You can try," she said primly, "but you will find yourself rejected." Then she hooked her arm through her sister's, and the two of them turned to walk away.

But she shot him one last look over her shoulder.

"You two are absolutely sickening," Zach said.

"Thanks."

"Actually, *you're* sickening. I'm not sure if she even likes you."

Evan felt a slow grin spread over his face. "I'm sure. I'm very, very sure."

"Right." Zach gave him a baffled look. "Shall we sit down?"

They made their way to a table not far from where the sisters had settled. Close enough for Evan to keep an eye on them—or rather, on anyone who might approach them. But not close enough for him to hear a word of their conversation, especially over the pub's cheerful din.

Ruth caught sight of him and gave a slight smile. She'd asked him to come with her tonight. Not *with* her—she wanted to spend time with her sister. But to be there, in case. She hadn't said in case of what, and he hadn't had to ask.

She was nervous. So he'd do this as often as it took, until she wasn't nervous anymore.

As time passed, Evan relaxed into his seat and into his conversation with Zach. He nursed his Coke, Zach nursed his lager, and hours ticked by while they talked shit about work, T.V., childhood—anything. It was the kind of easy friendship Evan had found in the army, but beneath it lay a foundation of trust that had snuck up on him. Zach was a good guy. A really good guy, the type that was hard to find. He was also fucking hilarious.

Until he paused mid-joke, the laughter fading from his face, and said, "Evan."

Evan didn't have to ask. He followed Zach's gaze to the pub's back door, saw Daniel come in from the beer garden with a group of laughing men. They all had drinks in their hands, smiles on their faces, except Daniel. He was subdued, glowering—much as he had been at work, recently.

Evan saw the exact moment that Daniel caught sight of Ruth. The man jolted as if he'd been bitten, his pale cheeks flushing.

Without a second thought, Evan stood. But then Ruth looked over at him, and instead of the worry he'd expected to see on her face, there was only calm. Not the forced blankness that set his teeth on edge, but real, actual calm.

She gave a slight shake of her head.

Evan dragged in a breath. And then, feeling as if his every joint was suddenly stiff, he forced himself to sit back down.

"Take a breath, mate. Relax."

He didn't even look at Zach as he answered. His eyes narrowed, pinned to Ruth's table, Evan said, "No."

～

"You okay?" Hannah murmured.

Ruth straightened in her seat, because a month ago she would've slouched. Would've made herself small to shrink away from the men approaching their table.

Things were different. She was different. She said, "Yes." And then she added, "Are you?"

Hannah's gaze darkened. "You mean, will I control the urge to glass him?"

"Hannah!" Sometimes, out of nowhere, Ruth's proper, sensible, caring sister would come over all terrifying. It was, frankly, fantastic.

"What?" Hannah demanded, feigning confusion. "Glassing him would be quite restrained, all things considered. Don't you think?"

And so, when Daniel and his gang finally arrived at their table, the sisters were laughing.

Daniel glared down at them, arms folded, as if he were a teacher catching out unruly students. Ruth felt the carefree humour coursing through her fade away, like champagne going flat.

But fear didn't arrive in its place. No; the emotion that filled her at the sight of Daniel's sharp, green eyes was anger.

She stirred the straw through her vodka and orange, and said calmly, "Can I help you?"

Daniel couldn't have looked more furious if she'd insulted his long-dead mother. "What on earth do you think you're doing?" he demanded. His voice, already deep and strong thanks to his barrel chest, carried. He was drunk.

Oh, great.

Ruth raised her brows. "I'm having a drink with my sister. You know Hannah, Daniel. You identified her—"

"We were at school together," Daniel interrupted sharply. "Obviously, I know Hannah."

Hannah, who was currently staring at him with more

disgust than she would stare at dog shit on the pavement. Hannah, whose gaze he studiously avoided.

Ruth didn't miss the feverish gleam in Daniel's eyes or the slight flush on his cheeks, the one that spoke of panic, of pressure. She took a sip of her drink, watching him closely.

Then she said, "Anything else?"

He shifted. Around him, his friends hovered like dandelion seeds half-blown from the clock. Usually, Daniel surrounded himself with men who made their presence intimidating, men who punctuated his every word with supportive jeers and pats on the back.

These men were familiar faces to Ruth. But they weren't acting in a familiar manner.

He set his jaw and took in a deep breath—which meant he was searching for the best possible insult. But he must be very drunk indeed, because all he managed to come up with was, "I know you spoke to my father."

"I'm sure," Ruth said. "It wasn't a secret."

He appeared nonplussed by that. And Ruth noticed, slowly, that the pub had grown quiet. Tense. Whispers bubbled beneath a thick film of silence, and all eyes were pinned to the town's live melodrama.

Let them watch.

Across the table, Hannah put down her gin and tonic with a sigh. "Look," she said. "I don't know if you can tell, but Ruth doesn't want to talk to you. And *I* certainly don't want to."

Daniel's flush deepened, until his cheeks were almost as red as his hair. "Is that what you've told her, Ruth?" he demanded. "That you don't want to talk to me?"

Ruth frowned. "I *don't* want to talk to you. Why the hell would I?"

His mouth worked for a moment, his nostrils flaring, before he stepped closer. He leaned over the table as if wanting privacy, but when he spoke, his words were embarrassingly loud.

"I know you told me to stop," he said. "But that's what you said before! And I kept trying. I waited—"

"This isn't like before," Ruth clipped out, awful understanding washing over her. "We were kids. It was pathetic. But I'm not playing hard to get right now, Daniel. I don't want you to convince me. I want to be left alone."

Without warning, Daniel slammed a hand against the table, knocking over her drink.

She heard the scrape of multiple chairs as people rose to their feet, heard voices overlap.

"Come on, now, mate—"

"Calm down—"

"Just leave her be—"

Ruth wasn't paying attention to any of it. She wasn't even paying attention to the slow drip of liquid spilling from the table's edge onto her legs. Instead, she sought out Evan, found he and Zach both on their feet, and glared. Hard.

Don't you dare come over here.

Evan glared right back. *You can't be serious.*

She mouthed, clear as day, "*Sit.*"

He stared at her for a moment, his chest heaving. Then, slowly, he sat.

Relieved, Ruth turned back to Daniel. His friends had hold of him now. One man gripped his shoulder firmly, murmuring soothing words. Another grasped Daniel's wrist, stilling his right hand, speaking sharply under his breath.

Daniel pulled away and muttered, "I'm fine. I'm fine." Then he narrowed his eyes at Ruth and spat, "You think I don't know your latest victim is in here? Watching you like a lapdog?"

Ruth arched a brow, unimpressed. Daniel had always had a way with words, and with metal, and not much else. "I'm assuming you mean Evan," she said. "My boyfriend."

Daniel spluttered. "Boyfriend?"

"Yes. It means a man with whom I am in a committed relationship. It's kind of like how Laura is your *wife*, only without the legal aspect."

"You're jealous," Daniel accused. "You're jealous, and it's petty."

"I'm tired," Ruth corrected. She wouldn't bother pointing out the irony of his words, because he'd never realise it. He'd said them to her years ago, over the phone, when he'd told her about the engagement—casual as anything—and she'd told him to go to hell.

God, this man was exhausting.

"I'm tired of you," she repeated. "I'm tired of your gifts. I'm tired of your insults. I'm tired of your pathetic, teenage attempts to hold power over me, and I'm tired of telling you no. If you don't leave me alone..." She took in a deep breath and felt Hannah's foot nudge hers beneath the table. A reminder. *I'm here.*

Everyone was here. The pub's occupants stared openly now, straining to hear every word. Let them.

Clearing her throat, Ruth said loudly, "If you don't leave

me alone, I will report you to the police for harassment. For —for stalking."

Daniel clenched his jaw, rising up to his full height despite the fact that he was swaying on his feet. "You wouldn't do that to me."

Ruth couldn't bite back her astonished laughter. "Why the fuck wouldn't I? You pressed charges against my *sister*."

"She destroyed my *Porsche*," he replied, painfully serious. "What the fuck was I supposed to do? That was a vintage 911, Ruth!"

"Oh, for God's sake," she snapped. "Shut up about the fucking car. I am asking you, *nicely*, to leave me alone. Stop embarrassing yourself."

Daniel straightened up, his jaw tight, his eyes flicking around the pub. Apparently for the first time, he realised that almost every patron was staring at their little table. She saw the gleam of sweat on his pale brow before he adjusted the cuffs of his designer shirt.

Then, turning on his heel, he barked at his friends, "Come." Without waiting for their response, he strode off toward the door.

For a moment, the men he'd come in with stared after him in shock. Then, one by one, like trickles of water, they trailed out after him.

The last, a tall, dark man Ruth only vaguely recognised, paused. He nodded at Ruth, then at Hannah, and said roughly, "Sorry about that, girls. One too many." And then he left.

The sisters stared after him in shock.

"Did he—did he just apologise to us?" Ruth asked, her voice dreamlike.

"He did," Hannah said slowly. "Holy shit. What the fuck?"

"I don't even know. Jesus, that was weird. Wow." And then, after a moment of dazed contemplation: "Poor Laura."

Hannah snorted. "Poor Laura?! Laura, who tells everyone who'll listen what a man-eating slut you are? Laura, who campaigned to have me banned from the town centre as an *unsuitable person?*"

"You know, I'm sure that was just a rumour," Ruth soothed.

"Was it fuck. She's bonkers."

Right. She was also with Daniel. And Ruth had never convinced herself that he'd treat a wife better than he'd treated her. It wouldn't matter who he was with, how he was with them, what 'kind' of woman she was. Daniel was Daniel. Daniel hurt people.

She imagined being his wife, carrying his child, and felt slightly sick.

"At the end of the day," Hannah said decisively, "she treated us like crap."

"Yeah," Ruth murmured. "And I bet it didn't improve her life one bit."

Hannah stared at her as if she'd lost her mind. Then she opened her mouth, probably to say as much—but was interrupted by Evan's arrival.

"You okay?" He loomed over the table, reaching out to run a knuckle over Ruth's cheek. Another casual touch that felt anything but casual. There were so many. She'd never expected to love them or need them like this.

"I'm fine," she said, and realised that it was true.

"Do you want to leave?"

She looked past him, her eyes circling the room, meeting

the gaze of anyone still staring. And, one by one, they all looked away.

"No," she said finally. "I think I'm having fun."

A smile spread over Evan's face, and he squeezed her shoulder. "Okay. Good."

As the evening went on, that word turned out to be fitting. *Good.*

CHAPTER THIRTY-THREE

RUTH WATCHED the sun rise through the gap in Evan's curtains.

She'd woken up at first light, her head resting on his chest, her heart full. Mornings like this had become a habit over the last weeks.

Well, except for the part where she watched the dawn. What a God-awful hour to wake up at.

But sleep had been difficult last night, even after Evan loved her to the point of physical exhaustion. Her mind hadn't been able to shut off. She was somewhere between excited and nervous, and that had always interfered with her ability to sleep.

Ruth didn't want to check the time, didn't want to move at all in case she disturbed the gentle rise and fall of Evan's chest. But the sun was up now, so it would soon be time for the Easter service. Which she'd promised Mum she would attend—and which she'd invited Evan to, along with Sunday dinner afterward.

She'd never introduced a man to her mother before. Actually, she'd never really had the chance. Never really had the *choice*. Now she did, and she'd chosen, and if it all went horribly wrong somehow, she'd only have herself to blame.

How, exactly, would it go horribly wrong? She had no idea. Her mother was the most laid-back person on earth. Hannah, the real test, already knew and reluctantly liked Evan. Evan liked Hannah, and he could probably charm Mum more thoroughly in a day than Ruth had managed in a lifetime. Logically, absolutely nothing could go wrong.

But she worried anyway, because all three of those people were more important to her than anything in the world and bringing them together seemed like a risk. If there were such a thing as heart insurance, putting her mother, sister and boyfriend in the same room would double her premium.

Beneath the nerves, though, she felt an unexpected sort of joy. Evan was hers. He was proudly, publicly hers, and she was his, and everything was simpler than she'd ever dreamed it could be. Ruth trailed a finger over the warm, soft skin of his shoulder, tracing out the same three words again and again.

I love you.

He woke up slowly. He always did. First his breathing changed, went from deep and unconscious to something less steady. Then his heart would speed up slightly beneath her ear. And his hands, which would invariably be resting on some part of her—her waist, her hips, her shoulders—would tighten.

This morning, he grasped her thigh gently with one hand, her forearm with the other. Then he slid both hands over her skin, and they met at her waist. He said, his voice slow and rasping, "Happy Easter. Is that what you say?"

She kissed his chest and stilled her tracing finger. "Yes, you heathen. What, you don't read the icing before you eat your chocolate?"

"I glance," he murmured dryly. "The eating part has always taken priority."

Apparently, the hours of conflicting nerves writhing around in her stomach could've been dealt with hours ago, if she'd only woken Evan up. All of a sudden, she felt just fine.

"Evan," she said. She had no idea what she was doing. Something close to panic rose in her like a flood, except it *wasn't* panic, not at all—it shared the same sharpness, but it held delicious sweetness too.

He raised his brows. "Yeah?"

And, since she wouldn't say it at all if she didn't blurt it out, Ruth mumbled, "UmmmmIloveyou."

She'd expected him to look at least a little surprised, but he didn't; not at all. She might have been insulted by that, if it weren't for the pleasure spreading over his face, as warm and unstoppable as the morning sunrise had been.

"What was that?" he asked, his eyes dancing. She slid her fingers into his beard and pulled. He twisted his head to bite gently at her hand. "I didn't hear you," he insisted. "Go on."

"Bugger off."

He tweaked her nose. "Is *that* what you said? It sounded more like—"

"Oh, be quiet."

He shook his head, smile wider than ever. "I don't think that was it, either."

"I love you! Okay?"

Evan's eyes were all soft heat, his movements slow. He wrapped an arm around her waist and dragged her closer, until their faces were level. Then he whispered, "That's good. Because I am hopelessly in love with you too."

And then he kissed her. He kissed her hard, for a very long time, and eventually the kissing became touching, and the touching became sighing, and stroking, and rubbing, and gasping. And by the time all was said and done, they'd wasted a solid hour being desperate, love-sick fools, which she'd very much enjoyed.

But Ruth made herself push away the vestiges of worn-out pleasure like a comforting blanket, one eye on that slice of sunlight streaking through the curtain.

"Come on," she said, sitting up reluctantly. The loss of his firm, comforting muscle against her side was eternally sigh-worthy, but needs must. "Let's get ready."

He slid a hand over her belly. "We've got time."

"*I* haven't. If I don't do my hair before church, Mum will kill me."

"About that," he said slowly, sitting up.

Ruth raised her brows. "About my hair?"

"No," he smiled. "About your mother."

"What about her?"

"Well, is she—? I mean, should I…"

Ruth watched him search for words, affection spreading through her chest. He looked quite adorably hesitant. She took pity on him and said, "Are you trying to ask if she's like me and Hannah?"

He was visibly relieved. "Yes, actually."

She laughed as she stood, not bothering to cover her

nudity. His eyes slid over her body as she searched the floor for her pyjamas. She bit back a smile. "My mother is very nice."

"What does *that* mean?" he asked, scepticism dripping from his voice.

"Honestly, take it at face value. She's nice." Ruth found her pyjamas and went to the bed, pressing a quick kiss against his furrowed brow. "You'll be fine. Now I'm going next door to sort my hair out."

He laid back against the pillows. "See you in a sec, kitten."

"Bye," Ruth called over her shoulder. She checked her phone as she made the increasingly unnecessary journey from Evan's flat to her own.

Of course, it wasn't Ruth who'd started bringing her things to Evan's. It was him.

You'll need them in the morning, he'd say, and grab some pyjamas from her drawer. Or, *Might as well keep it at mine,* and then he'd pick up something like her toothbrush or her phone charger, and the best part was that he *thought* he was being subtle.

She'd never thought a man would want her things littered across his space, but apparently Evan did.

Ruth checked her texts with one hand as she headed to the bathroom, unwinding the band from the end of her braid. She had a text from Penny, which had been a regular occurrence since Ruth had written her number on that volunteering form. The first text had said:

Ruth,

Just to let you know, your DBS check is ongoing. :) Once it's done you can start right away!

Penny :)

Ruth had replied, with coaching from Evan—because texting Marjaana, her best friend, was one thing, but texting someone *new* felt like a test she'd almost certainly fail.

Penny had responded, and now they *talked*. Penny maintained her oddly formal texting style and excessive use of smiley faces. Ruth maintained her disbelief at the fact that Penny actually wanted to interact with her, for fun. Or something. Whatever.

But Penny's Happy Easter :) wasn't the only message. There was one from a number Ruth hadn't saved, which made her pause in the act of ferreting out her Shea butter.

Here it bloody goes, then.

Ruth's breath caught in her chest.

"You don't know how lucky you are."

Hayley rolled her eyes. "That my parents never take me anywhere?"

"That your parents never take you to church," Maria corrected. "Tell her, Ruth."

Ruth grunted.

"You're ungrateful cows, the both of you," Hayley muttered. "Youse get Sunday dinner after. What do I get? Fish fingers, if Laura's about."

"So learn to cook," Maria winked.

"Cooking's for suckers. Tell her, Ruth."

Ruth wrapped her tie around her finger, as tight as it would go, until the school's burning torch logo disappeared. Then she let it unravel and felt the blood return to the digit.

"Are you listening, Ruth?"

Ruth grunted.

The school bell rang, signalling the end of the day, and she pursed her lips. She'd go straight home, get changed, Mum would drag a comb through her hair, and then they'd be marched down to church for Good Friday. Maria would go through the same process at the Catholic church in the next village over, and Hayley would get to go home and watch TV.

She caught Maria's eye and sighed. "Here it bloody goes, then."

"Oh," Maria laughed. "She speaks."

Ruth stared at the text for what felt like a painfully long time. Then she remembered that she had things to do, an important day to prepare for. Really, she should ignore the text completely.

Instead, she typed out:

Oh. She speaks.

Then she put her phone face-down on the counter and got on with her hair.

CHAPTER THIRTY-FOUR

ONE THING EVAN could not have predicted about Ruth was her extensive knowledge of hymns.

She appeared to have memorised at least ten, by his calculation. Of course, it could have been a hundred. At this point, they were all blurring into one, and Evan was staring down at the dogged, old hymn book he'd found in his pew and mouthing along silently.

Hopefully, he looked enthusiastic enough to convince Patience Kabbah. The tiny, brightly-dressed woman seemed utterly serene, but he still didn't completely trust that. She had produced both Ruth and Hannah. She had to be secretly terrifying, somehow.

Right now, in an enormous hat with a beatific smile on her round face, Patience seemed anything but terrifying. That made him even more suspicious.

But at least she seemed, thus far, to like him. He really, *really* needed Ruth's mother to like him.

When the service was finally over, Evan realised that the

hard part had only just begun. Standing beside someone during church was an easy interlude of occasional friendly eye contact. But now he'd go back to Ruth's family home, and have dinner, and Ruth loved her family more than anything so if he fucked up somehow...

"Hey." Ruth's voice was soft, her hand capturing his. "Let's go."

Her mother and sister were making their way through the milling crowd of churchgoers, moving leisurely toward the huge, wooden doors. He found himself studying the metalwork of the door's hinges, analysing how they'd been designed. Then he pulled himself together, his fingers tightening around Ruth's.

"You seem slightly dazed," she murmured, her lips pursed in that almost-smile.

"I've never been to church before," he replied under his breath. "I didn't think there'd be so much... singing."

"Lucky for you, we only have to go twice a year."

Evan tried not to grin wide, or squeeze her hand, or do anything to give away how those words went straight to his heart. If he did, she might realise the implications of what she'd just said and come over all embarrassed.

But really—who knew twice-annual obligations could feel so romantic?

"Twice?" he said. "Easter and...?"

"Christmas." She shot him a smile, a real smile. "You're bad at this."

"I know." He smiled back, not even caring that they'd stopped walking, that they were standing in the middle of the church, hands joined, staring at each other like happy little lemmings.

Then a familiar voice said, "Miller. Ruth."

Evan drew in a deep, deep breath. He hoped that by the time he was ready to exhale, he'd be less pissed off than he currently was.

It didn't work, exactly. Instead, Evan and Ruth turned as one to find that the voice he'd assumed was Daniel's belonged to Mr. Burne.

The older man stood stiffly with a tall, dark-haired woman at his side. Behind that woman, resting a hand on her shoulder, was Hayley, the girl who'd been so rude to Ruth.

Which would, logically, make the dark-haired woman Laura Burne.

"Hello," Ruth said cautiously.

Evan said nothing. Tension seemed to thrum between the three women in an unbalanced sort of triangle. He had the unmistakable feeling of being utterly superfluous. Whatever was happening here would go on well enough without him.

Burne seemed to have a similar idea, because he said, "Well. I shall see you at work, Miller, I'm sure." And then, after a slight hesitation, he added, "Goodbye, Ruth. Happy Easter."

Evan could almost *feel* Ruth's shock, but it didn't show on her face—or in her voice when she murmured, "Goodbye, Mr. Burne."

The man wandered off, leaving Evan and Ruth, Laura and Hayley, standing opposite each other in the middle of the stone floor.

Evan studied the woman who, for better or for worse, had ended up tied to Daniel.

She was tall like her sister, with the same long, dark hair and unobtrusive prettiness. There was a firm set to her shoulders and a sharpness to her jaw that reminded him of women he'd known in the army. She stood close, very close, to her sister, and was resting a hand against her own belly. He remembered hearing somewhere that Daniel's wife was pregnant. She wasn't showing. But two rings gleamed on her fourth finger, one bearing an enormous, tear-drop diamond.

"Ruth," Laura said. There was no animosity in her tone, or in her face—though, just behind her, Hayley was scowling awfully.

Ruth nodded slightly. "Laura."

"It's nice to see you." The woman's pale, grey gaze flickered down to Evan and Ruth's intertwined hands.

"It's nice to see you too," Ruth said. "I hope you're doing well." She sounded careful, which meant that she had no idea what the fuck was going on. Frankly, neither did Evan. But it was certainly… interesting.

The rest of the churchgoers seemed to think so too. Those who had been hurrying toward the exit found reason to slow down, to dawdle, all of a sudden. Evan resisted the urge to roll his eyes. He wondered where Daniel was, then decided he didn't care. The fucker was probably allergic to places of worship, being a demon and all.

"I'm as well as can be expected," Laura replied with a hint of wry humour. Then she smiled with an unaffected ease that could only be the result of years' practice. "Perhaps we might meet for coffee," she said. "At some point."

Behind her, Hayley's face was stiff. Evan saw Ruth flash a look at her old friend before murmuring, "Alright."

And that, apparently, was that. Laura inclined her head with a matronly grace that seemed too old for her. She couldn't be more than 35, but she was almost stately as she left.

Evan squeezed Ruth's hand, ignoring the low murmurs and interested looks around them. "So that was weird."

"Yeah," she said. She was frowning slightly, and he could almost see the cogs whirring inside her mind. But then she shrugged, and the frown cleared, and she said, "Let's find Mum and Hannah."

It didn't take long. Patience Kabbah's enormous, pink hat was visible above the crowd. She stood by the door, pressing the vicar's gnarled hand with her own. The two of them were speaking very seriously, but as he grew closer Evan realised that the topic of discussion was, apparently, hot crossed buns.

As they waited for the baffling conversation to finish, Ruth and Hannah communicated with that series of significant, eye-widening looks they shared so frequently. Then, after a few moments, Patience turned.

"Well," she said, her lyrically accented voice bright. "Let's get home and eat, shall we? Are you hungry, Evan?" She didn't wait for his response. "I bet you are! Come, girls."

She floated out of the church, Hannah following dutifully behind.

Ruth and Evan stepped out into the church's riotous gardens together, the sun beaming gently down on them. They walked slowly, and Evan took the opportunity to study the woman by his side.

She was focused on the daffodils lining the concrete path, simple pleasure all over her face—which was to say, her lips tilted slightly, and her eyes sparkled, and her cheeks plumped. Her dark skin gleamed in the light, and fine tendrils of frizz escaped her braid. She was wearing the most formal clothes she owned, which amounted to a black pair of leggings, boots, and a T-shirt that didn't bear a fictional character's face.

She was painfully perfect.

Evan hung back slightly, tugging on Ruth's hand. She paused, looking up at him, her brows raised in question.

"What's up?" she said.

"I love you," he replied, his voice soft.

Her face split into a smile, and she said without an ounce of self-consciousness, "I love you, too. A lot. I mean, a worrying amount. I'm not quite sure how it happened, actually—"

With a laugh, Evan grabbed her by the waist and dragged her to him. She came with a sigh, batting at his shoulder. But when he bent down to kiss her, right in front of the church, she didn't complain.

Not at all. Not even a little bit.

EPILOGUE

FIVE YEARS LATER

"WHAT ARE YOU DOING?"

Ruth jumped, dropping a packet of rice on the floor.

It split.

"Oh, fuck," she sighed.

Evan laughed, padding into the kitchen on bare feet. He held out a hand as she started to bend. "Don't you dare."

Ruth didn't argue. He was probably right. She'd fallen over enough before, without the added burden of an enormously round belly. Now, she was a disaster waiting to happen.

Evan put the rice on the counter, cupping his hand over the place where the bag had split. Then he caught her hand in his and tugged her from the kitchen—but not before casting a speaking glance at the food she'd lined up on the side.

"So," he said, leading her back into their bedroom. "You decided to get up in the middle of the night and cook dinner?"

"We should sweep up the rice," she mumbled.

He pushed her gently back into bed, on top of the rumpled blankets. "That can wait 'til morning. It's 1 a.m."

She huffed, because his calm reason was vaguely annoying. Then he lay down and wrapped an arm around her, and Ruth, weak as she was, forgot all irritation and purred like a kitten.

Evan kissed her cheek and murmured, "Are you nervous?"

She snorted. "Why would I *possibly* be nervous about our first time hosting Sunday dinner? About taking responsibility for the tradition and trying to live up to my mother's half-a-century of experience when I can't even cook—"

"You're not doing the cooking," he reminded her gently. "I am. Which makes me wonder what, exactly, you were doing in the kitchen."

"Well," Ruth said, feeling her cheeks heat. "I thought it might make things easier for you if I laid out all the ingredients and so on."

Evan laughed. "I see. Thanks for the support, love." He rubbed slow, soothing circles over her belly, but she knew that wasn't just for her. He put his hands over her bump whenever he could.

Ruth looked down and watched him stroke the swell of her stomach and felt herself relax. Somehow, he smoothed away her hours of lying awake, feeling ridiculously nervous, worrying that she'd ruin everything by... well, by setting the kitchen on fire despite *still* being banned from using ovens. Or something along those lines.

The tension drained from her with every circle of Evan's hand. The glow of their bedside lamp shadowed his features, but she could still see the glint of his golden beard, his sky-bright eyes.

"Everything's going to be fine," he said. "It's not a big deal."

"Not a big deal?" The Kabbahs and Davises all crammed into she and Evan's three-bedroom house expecting a perfect meal seemed like an enormous deal to her.

But then Evan said, "We're family. So even if we fuck it up, everything will be fine."

She relaxed again, just a bit. "Hm. I suppose that is technically true."

"*Plus*, we're not gonna fuck it up. I've been watching your mother cook for years." He smiled down at her. "And I know you're not questioning my skills."

Ruth rolled her eyes. "Would I ever, Great Husband, O Master of the Kitchen?"

"You *shouldn't*," he said haughtily, mimicking her tone. "But you've always been impudent."

"Impudent?" She snorted. "I don't even know what that means."

"Guess." He lowered his head and kissed her, his lips gentle and familiar and electric all at once. His hand stopped circling and started rising, sliding up over the curve of her belly until it reached her full breasts.

Ruth moaned as he pushed up her T-shirt to pinch one thick nipple. She reached down to the waistband of the boxers he'd been sleeping in, shoving them down without much grace. When she felt the growing hardness of his cock against her palm, she shuddered.

Evan pulled her underwear aside and slid a finger through her wetness. She was almost always wet, now.

Always desperate for him. And she'd thought she had it bad *before* she got pregnant...

"Again?" he asked softly, a teasing light in his eyes. "You'll wear me out."

"Liar." She squeezed his erection as he pulled off her knickers, and then released a choked gasp as he thrust two fingers inside her.

"Come on," he said calmly, even as his hand worked over her mound. "Sit up for me, love."

Because she wasn't supposed to lie on her back for too long, now, and definitely not during sex. As Ruth pushed herself into a seated position, helped by Evan's strong arm, she moaned. Every shift brought his fingers into contact with that delicious spot that sent her eyes rolling back.

Evan pulled her into his lap, so that her back rested against his chest. She spread her legs wide and looked down to watch his fingers thrusting into her—but his rigid cock blocked the view.

"On your knees," he said softly, and she adjusted until she was straddling his thighs. He pulled his fingers from her pussy, and she tried not to whimper—but it was hard, so fucking hard, when she could feel his naked skin on hers, his body surrounding her, his laboured breath against her neck.

"Evan," she moaned softly, and he bit gently at her throat.

"Shhh, love. It's okay. I have you." He gripped her thighs, pulled her up slightly, and she reached down to guide his cock. When the swollen head pushed into her, they both released a tight breath.

Evan wrapped an arm around her hips, slid the other

over her gently swaying breasts. As his fingers pinched one taut nipple, hard, Ruth let her head fall back against his shoulder.

"There," he whispered. His beard brushed her throat, his lips grazing her ear. "Is that what you wanted, my love?"

"Yes," she panted, but it wasn't completely true. Ruth shifted her hips, clenched her muscles around him, chased the growing pressure within her.

He laughed. "Are you sure?" And his hands moved, cradling her hips, holding her tight, lifting her—*fuck*. He pulled her up, and delicious friction burst to life inside her. Then he pushed her down again, onto his cock, and said, "You don't want that?"

"I do," she gasped out, her voice almost a sob. "I do. Please, Evan—" She broke off as he repeated the movement, his strong arms lifting her, letting her fall again, sliding her up and down his length. "Oh, Jesus," she moaned. "Fuck, fuck, *fuck*."

His fingers dug into the flesh of her hips as he moaned too, low and raw and deep in his throat. He sounded like an animal. The heavy pants of his breath felt almost feverish against her skin, and then he *bit* her, sinking his teeth into her shoulder, and Ruth had to reach down and rub her clit because this was too fucking much.

"You're so beautiful," he rasped out, his hips jerking beneath her. "You're so beautiful and perfect and you're mine."

"And you're *mine*." Ruth rubbed harder, tried to ride him even though it was a struggle, even though he set the pace and moved her body for her, because she was reaching that desperate, frantic point when lust surpasses reason. "Fuck, Evan. Christ, I love you."

"I know." He slammed her down harder onto his cock, bit her shoulder again.

And she came. Screaming, sobbing, breathless, sated. That was how he always left her, any time she asked for it.

Evan came too, with a choked moan that always made her smile, because it belonged to moments like this. And then they sat there for a while, his arms wrapped around her, Ruth's hands clinging to him. She could feel his length softening inside her and even that, weirdly enough, made her happy. Everything made her happy.

"Perfect," she murmured, her body still soft and liquid with pleasure.

He roused enough to press a kiss against her cheek. "I love you. Will you sleep, now?"

"Oh, is that what that was? You putting me to sleep?"

"Depends. Did it work?"

Ruth closed her eyes, resting her head against his shoulder. "Maybe. Possibly."

"Good. You need your rest." Which was an ironic statement, considering what he'd just done with her, but Ruth would let that slide. He murmured, "Don't worry about tomorrow, okay?"

She nodded. "Okay."

"You know I won't let you down."

"I've never worried about that," she said. "You're perfect."

Evan raised a hand to her forehead. "Are you okay?" He asked incredulously. "Feverish at all? Hysterical? No?"

"Shut up." She pulled his hand away, then kissed his palm. "I wasn't worried about you. I was worried about me."

"Well, don't. Because you're perfect too."

"I most certainly am not."

Evan tutted. "Don't insult my wife. I take it very personally."

There was a point when Ruth would've brushed those words away. When she would've been uncomfortable at the pure love in his voice, in his eyes, in the way he held her.

But she was used to it now. She was happy with it. And she deserved it.

So instead, she turned her head to kiss him, soft and chaste. Then she said, "You are correct, I suppose. We're both perfect for each other."

He smiled. "That sounds about right."

The End.

AUTHOR'S NOTE

A little while ago, I saw a GIF of a very handsome man. And the moment—the *second*—I saw it, I also saw Ruth Kabbah.

She was sitting in her living room with a cup of tea, and the handsome man was there too, and she wanted to kiss him but would also rather die than make the attempt. I liked her a lot, so I wrote the book.

It was a lot of fun to write a main character with Autistic Spectrum Disorder, as someone with ASD myself. I hope that my neuroatypical readers find in Ruth the sort of representation we rarely get: an autistic character with a personality and a life, rather than an animated stereotype. An autistic character who isn't an alien or a changeling or even a theoretical physicist.

In the words of that one meme, it's what [we] deserve!

This book is the first of three set in the town of Ravenswood. The next book will be about Hannah, and the final book will be about Rae. Who's Rae? You'll find out in book 2! But enough of me trying to be mysterious.

If you or someone you know is experiencing, or has experienced, intimate partner violence, I recommend the U.K. charity Women's Aid. They are helpful, trustworthy and genuine.

You can visit their website at https://www.womensaid. org.uk or use their free, 24 hour helpline: 0808 2000 247.

(I often recommend charities and resources in my author's note—but never for countries other than my own, because I only promote charities I 'know'.)

As always, thank you so much for reading this book. It really does mean a lot to me.

Love and biscuits,

Talia xx

~

Read on for sneak peek at Ravenswood book 1.5, a bonus novella starring Laura Burne, her childhood sweetheart, and the unborn baby she's desperate to protect…

DAMAGED GOODS

CHAPTER ONE

The stranger arrived on a Saturday night.

Her great, sleek Range Rover rumbled into the seaside village, gleaming like whale skin under the full moon. A young lad walking his dog watched it pass in awe, his jaw slack. Not even during the season, when the middle-classes descended upon Beesley-On-Sea for their summer holidays, had he seen such extravagant rims on a car. And he'd certainly never come across a private plate like that.

Burn3, it read.

The car drove past the astonished youth without pause. Its driver barely saw the boy, just as she'd barely seen the *Welcome to Beesley-on-Sea!* sign she'd passed five minutes ago. It didn't matter, though; she knew exactly where she was. Even after all these years, the briny tang of seawater on the breeze made her muscles loosen and her heart rise. By the time she reached her destination, the old beach house, she was grinning like a ninny.

The driver's name was Laura, and she left her rings in

the glovebox.

They were irritating, anyway, you see. The teardrop diamond of her engagement ring always dug into her other fingers. The wedding band was alright—if one forgot the part where it symbolised her legal attachment to the biggest piece of shit on earth. But, she reminded herself, that attachment would soon be dissolved. Thank fuck.

The beach house of Laura's memory was a grand old thing, but fifteen years later it was simply… well, an *old* thing. Her father-in-law's monstrous Range Rover looked ridiculous on the driveway, gleaming smugly beside the house's battered wood panelling and chipped, white window frames. And yet, in an instant, she loved the beach house quite unreasonably. The car she loved far less, even if it *had* allowed her madcap escape.

The house keys had been left in the old post-box by the door, because the estate agent overseeing this rent was an older, small-town man. The older, small-town man, Laura knew, was a curious specimen. They tended to lack the proper survival instincts, so they did ridiculous things like… well, like leaving the keys to a house in said house's post-box and trusting that no-one would steal them.

Thankfully, no-one had. Laura glanced over her shoulder as she fished them out, squinting into the moonlit darkness, searching for potential home invaders. All she saw was leafy isolation across the street and scattered stars lighting up the night. All she heard were the familiar sounds of night creatures hooting and rustling and whispering on the breeze. She could almost pretend she was back home in Ravenswood.

But not quite. There were three key differences, so far,

between Ravenswood and Beesley. The first: Ravenswood didn't have a beach, and thus its breeze lacked the raw, wild, salty scent of Beesley's. The second: in Ravenswood, she would've been secure in the knowledge that her friends—or at the very least, her father-in-law—were within walking distance. The third: she would also have been terrified by the knowledge that her *husband* was within walking distance.

That last point alone made Beesley far preferable to Ravenswood right now. She hurried into the house.

Its interior was as charmingly faded as its exterior had been, filled with mismatched furniture and outdated appliances. Laura hadn't brought much with her, so it didn't take long to unpack. Everything had its place: designer clothes stuffed into the bleached-wood wardrobe, La Mer arranged on the eighties-style tiles of the en-suite's counter, phone charger plugged in by the dusty-rose divan. She wandered downstairs, stomach growling, and found the kitchen fully stocked.

The sight of fat, round grapes by the sink, a floury bloomer in the pantry, and a slab of white cheese in the fridge made Laura nauseous. This was the food she'd requested. This was the food that, five minutes ago, she'd been desperate to shovel down her throat. Now the mere idea made her stomach roil. The midwife's pamphlets had totally lied, and Laura was still bitter about it. Morning—or evening, or afternoon, or *midnight*—sickness did not fade after the first trimester.

"Alright then," she murmured, looking down at the swell of her stomach. "What do you fancy?"

The bump remained silent. *Typical.*

She wandered over to the kitchen sink and ran her sweaty palms over its cool steel. Still fighting the queasy lurch in her gut, Laura glanced out of the window at the stars, then studied the narrow scrap of beach outside, untouched by the high tide.

That was the ocean she saw, winking at her like an old flirt, just beyond the sand. Oh, how she loved the ocean.

"A walk on the beach, perhaps?" she suggested to her own abdomen.

The foetus within held its tongue. Did they have tongues, at this stage? She'd have to consult her pamphlets again.

Oh, whatever. The baby may not have an opinion, but Laura knew exactly what she wanted.

And for the first time in a while, she was free to go for it.

~

Samir didn't *think* he was being spied on.

On the one hand, people were often spied on here in Beesley—especially during the off-season. Folks had too much damned time on their hands. The elderly in particular became vampires in their old age, always thirsty for someone else's drama.

But on the other hand, whoever had just joined him on the beach was far too noisy to be a spy. Surely, if they were trying to be sneaky, they wouldn't blunder over the stony shoreline like the world's loudest bulldozer. And they certainly wouldn't be tossing pebbles into the silky ink of the ocean with a successive *plop, plop, plop* that yanked him right out of his evening's angst-fest.

So they weren't going to pinch his cheek and call him a lovely boy, and they weren't going to tell the whole town that Samir Bianchi had been staring out to sea, grim-faced and resentful, like some wannabe Batman. Those were good things. Very good things.

But Samir still wasn't feeling charitable towards the person who'd intruded on his solitude—and never mind the fact that this was a public beach. It was the middle of the night, for goodness's sake. A man should be able to brood without interruption on a beach in the middle of the night. An hour or two of self-indulgence wasn't asking for much.

Clearly the bulldozer disagreed. They came ever closer, ever louder, ever clumsier, until it became suddenly and painfully clear that Samir was going to have to announce his presence. It was dark enough that, if he didn't, this bulldozer of a human being might just bulldoze him.

"Hey," he said, his voice breaking the gentle, wave-tinged silence.

"Argh!" the bulldozer said and fell on top of him.

What followed was an alarming series of shrieks, grunts and mumbled apologies that Samir really could've done without.

"Bloody hell," he blurted as the bulldozer collapsed over him like a sack of bricks.

"Oh!" the bulldozer cried. "I'm so sorry!" She—it did *seem* to be a she—accompanied those words with what felt like a shoulder to his throat.

"Bloody *hell!*" he spluttered, this time with even greater feeling.

A small storm of sand was kicked up as the two of them shuffled apart like crabs on speed. He felt the grit against his skin, scratching his dry eyes, and even sneaking into his open, panting mouth. *Delightful.*

Eventually, despite all the scuffling and swearing and shrieking—this bulldozer operated at a rather high pitch—they managed to put a decent amount of space between them. Samir could see the outline of a person in the moonlight, just a few feet away. The gentle *whoosh* of the wind over the waves should've made the silence between them peaceful. Instead, it felt painfully awkward. He should say something, really. The only problem was, he thought his voice box might be damaged. The woman's shoulder must be made of bloody brick.

"I'm sorry," she said, the words sudden and disarmingly earnest. She sounded absolutely mortified. In fact, it was more than that; she sounded ready to throw herself down a well. The abject discomfort in her voice was so intense, it was making *him* uncomfortable. And there was something else, too—something in her tone, or maybe her accent, that tugged at a thread in the back of his mind. It was a weird sensation.

He decided to ignore it.

"It's okay," he managed, his voice far too cracked and hoarse to be convincing. "Don't worry about it."

She snorted. It was a soft, horse-like sound, and something about it tugged on that thread again. "It most certainly is *not* okay," she said. "I must've squashed you."

This was the part where he lied gallantly. "I wouldn't say *squashed*—"

"*I* would."

"It wasn't that bad."

"I might believe you," she said wryly, "if you weren't still wheezing like a donkey."

Samir managed to choke out a laugh in between wheezes.

Maybe his eyes were adjusting, or maybe some of the cloud cover had passed. Whatever the reason, he suddenly caught a glimpse of his strange companion: the gleam of moonlight on long, dark hair as she tipped her head back; the outline of a sharp, rather no-nonsense nose; the curve of the impressively substantial shoulder that had found its way to his throat. No wonder he was still a bit winded.

"Please," she said, sounding oddly, subtly urgent. "Let me be sorry. I'm very, very sorry."

He recognised something in her voice—something self-flagellating and hopeful all at once. Something he'd heard in his own voice, once upon a time. Or rather, he *thought* he did. He was probably imagining things.

"If it matters so much," he said lightly, "you can be as sorry as you like."

"Oh, thank you," she murmured, a slight smile in her voice. "I appreciate it."

And wasn't the human mind such a strange thing? Because, out of everything she'd said over the past five minutes, it was that single phrase—those three little words —that pulled loose the insistent, tugging thread in his mind.

"*I appreciate it,*" she'd said fifteen years ago, after he'd given her a stolen Cornetto. She'd been all prim and proper while she unwrapped his ill-gotten goods, and for some reason it had made his teenaged heart sing. He'd wanted to steal a thousand more Cornettos, just for her.

Over the course of the summer, he probably had.

Samir sank his fingers into the gritty sand, grounding

himself even as strange hope ran wild. Surely not. *Surely not*. This woman, whoever she was, dredged up old memories for some other reason. She just happened to have the same accent and that same arch tone. It was a coincidence. Because the chances of meeting *her* again, here, after all this time...

It wasn't possible. That sort of thing didn't happen.

But Samir found himself squinting at her in the darkness, anyway, as if he could will himself to develop night vision.

"Are you okay?" she asked. She might as well have whacked him over the head. *Now* he was sure. He was positive. He could've predicted every inflection in that sentence, from the way she glided over the *you* to the wobbling lilt on *okay*, as if she really gave a shit. Because she did.

"Laura?" he asked slowly. And, though he'd been certain a second ago, just saying her name made it seem so impossible. Made him think that he must be mistaken.

Until she stilled, her shadowy outline stiffening. Her voice was hard as glass and twice as fragile when she demanded, "Who are you?"

Because of course she'd be freaked out by a strange man knowing her name. Who wouldn't? Through the flood of disbelief rushing over him, he managed to say, "It's Samir. Samir Bianchi. Do you remember me?"

For a single, stuttering heartbeat, he thought the answer might be *no*. But then she spoke, sounding as astonished as he felt. "Samir? Seriously?"

It was her.

DAMAGED GOODS: Available Now

ABOUT THE AUTHOR

Talia Hibbert is an award-winning, Black British author who lives in a bedroom full of books. Supposedly, there is a world beyond that room, but she has yet to drum up enough interest to investigate.

She writes sexy, diverse romance because she believes that people of marginalised identities need honest and positive representation. She also rambles intermittently about the romance genre online. Her interests include makeup, junk food, and unnecessary sarcasm.

Talia loves hearing from readers. Follow her social media to connect, or email her directly at hello@taliahibbert.com.

BB 🐦 f 📷 g a

CPSIA information can be obtained
at www.ICGtesting.com
Printed in the USA
FSHW021817290419
57683FS

9 781916 404304